The Stones of Petronicus

Peter Tomlinson

BeWrite Books, UK
www.bewrite.net

Published internationally by BeWrite Books, UK.
32 Bryn Road South, Wigan, Lancashire, WN4 8QR.

A CIP catalogue record for this book is available from the British Library

ISBN 1-904492-76-2

Also available in eBook format from www.bewrite.net

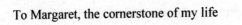

To Margaret, the cornerstone of my life

As well as being a novelist Peter Tomlinson is a well-known poet and short story writer. He has had various careers including radio telegraphist, soldier, teacher and overseas cultural guide.

The Stones of Petronicus

Prologue

Petronicus always avoided the town of Bedosa if he could. He found the place unwelcoming and the people mean and aggressive. The Ruler of Bedosa was old, bitter and known for his intolerance.

Petronicus heard a crowd of people approaching, pushing a prisoner in front of them.

"Another unfortunate," said Petronicus to the woman whose infected arm he was treating.

"A thief," she said with contempt and spat onto the ground. "He deserves to hang."

"Men will steal if they are hungry. There are many hungry in Bedosa, I hear." But he did not want to argue with her. All he wanted was to earn enough from selling his cures and potions to be able to leave for the Land of the Tall Trees before the rains came.

"Use the salve every day and say these prayers every night. The town scribe will read them for you and teach you the words."

He took the coin she grudgingly offered and watched the wretched prisoner being manhandled into the stone-built prison next to the scaffold. Petronicus made his way through the crowd intending to set up his stall in the market place. He was pushed out of the way by one of the Ruler's men carrying a small baby. The child was being handled very roughly and crying loudly.

"Whose child is that?" asked Petronicus.

"The child of the thief. The mother cannot be found."

"What will become of it?" asked Petronicus, knowing little about the customs of Bedosa.

"Exposed on the wall by the prison to die. Nobody wants the child of a thief."

"Well, if that is your custom …" He did not finish his sentence but hurried away in disgust.

Petronicus found a good place near the town well to set up his stall. His first patient was a rich man, whose servants brought him on wooden boards. A woman who might have been his mother explained that he had severe stomach pains and could pass nothing.

"Vomit for me, please," said Petronicus, but the man could not.

"There is no more to come," said the woman.

"There is always more to come. Show me your hands, woman."

Petronicus scratched a little of the vomit that clung to her hands from caring for the man. He smelt it and moistened it with his own spit before tasting it.

"Hmmm. Wait here. I will go and find the things I need to treat him."

"Will you cure him, Petronicus? We know of your fame as a healer."

"The medicines will work if he is an honest man. If he is not, the gods will let him die."

Petronicus found the grubs he needed in some putrefying offal in the gutter near the prison. He carefully collected it up and selected the tiny grubs for his potion. He mixed them with a little water and crushed leaves taken from small plants growing in the walls and was about to return to his patient when he heard the child crying. It was lying naked on top of the wall in the full glare of the sun. Some people had spat on the child and its crying was pitiful. The prison guard was dozing at the base of the wall. Petronicus touched him with his foot to wake him.

"The child," said Petronicus. "It is hot and needs food and water."

"Then feed it yourself. Do you want it? Show me your coins and you can have it."

Petronicus could only think of soothing the child. He put his straw hat over the tiny body to shield it from the sun and said to the guard:

"If I give you coins, will you buy food and water for the thief? I will also give a coin for yourself. But remember, do not cheat me for if ever you are sick and ask for medicines they will only cure you if you are an honest man."

The guard stood and looked at Petronicus with gratitude. Healers were usually respected throughout the world, but not always in Bedosa. The guard touched his hat and bowed slightly as Petronicus gave him three small coins.

"Remember now," said Petronicus, "be an honest man and the gods will look kindly upon you."

"Yes," said the guard. "I promise you, Petronicus. You are welcome to the child; nobody wants the child of a thief. But what will you do with it? Try and sell it?"

Petronicus did not answer. He rummaged in his pouch for some blue leaves.

"Here," he said, "crush them up and put them in the prisoner's drink. They will dull his senses before he hangs."

The guard picked up the child roughly and handed it to Petronicus, who put it into the fold of his cloak and returned to his stall in the market place. The sick man was lying on the floor with a small crowd around him. Healers were a popular distraction for the people who hoped he would undertake some bloody surgery or impose some other unpleasant treatment.

Petronicus said: "He must drink this solution without chewing. Tell him he must not kill the small grubs in the water with his teeth."

"Do not concern yourself, Petronicus, he has had no teeth for years." The crowd laughed and some old men opened their mouths and showed their empty gums. They all watched as the woman poured small portions into the man's mouth, held his lower jaw up and made him swallow.

"Now, we must wait a while," said Petronicus. "They will clean out his inside and eat the poison in his stomach. Keep the sun off him woman! And stand back, you people; let him breathe."

The crowd pressed forward hoping to watch the patient writhe in pain on the ground. Petronicus did not like the people of Bedosa so he tried to ignore them and busied himself preparing the next part of the treatment. He took a small, blackened root from his medicine box and scraped away some fragments and mixed them with his own spit. The people watched in awe, as everyone knew that the spit of a healer was magical. Petronicus then mixed the root fragments with droppings from his own donkey that was tethered nearby. He told the woman to put the mixture into the man's mouth and make him swallow. A moment or two later the man vomited very painfully and Petronicus began to poke amongst the vomit on the ground with a small piece of rabbit bone.

"That's better out than in. He will be well by morning. The poison has come out."

Two large coins were placed in Petronicus's hand. The baby, still wrapped in the cloak, began to cry.

The day of the hanging brought much trade to Petronicus. He set up his stall by the temple steps, paid a woman to cleanse and nourish the child and sat back waiting for his first patients. A roar of sadistic appreciation came from the crowd around the scaffold as the thief was hanged and then there was drinking of wine, and fights broke out. Petronicus earned many coins treating bruised heads and straightening broken arms and legs.

He left the child with the woman until the next moon appeared, whilst he accumulated sufficient coins for the forthcoming winter. The journey to the Land of the Tall Trees would be long and arduous but the winters were warmer there and food was usually plentiful.

The woman smiled as she handed the small bundle to Petronicus.

"It is a boy of early summer," she said.

"Then that is good. A boy of early summer grows strong and is free from disease."

"Aye," said the woman, "you know what has long been said; avoid the winter's child for it is born weak and sickly."

Petronicus was glad to shake the dust of Bedosa from his feet as he left the town. He still carried the child in his robe but there was no crying and it seemed to sleep contentedly.

They camped that night by a lake and Petronicus started to make a basket of reeds and grasses to tie onto his donkey for the child to ride in. Feeding was difficult and he had to chew the bread in his own mouth before giving it to the child.

"And what shall become of you, I wonder?" Petronicus asked as they lay down for the night.

The darkness came over them but it was still warm with only a slight hint of approaching winter in the night air. They continued their journey the next day with the child safely in the basket on the donkey's back.

"Bobbing about makes the brain work," said Petronicus to the smiling child. "The guard asked me what I should do with you. Well, child, whoever you are, I will teach you the thoughts of Man and the words that tell of them. I will teach you my trade and you will be a man when I am old and I will die on clean straw that you will bring for me."

Petronicus, the child and the donkey headed for the Land of the Tall Trees where the winter's snow seldom fell and the wind blew warm from the Inner Lands.

One

I have often tried to remember my earliest childhood and my life with Petronicus. There is so much I have forgotten but I can remember some of the more important events. Petronicus was always there and maybe the oldest picture in my mind is of him, his warm face, his full smile and long beard. Perhaps my memories are not real memories at all; perhaps they are things Petronicus told me about later and that I made into pictures in my head.

Of my first four or five years I remember nothing. But then into my mind happy pictures appear of when we spent the warm summer moons in the Land of the Tumbling Waters. There were many fish for us to catch and small animals to hunt so our bellies never ached with hunger. We have returned to that place many times since so maybe I find it easier to remember.

I see a day in my mind when I was so happy I ran about shouting with joy. It was the day Petronicus said I was old enough to have my own blanket.

"You are too big to curl up inside the sheep pelt now," he said as he showed me some coins that would buy a blanket from a weaver in the next town we visited. And that was the day he also said I was to have my hair shortened and I would not have to tie it up with straw every day as we set off on our travels.

He started by cutting my hair with a sharp stone and then he held it tightly in one hand and singed it off with hot embers from the fire. I remember screeching and laughing at the same time, trying to make Petronicus think he was hurting me. And then he lifted me up and walked into the river with me and let me down with a splash. It was a happy time!

At night we would sit by our fire and he would tell me of many wondrous things he had seen on his travels. The firelight shut out the world and wrapped Petronicus and me in our own small safe place.

We had to travel most of the time so that Petronicus could earn coins or food from the medicines he sold to sick people. We went from town to town and wandered as far as the birds fly and I often fell asleep before we made beds for ourselves amongst the trees and bushes at night. We always lit a fire to keep the wolves and other animals away. Petronicus would let me watch as he scratched a flint against a small hard stone he always carried in his pouch. And then to my delight a small spark came and he carefully breathed on it to light the dry moss; Petronicus always carried some dry moss in a pouch tied to his waist. I thought it was magical but I understand it now.

"And as you add years to your life, child," Petronicus used to say, "the more things you will understand."

I shall always remember those words and the ones that came next.

"Words," he said, "are spoken thoughts that give understanding."

I must have looked puzzled and Petronicus added: "You will not understand everything at once but as you grow older, more and more understandings will come to you."

I think it was the next day when he tried to explain further: "In autumn when the leaves fall, they are often blown about by the wind. Think of the words as leaves all blowing about in your head. Sometimes they settle, sometimes they don't."

I ran about picking up bundles of dry leaves and threw them into the air and watched them blow about in the wind. I remember laughing and Petronicus laughed with me.

"You see how the leaves blow all around the trees? Some are lost and just blow away and we lose them. Well," he said, "words are like that. Some settle quickly and become part of your thoughts but some just blow away and are lost. That is what I mean by understanding words."

I seem to remember that I spent most of my life riding on the donkey. I asked Petronicus if I had been born on the donkey and if it was my mother. He stopped on the trail by a small lake and lifted me down.

"Come," he said, "and answer your own question."

We walked to the lake and we both lay down to see our faces in the waters and that was the first time I can remember seeing my own face. And then the donkey came to drink beside us. I could see that I was quite different from the donkey and we both laughed.

"Always ask questions," Petronicus said to me. "But always try to answer them yourself first."

That was the way Petronicus taught me.

It was during these early years with Petronicus that I began to realise that my master was the wisest of men. We watched the moon each night and Petronicus told me how it grew bigger and then became smaller as the days passed. He told me about the seasons and the signs to watch for. He told me that we would feel colder when the leaves were falling and warmer when they grew again. Petronicus tried to ensure that we had fire each night, especially during the winter moons but it was sometimes difficult to make, especially in the wind and rain.

There was a custom on the trails of sharing fire with fellow travellers. I had always known that fire was the gift of the gods and that all men shared it freely with each other. I don't know how I knew that; perhaps I had been born with that knowledge. But there is one very cold and wet day that I remember well. We had travelled a long trail and we were very tired. Petronicus looked round for signs of smoke from other men's fires. We saw some on the side of the hill so we went up to them.

"Greetings, Petronicus," the leader of the men said. They were merchants who travelled between the towns trading goods. "You are always welcome to share fire with us."

Petronicus was so well known on the trail that everyone hailed him and stopped to talk. That night we stayed with the merchants and then other travellers came to share fire with us. There was also another healer who was on his way to the coastal towns. The men were talking about the gods and I sat by Petronicus but I had to be silent. It was inappropriate for a child to speak during their conversations but Petronicus pulled my ear very gently and whispered: "Listen, child. Always listen when wise men speak and some of their wisdom will come to you."

That was the first time I had been allowed to sit with the men and listen to them talking. There was so much I did not understand about the gods. I tried to listen but I think I fell asleep long before I could learn very much from them. It was cold that night and Petronicus had covered me with leaves and placed warm stones from the fire around me. When I awoke the men were making preparations to leave. They were loading their donkeys and saying goodbye to each other.

We returned to the trail just as the first snows began to fall. Petronicus said: "It is time to seek shelter for the winter."

We worked hard for the next moon catching fish and smoking them over our fire so we could eat them later. We collected furs and bones and the fruits of autumn and we found a good dry cave in the Land of the Tumbling Waters. There was a small town nearby so Petronicus and I could go there and set up his medicine stall. We seldom stayed in the town because the inns demanded coins and Petronicus preferred the open air. The donkey would lie close to us at night and keep us warm. I remember asking Petronicus one night as our fire burned brightly and we felt secure and warm: "Who are the gods, Petronicus? I have never seen them. What do they look like?"

"They look like all of us and they look like none of us," he said, but I didn't understand. He went on to explain in words a child could follow: "They make things happen. They make the rain fall and the wind blow. They show the sun where to go each night and tell the stars when to twinkle. The gods are in the breeze that cools us on the trail, they are in the fire that warms us at night." I smiled and looked up at the stars. Many of them had gathered around the moon, which shone much brighter.

Petronicus waited for me to think about what he had said and then added: "There is a little of the gods in all good men."

"What about wicked and dishonest men?"

"No, the gods leave them. I once heard it said that the gods sometimes sleep for a hundred moons and then there is great wickedness in the world."

I was sometimes frightened by things he told me, but I knew that if I stayed close to Petronicus and the donkey I would be safe.

When spring came we still felt winter's hunger so we took to the trail again and entered a big town. I was amazed by the size of it; there must have been two or even three houses for every finger and toe a man had. In the centre there was a big open space and more people than I had ever seen in my whole life. I tethered our donkey and stroked its head because it was not used to so many people. Petronicus placed his big medicine box on the ground and opened it so that the people could see he had powders and potions that would make sick people well. People came with all sorts of ailments and Petronicus treated them all. People who had no coins gave us food or pieces of cloth in return for medicines and Petronicus also wrote down prayers for them to say. He wrote on reeds, which we had dried in the sun and stuck together with sap, and taught me to wade out into the lakes to collect them.

We left the town as darkness came and made our camp for the night by some trees. After we had eaten our meal I asked him why he gave the people prayers as well as medicine.

"They cannot read the prayers themselves," said Petronicus, "so they take them to the town scribe who reads them for people. If they are sharp of mind they remember the prayers themselves and don't have to go to him again. Only healers, scribes and priests can read and write, you see."

"But why do they need prayers as well as medicines?"

Petronicus sat back and leaned against a tree. He poked the fire with a stick to make more light and looked at me. I think he was wondering if I was old enough to understand what he was going to say.

"As I told you once there is a little bit of the gods in all of us. Even in children. The gods help us to think good thoughts."

"Is there a god inside the donkey?"

"No, I don't think so, although sometimes I wonder about that. You will not remember this because you were too small but one year the donkey was stolen. You cried and cried but we just stayed where we where and eventually the donkey came back to us. As soon as the thieves put him out to grass he ran off and found his way back and you were happy again."

"You mean, the donkey's god guided him back to us?"

"Oh, I don't know. I don't really think so, but nobody really knows."

"Do the priests know these things, about the donkey I mean?"

"No, I don't think they do."

That was how Petronicus taught me when I was quite small. He let me ask questions but I didn't always understand his answers and then I thought of the leaves blowing about in my head.

One day we found a merchant who was lying by the trail very sick. I watched as Petronicus examined his stomach. It was pushing in and out and the man was in great pain.

"I have some powder which I shall mix with water and you must drink it down all at once. Do you understand?" The man nodded and I watched as Petronicus mixed the powder but just before he gave it to the man he asked: "Are you an honest merchant?"

"Yes," said the merchant and then he added: "But like all men perhaps not always."

"Then I will write down a prayer for you to say when next you take the medicine and I will give it to you. If you cannot read or find a scribe put the prayer under your head when you sleep."

We left the merchant in the care of his family and set off on our way again. That evening when we had eaten our meal I asked Petronicus again: "Why do the sick need a prayer as well as your medicine and why did you ask him if he was an honest merchant?"

"When a person is sick his body needs medicines but we must make a prayer to the god within him to help make him better."

"Is that why you always ask if they are honest men?"

"Yes, that is right. If they are dishonest or wicked the god leaves them. They will not dwell within such men. Sometimes the medicines work with bad people but often they don't. If the man has not been too dishonest, the medicines will keep him alive until the god comes back to give him another chance."

"If the man becomes honest again the god might come back?"

"Yes, sometimes. I'm fairly sure of that." I remember Petronicus smiling at me because my mouth was wide open in wonder. But then he became more serious and said: "To kill an honest man is the greatest wickedness. Do you know why?"

I thought for a moment and listened to the crackling of the fire. I looked out into the night sky and could see the stars shining brightly in the heavens. "Because you hurt the god who lives inside him?"

"That is correct, child."

I went to sleep that night knowing that Petronicus was well pleased with me.

Two

It was the year we journeyed to the Land of the High Valleys through the Land of the Boar Hunters. I remember it well, because it was the first journey when I was old enough to walk and not add to the burdens of the donkey. Petronicus was pleased with my growing because it meant he could ride sometimes.

That summer we had spent our time selling the potions which Petronicus made to the people in the towns of that region. And it was that summer he told me who I really was. I had always thought that I belonged to him just like the donkey, but I learned that it was different with people.

"Your real father," he told me one evening, "was to be hanged by the Ruler of Bedosa for stealing."

"Was he a thief then, my own father?"

Petronicus said that was true, although my father had only stolen food because he was hungry. "But that was against the laws of Bedosa and he was to hang for it."

"Was I there?" I asked him.

"You were so tiny that I could hold you in the folds of my robe and you ate so little that I could hold your meal in the palm of my hand."

"Then I was really small."

I remember being much troubled as we lay down to sleep that night. I cannot remember the name of the town we were in because Petronicus and I visited so many. It was a large town with a wooden stockade all around it. Petronicus told me there was a house within the stockade for every finger and toe I had. That was the clever way he taught me to count. But we were not of their people and could not sleep inside the stockade. The safest place for us was just outside the gates. The guards were pleased that we should lie there because one of them was sick and they knew Petronicus could make him better.

Sleep did not come to me that night. It was not because of the cold for I had my own blanket and I lay close to Petronicus. It was just after the Guard of the Watch had called the midnight hour that I asked: "Is it wrong to steal if you are hungry, Petronicus?"

The old man said nothing. I thought he was asleep or sick so I repeated my question and he answered: "It is well with me, child. I heard you."

He was silent for a while and I thought he had returned to sleep. And then he said: "That, child, is for each man to decide for himself."

I did not understand, because Petronicus had always told me what was right and what was wrong.

I remember the next day well because a woman came and swore at Petronicus and kicked his medicine box. I think it was because her husband had died. She had bought a potion from Petronicus, and the prayer to go with it but her husband had died all the same.

Petronicus and I left the town quickly that morning. Petronicus was an honest man and a good healer but sometimes the people who bought his medicines were so wicked that the prayers were ignored by the gods.

As we walked away from the town that day Petronicus told me more about myself: "Your father was to be hanged the next day and you were to be left on the town wall in the sun. That is what they do in Bedosa when there is a child nobody wants."

"And is that where you found me?"

"Patience, child, I will tell you all." We had been walking fast to get away from the town and Petronicus found his breath did not come easily. "I gave the hangman money so that your father could have water and food that night. Your mother was nowhere to be found and no one knew who she was. So the executioner gave you to me."

"That was kind of you, Petronicus." I remember he rubbed my head gently and smiled.

"I got the best of the bargain," he said.

After we left the town we journeyed towards the Land of the Tall People and the way was long and arduous. The Tall People were not very friendly to strangers but they always treated Petronicus with respect; the Tall People always treat healers with respect.

"Petronicus," said I one morning as we journeyed towards the setting sun. (We hoped to reach the river before nightfall so that we could fill our vessels with water for the next day.) "If my father was a thief, will I be a thief also?"

"What a question, child," he said. "That depends on what kind of a man you become."

"But how will I know what kind of man I will become?"

Petronicus was always patient with me and that night as we lay down to sleep by the river he started to tell me a story: "There was once a man who lived long ago, so long ago that the sun and the moon were very young and shone much brighter than they do now. And this man was blind and could not see his own hand in front of his face. That was his first misfortune. The second misfortune was that he was in prison."

"Clearly," said I, "the gods had heaped misfortune upon him."

"Yes, child, they had."

"But what was his wickedness that the gods should treat him so?"

Petronicus always spoke slowly to me so that I could understand his words more fully. He just smiled and told me to be patient as he continued: "And then one day he woke up and opened his eyes and was amazed to discover that he could see. So amazed was he that he began to think that his blindness had been only a dream."

"And was it?" I asked. "Or had the gods forgiven him for his wickedness?"

"I do not know, child. I don't think anyone knows these things. Truly I know of no potion that can restore the sight of a man."

"What happened then, Petronicus?"

"The prisoner stood up on the floor of his dungeon and wailed and began to punch his head with his fist."

"That was strange, Petronicus. Surely if …"

"Patience, I tell you. Young ones know no patience. You want to know everything at once."

"I am sorry, Petronicus. I will learn to be patient."

"Well, as I told you, he wailed and shouted and punched his own head with his fists and bemoaned the wickedness of the gods. He thought the gods had played a cruel trick on him you see, restoring his sight and yet keeping him in prison where he could see nothing. 'Here I am,' he said, 'able to see after all these years but I am in a prison. I cannot look at the blue in the sky. I cannot see the trees or the colours in the flowers. I cannot see people or the animals because I am confined within these dark walls. Oh, how sad I am'."

"Truly he was unfortunate," said I. But I could see Petronicus was tired and I had promised to be patient. I knew he would continue the story the next day.

I let Petronicus sleep long after the sun rose the next morning. I wanted to make amends for my impatience. By the time he awoke I had cleaned the bowls with fine sand and filled the water skins. I had made holes in the bread with my thumb and pushed in the small pieces of meat we had left over from the previous night.

Petronicus was pleased and gave me a small piece of sweet leaf to chew. It was very sweet and only Petronicus knew where the plants grew.

We left our camp and followed the sun. He said we must reach the Valley of the Whispering Rocks before nightfall.

"Now, do you remember the story so far?" asked Petronicus. I replied that I did. I was very impatient for him to continue the story.

"And so he had his sight restored and yet he could see nothing because he was in prison," said Petronicus.

"Truly a cruel event," I said. Petronicus never gave me my lessons just with words and stories. Often he showed me the meaning in other ways. He told me to pull my body blanket up over my head and cover my eyes. All I could see were some specks of sunlight trying to poke through the woven wool. I said: "Oh yes, Petronicus. It is truly a bad thing to be able to see and yet be confined." Petronicus merely smiled at my childishness and fell silent whilst I thought about it.

We journeyed until we felt the pains of hunger in our bellies and he said: "Let us rest while the sun is high and very hot for I have no hair on my head to protect me. We will sit under that tree and rest until the shadow is behind us and I will tell you more."

When we were resting, Petronicus continued: "Well, you seem to think that the prisoner was correct to curse the gods for his fate."

"Yes," said I.

"And would you have done the same? Would you have punched your own head and wailed lamentations to the gods?"

I paused before answering because I knew his ways of teaching me.

"I will not say yet, Petronicus. I will say when you have finished the story."

"In truth, a good thought you have there. Now let me tell the story in a different way. Imagine the same prisoner in his dungeon and suddenly his sight is restored. Only this time when he stands up in his dungeon he does not punch his own head and bewail his fate."

"He does not, Petronicus?"

"No. He stands up and looks up at the tiny window near the ceiling of his cell. He sees the golden sunlight shining through. He smiles in wonderment as he traces its shimmering path on the smooth stones of the dungeon floor. And oh, those shining stones, they are like silver and gold to him."

"Truly, Petronicus, this is different thing to do."

"He pours a few drops of water from his jug onto his hand and just looks at the droplets; they shine wondrously and he gazes at the beauty before him. And then he walks over to the huge wooden door and lets his fingers trace the intricate pattern of the wood."

"Truly a different man, I think."

"No, child, the same man. He then sits down on his wooden bed exhausted with joy and picks up the rough blanket. He gazes in wonder at the intricate weaving and looks with delight to see how each thread worms its way through the next and forms such a beautiful pattern."

Petronicus fell asleep in the shade of the tree when he had finished the story. He often did this when the sun was high in the sky. I sat close to him and kept the flies away from his face with a brush made from the donkey's tail.

We did reach the Valley of the Whispering Rocks before nightfall and Petronicus told me to sit quietly and listen as the wind sang to us when it wafted through the stones high above us.

"But how does the story of the man in the prison tell me what kind of man I will be, Petronicus?"

"Well, child. Firstly you must decide which story is correct for you. If you were that man, would you have wailed and punched your head and cursed your fate? Or would you have looked excitedly about you admiring everything you saw?"

"Admiring every little thing in the prison you mean?"

"Yes."

"Even the insects … the flies … and everything?"

"Yes, everything. Even the dirt on the floor."

"Well ..." said I, but Petronicus put his hand on my lips and said: "No, don't tell me, child ... tell yourself."

I never told Petronicus which of the two men I was. But I told myself and that was how I knew what kind of man I would become. Petronicus, I have often thought, already knew.

Three

It was the year of the great sickness that Petronicus and I left the towns by the sea and headed into the hills. I was taller now and Petronicus had to bend his elbow to put his hand on my head. I was pleased because my master could ride more and was less tired when we stopped for the night.

Two things happened to me that year; one gave me much joy but the other, much sadness. We had done well on the coast, selling the powders Petronicus made from drying and grinding flowers and herbs that grew secretly in the woods and amongst the rocks. Only men who had studied on the Mountain of the Year knew how to do this.

"What made the people sick?" I asked. "Are the gods angry with them?"

"No," said Petronicus. "It is eating winter's meat that has caused the sickness, nothing to do with the gods."

One day we looked down from the hill and saw the people leaving a town, trying to escape the sickness. They were weighed down with possessions and travelled very slowly.

"No man should possess more than he can carry on his back or on his donkey," said Petronicus. "He will never be free if he does. Possessions trap a man and tie him to one place. It is a godless place where possessions are the measure of a man."

I did not always understand what Petronicus said but his ideas lodged in my mind.

"And robbers?" I asked. "Will robbers come for them?"

"Yes, probably, but we will be safe even in the Hill Country."

"Why will we be safe?" Petronicus liked me to try and answer my own questions; that was the clever way he taught me. "Is it because we possess nothing?"

"That is correct, child," said Petronicus. He was a wise man and taught me well. "All we possess is in my head and they cannot steal from there." He meant the knowledge he had of the herbs and flowers that made people well. And of the prayers he gave people to say during the treatment.

Three days into our journey to the Hill Country we camped for the night beside a large arabak tree. The event that gave me so much joy all began with that arabak tree.

But before Petronicus explained it to me he said something that made me sad and fearful. He told me that he would put me to a scribe and we would be separated for the first time since he found me on a town wall as an infant. He said that he would leave me with a scribe while he himself returned to the Mountain of the Year.

"Only scribes are permitted to teach the letters," Petronicus said. "Some young ones take many moons to learn the letters but your head is well shaped to learn. And you must learn the prayers. We have different prayers for different ailments and you must know what they are. But you are a quick boy and will learn swiftly."

I had thought Petronicus would teach me all I needed to know to take the medicine box and the donkey when he died. I think I remained silent for a long time that evening. Petronicus tried to talk with me but I could not help feeling sad and fearful. I had never known a time when I was not with Petronicus.

"When I am dead," he said, "you will need to earn your bread. You will be a healer but first you must learn your letters so you can write down the prayers. Only people like us can read. The sick people put the prayers under their heads when they sleep or ask scribes to read the prayers for them and teach them the words. Only scribes are allowed to give the letters; that way the words remain pure. Words are written thoughts and if the letters are pure the thoughts will be pure."

"But how long will we be separated?" I asked, feeling my face swelling with tears.

"Long enough for you to learn the letters and long enough for me to return to The Mountain of the Year."

"But why can't I come with you to the Mountain?" I think that was the first time I had ever made protest, however childish, to Petronicus.

"Because only healers and novices can go there and you cannot be a novice until you have learned the letters."

Petronicus was wise and patient. He knew how sad and afraid I was.

I woke several times in the night and reached over to Petronicus to make sure he was still there.

"Hush, child, I'm still here. Sleep now."

In the morning when I had taken the donkey to new grass and helped prepare our breakfast, Petronicus tried to reassure me. "We will not feel lonely when we are apart because we can still speak to each other through the trees."

I knew Petronicus spoke to the trees and plants as he collected The Gatherings, as he called them. He often thanked the trees and plants when he cut a piece of bark or a stem for his medicines.

"How will we do that, Petronicus?" I asked.

Then he told me why we had slept by an arabak tree.

"Trees have very long roots; they journey deep into the soil."

"Yes, I know that Petronicus, but why will that …?"

"Patience, child. Young things want to know everything at once." I bowed my head a little but looked up into his face. "Trees of the same family talk to each other through the soil. Their roots spread out and search for one another. The greatest family of trees is the arabak."

He told me to put my hand on the rough bark and slowly press downward. Petronicus did the same. "When we are apart we will each find an arabak tree and touch it at the same time and we will know if we are both well."

"How will we know that, Petronicus? Will I hear your voice?"

"No, child, you will not hear my voice but you will *know* I am well. No matter how far apart we are, the trees will find us and we will be together." Petronicus knew I would think deeply about what he had said but the next night I found sleep slow to come.

That night we huddled between the rocks on a moss bed I had prepared. The donkey came and slept by us and shielded us from the cold wind that blew from the hills. I was nearly asleep when I suddenly had a frightening thought. I sat up and touched the shoulder of Petronicus in alarm.

"What is it, child? Why have you brought me back from sleep?"

"But Petronicus!" I said, now sitting straight upright and trying to find his face in the dark. "How will I know *when* to touch the arabak tree and know that you are well?"

Petronicus sent his sleep away into the far corners of the night and sat up. He felt the cold round his old shoulders so he pulled the blanket up and wrapped me up in it as well.

"Look up into the night sky, child, and tell me what you see."

I looked up and saw the stars. I knew they were the children of the sun and were left behind each night when the sun went to rest. The moon was there to watch over them and to make sure they didn't move about too much. I could see the stars reflecting in his eyes as he looked up with me.

We had often sat at night gazing up at the wondrous sight of the night sky. I knew that the moon curled up when it was tired and made itself small and then became big and bright when it was fully awake. Petronicus told me all these things. He also told me that winter is when the sun hurries across the sky to reach the great fires in the sea more quickly because the world is so cold. He said too that other wise men think that the winter is something quite different and nothing to do with the sun. That night, as we sat by the arabak tree, he told me more about the stars.

"There are so many stars in the night sky that everybody can have one for himself. That is known as your naming star."

I was silent for a few moments and began to feel the excitement rising up inside me. Petronicus had always told me that one day he would give me a name and I would not always be known as *child*.

"You can choose a star for your own," said Petronicus, "and we will call it after you." I shivered with excitement. Perhaps he would give me a name that night! Having a name meant that I could climb the steps of the temple and shout my own name to the priests as I entered. I could walk in the market place as a free man and tell people who I was.

"Which is your star, Petronicus? I want mine to be near yours."

"If you look carefully you will see some stars which look like a stick sharpened to a point. Can you see?" He told me to rest my head on his arm by his shoulder and look along it to his pointed finger. And then I saw it, a group of stars that formed a point in the sky. "Now," said Petronicus. "Look just a little further forward and you will see a bright star standing on its own."

"Yes, I see it," I said excitedly. "Is that your star? Is that the star of Petronicus?"

"Yes, that is the star my father gave me when I was about your age."

"I want mine to be near yours."

"Yes, I am pleased you do. Now if we wait a little while another star just by it will begin to twinkle. It is smaller and not as bright. That is because it is very young and further away. Wait a little while longer and you will see it."

"Is it far away from yours?" I asked

"About as far as we could walk in a day, I think."

"And how far away is the moon, Petronicus?"

"Nobody knows for sure because nobody has been there. Sometimes I think the Mountain of the Year is so high I could step right on to the moon, but that is a fanciful thought."

"But how high is it?"

"Further than we could walk in a year."

"If we could walk in the sky," I said, and Petronicus laughed.

"Yes, child, if we could walk in the sky." He looked at me very closely and I could see his smiling face in the moonlight. He pulled me nearer and said: "It is almost time. Watch closely. There, can you see it?" I felt his arm tighten around me and I saw a tiny speck of light begin to twinkle just by the star of Petronicus.

"And that star will be called Petronius – the son of Petronicus."

I was silent and gazed at my own star: the star of Petronius. I gazed at it for so long that it began to dance in the water of my eyes.

Petronicus whispered: "And just when your star begins to twinkle next to mine, we will both touch the arabak tree and know that we are safe."

That night I slept content, whispering my very own name into my sleep shadows.

My fears about being separated from Petronicus returned each morning. He always seemed to know what I was thinking and found little treats for me: sweet roots and tasty berries to suck.

We stopped in a small town called Biltis where there was much sickness. Many people had bad skin on their hands and legs and we had to search far and wide for the herbs to make the potions for them. They were also mean with their coins and we had to stay in the town until their skin healed, for only then would they give Petronicus his due.

At night we slept near the town well because it was very hot and Petronicus often felt thirsty in the night. The town was quiet as the Ruler was very strict and had people beaten if they made a noise during the dark hours. On our last night in that town I whispered to Petronicus: "Will you tell me about the Mountain of the Year?"

"Yes, child, but it is sleep time now. Soon we must begin a long journey to the Mountain of the Year because there are some plants and herbs we need. But before we leave this town there is something I want you to see."

The next morning we went to the market place and found the house of the Elder Scribe of Biltis. We watched from a distance as the scribe sat in the shade instructing three boys of about my age. Each had a flat piece of wood with some fine sand on it. The scribe would call out a letter and the boys made the shape of the letter in the sand with their fingers. The scribe then looked at the letters to make sure they were correct. Towards mid afternoon, the scribe took one of the boys who had been helping him instruct the others, up to the temple door and announced: "This is Balentius, son of Balenticus. He now has the letters."

The priest appeared, took a coin from the boy and placed a black cape across the boy's shoulders. The cape was from the pelt of a boar and was the sign of the scribe. The boy's name was entered on the list of scribes in the temple.

"One day soon, Petronius, your name will be on a list of scribes," said Petronicus. He knew that I became sad every time he mentioned putting me to a scribe. He smiled and added: "And then you will go with me to the Mountain of the Year. Soon I hope, for the mountain gets steeper every time I go there and I need your young legs to help me climb."

We left the town of Biltis and commenced our journey towards the Mountain of the Year. We walked together now that I was big enough, which eased the labours of the donkey. It was during that journey that he began to tell me things about the Mountain of the Year.

"And there is snow on the top all the year round," said Petronicus. "As you climb you pass through all the seasons of the year and all the plants of summer, autumn, spring can be found."

"Is that where you get the very special plants?" I asked

"Yes, that is where the best plants and cures come from."

He told me many things during the next two days and nights. He told how the world had been born out of the crater at the top of the Mountain. I asked him how long ago that was and he said: "It was so many years ago that even the wisest men could not count them."

"More years than there are sheep on the hills?" I asked in wonderment.

"Many more years than that. It was even before the sun and the moon were born. On the top of the Mountain is a huge crater. Its sides are covered in snow and that is where the world came from."

"Out of the hole?" I asked in disbelief.

Petronicus told me all about the Temple of the Healers which was on a small hill at the base of the Mountain. He told me about the House of Humility nearby where very sick people went to be cured or to die.

"Only healers and their novices can enter the temple or climb the Mountain."

"Have I been there before?"

"Yes," said Petronicus. "Several times but you were too small to remember. I had to leave you with one of the women, waiting for her man who was a healer to return from the Mountain. I was only away three days and had collected enough herbs and plants to last a year."

I slept very little that night. Every time I sank into the arms of sleep my fears threw me back into the cold night. The thought of being alone, of being away from Petronicus who had protected me and taught me since before I could remember made me so afraid. The nearest town with a scribe was Biltis, the town we had just left, and that was now two days away and I would have to make the journey alone!

"Do all the sons of healers become scribes and novices?" I asked the next day on the trail.

"No, some are content to just lead their master's donkey and carry his medicine box. They just sit at the bottom of the Mountain and wait for him. Some are not clever enough and that is very sad for the healer if his sons cannot learn his craft."

"But what becomes of them when their master dies?"

"Some pretend to be healers but when they are found out they are driven from towns with whips."

That night we lit our fire near the mouth of a cave. It was a good spot and we could crawl into the cave if the rains came. It was a warm night but I felt cold and fearful. I looked up and saw my naming star clearly as it began to twinkle shortly after the star of Petronicus. I felt lonely for the first time in my life and put my head under the blanket. Petronicus could feel how nervous I was whenever I thought about being separated and even his reassurance about the arabak tree did not help that night.

"I do not want to be alone," I said. "I want to stay with you."

He was silent for a moment or two and then he said: "You could be like the other boys who remain at the foot of the mountain until their masters return."

"Do they remain because they are afraid? I am afraid."

"Yes, I know. But the decision is yours and yours alone."

I remained silent and hid my eyes. And then I heard him say: "I will not think any the less of you if you remain. I remember a wise man saying: 'Better the bondage you know than the freedom you don't know'." He pulled the blanket away from my face and smiled.

I was about to speak when he began to tell me a story. "Once in the land far away towards the Mountains that hold up the Sky there was a slave who had lived on his master's farm all his life."

"Truly an unfortunate man," I said, "never knowing freedom."

"Yes, truly. And there were many other things he never knew."

"How did he come to be a slave?"

"In that part of the world a child could be sold as a slave if his father was in debt and could not repay it."

"How horrible, but surely that is wrong. Petronicus, why does that happen?"

"Patience, child, I will tell you all you need to know. Some details you do not need to know."

I held my head down and looked up to him, promising to be patient as the story was told. "Each night his master put him inside a hut made of stout logs and secured the door with a log from the outside. The hut was by the gatepost so that he could act as a watchman and raise the alarm should any robbers approach the house."

"Truly an unfortunate … sorry, Petronicus, I will be patient."

"And so each night after a hard day of labour in his master's fields, he lay in the moments before sleep and looked out through a small slit between the logs. He looked over the valley to places he had never been. He looked to the other side and saw how the valley sloped upwards covered in green trees. And beyond even that he could see white snow on the mountain tops and his last thoughts before sleep took him away were of running across the valley, climbing up through the trees and feeling the soft cool snow on his feet, and just running free."

"A wonderful dream he had. But did his master ever take him across the valley?"

"No, never. He never left the farm where he had been a slave since childhood."

"The gods must have frowned upon him all his life."

"Yes, but one night …" Petronicus now pulled me closer to him and became a little excited with the story. "One night, his master had drunk too much wine and did not close the door properly. The slave opened the door and looked out."

"His chance to escape!" I exclaimed excitedly.

"Yes, perhaps. But ponder awhile before deciding what he would do. Let us pretend you are that slave."

"But I am not a slave, Petronicus. You have always told me that. Even that year when there was so little food you never sold me."

"Of course not, Petronius. I would never sell you." I smiled and waited for him to continue. "Remember, all his life he was a slave. His master provided food and water for him. He gave him cloth to put on his back and sometimes old leathers for his feet. He never had to think for himself; he just did as he was told all his life."

I remember being thoughtful for a while and then I tried to give him my answer but he stopped me before I could speak. "No, child, think on it during the night and tell me in the morning what you would do had you been that slave. Tell me what the master found when he returned to the hut the following morning."

I smiled to myself many times the next day thinking how Petronicus would be surprised and very proud when he awoke and found that I had left. I had prepared breakfast for him and moved the donkey to new grass. I had put my blanket on his feet as I was younger and my blood would keep me warm at night. I set off alone on the trail back to Biltis. I knew Petronicus had doubts about me and was prepared for the disappointment of finding me still beside him that morning.

I rested during the heat of the afternoon and found some plants and roots to eat and then I found the coins in my pouch. Petronicus had put them there during the night for me to pay the scribe and the priest.

He knew all the time what I would do! And that night I slept beside an arabak tree.

Four

It was my tenth year and the year a great star soared across the heavens and fell into the sea just where the world ended and where boats fear to go. That was the year I left the house of the scribe.

On that glorious day of freedom I just ran and ran with my black scribe's cape flowing behind me in the wind. I was free once more: free to go and find Petronicus.

"But how will you find him?" the scribe called after me as I left his house for the last time. "He could be anywhere. Why did he not tell you where he would be?"

I was glad to leave the house of the scribe where I got little food and my belly hung loose under my cloak. I had to earn my keep by tending his sheep and goats, milking his cow and any other tasks he or his wife gave me. I had mastered the letters that told of men's thoughts and I had all the prayers in my head. There were different prayers for sickness in different parts of the body. There was a prayer for stomachs, for bad heads and for broken bones and I had to learn them all. But it was a proud day when my name was entered in the scrolls of the temple. I really wish Petronicus had been there to see it.

I had felt lonely during the time away from my guardian. I often remembered how I left him that morning sleeping beneath a tree before travelling to the Mountain of the Year to collect rare plants for his cures.

I just ran freely the morning I finally left the house of the scribe. I don't know how long I ran but I felt my legs wanting to grow long after so many moons of sitting cross-legged before the scribe's chair learning the shapes of all the letters and words. I stopped when all breath had left me and threw myself into the long grass still wet with the morning dew. I looked up at the sky and wondered if Petronicus would see the same clouds I saw: that would mean he was near.

For weeks I searched for Petronicus. I was often hungry and got little employment as a scribe in the small towns. I always went to the market place in the towns to look for him. I climbed the temple steps or sat by the town well where Petronicus always set up our stall but there was no sign of him. Often I slept by the town gate in the hope of seeing him approaching along the trail or leaving the town, but each night I slept with anxiety and loneliness my only companions.

I learned how to speak to strangers and ask for work, but only occasionally did anybody employ me. "Too young," they would say. "Go back to your master, boy."

Some days I earned a little food or a coin scratching prayers on the doorposts of people's houses. The prayers asked the gods to look kindly upon the people and keep their thoughts pure. People would tell me their fears and which gods they thought disliked them. On other days I earned food by writing the names of dead people on their shrouds in cow's blood. Their relatives wanted the names of the dead on them before doing whatever their beliefs required them to do with the bodies.

And then one night I lay down by a huge arabak tree. I waited until the star of Petronicus appeared and then when my own star began to twinkle I touched the arabak tree and thought about Petronicus. I made pictures of him in my mind and pretended he was with me. I lay down and fell asleep immediately and dreamed we were back together again.

In my dream I was sitting by a stream cleaning our bowls after our evening meal. It was a good summer and food was plentiful. Petronicus had taught me much that year; in particular how to gouge out the small stones that often lodged in the donkey's hoofs.

'If the donkey becomes lame,' Petronicus said, 'we will have to carry the box and things ourselves – until we can earn enough to buy another donkey.'

'Do donkeys cost many coins?' I asked.

'Oh yes, more coins than we earn in a year.'

I awoke suddenly and reached out to see if Petronicus was lying beside me as he always did. My hand touched a cold rock and I realised that I was still alone. But there was another thought just behind my head. A horrible thought that had been troubling me for a long time: why didn't Petronicus tell me where he would be?

I looked up at the night sky and saw my own naming star just above the star of Petronicus twinkling brightly and I remember asking my star: "Oh where is Petronicus? When will I find him?"

Then I remembered a tale Petronicus had told me that very summer when I learned all about the donkey. We had sat with our backs against a rock looking into the dying moments of our fire and Petronicus told me of the Trail of High Regard.

I asked: 'Where is the Trail of High Regard and where does it go?'

'It is anywhere and leads everywhere,' he answered.

'I don't understand, Petronicus. What trail is anywhere and leads everywhere?'

'Patience, child, and I will tell you all you need to know.'

I promised to be patient.

'Wicked people,' he said, 'leave only unhappiness wherever they go. They are like people walking along the trail dragging their blanket behind them.'

'To rub away their footprints?' I asked.

'Yes, that's right, child, wicked people leave no tracks.'

'That is because they are afraid of being followed,' I said. Petronicus always liked me to find explanations for myself. That was the clever way he taught me.

'That is a correct thought, child. But good men leave happiness behind them and everyone is sorry to see them go and people remember which way they went.'

I smiled at the stars and thanked them. Now I knew how to find Petronicus.

I visited many small towns on the trails, sometimes earning food or coins with small tasks of writing and reading, but at other times I lived off the country as Petronicus had taught me. I stood at crossroads and wore my scribe's cape in the hope of earning something, however little. I met other travellers on the way and talked with them but always I asked about Petronicus.

In each town I went into the market place and the temple and listened to people talking. They talked about all manner of things. I always listened carefully when they talked about their health but mostly it was about how many coins were needed to buy a sack of corn. Often they mentioned healers who had passed that way – I listened for the name of my guardian.

One day, in a very small village where two trails crossed, I overheard an old woman whose skin had been covered in sores. She was telling her sister about a healer who had given her a potion and a prayer and she was cured within a few days. I was excited when I heard her tell her sister that the healer had left for the hill town of Klynos. It was a long way off and would take me nearly a whole moon.

I travelled swiftly carrying only my eating bowl, the piece of rabbit bone I used as a stylus and two small stones that I used to grind down plants to make ink. I took what food I could from the bushes and trees and slept very little at night. And then one day, a day I will never forget, I saw in the distance the familiar figure of an old man leading a donkey.

I ran as fast as I could, calling out his name. He was bent forward and held a long staff in his hand. The donkey had our medicine box strapped to his back and in my excitement I nearly dropped my few belongings.

"Petronicus … Petronicus!" I shouted.

I was only a few paces from him when he turned and looked at me:

"Patience, child, I hear you!"

I ran to him and he swept me up in his robe – we were together again!

That night we had our first meal together for such a long time. We sat by the fire with a blanket around our shoulders and I asked Petronicus the one thing that had troubled me for weeks: "Why didn't you tell me where I could find you?"

He just smiled and said: "I knew you would find me sooner or later."

"But how did you know?" I asked impatiently.

"Well," he said, "tomorrow you must help me take some small stones from the donkey's hoof."

"You knew I would remember the story."

He smiled and said: "Now tell me, child, what did you learn on your travels?"

The days before the moon grew big again were the happiest of my life. Petronicus began to teach me the ways of the herbs and plants. He told me how to thank them for the small pieces he took from them and how to take leaf and bark without harming the plant. I now wrote down all the prayers for the sick people and learned how to make paper scrolls from reeds. He showed me how to make good ink from plants and he even explained how to make the more simple potions. Petronicus was pleased that I could write the prayers for him.

"I think my eyes are older than my head," he used to say. "I cannot always see the letters."

And then one night I asked: "When can I come with you to the Mountain of the Year and become your novice?"

"There are times," he said, "when impatience is a good thing in a young one. But remember, being a healer means more than understanding the secret of the plants. You have to seek wisdom."

I slept that night with anxiety once again my companion. Would Petronicus put me to a wise man as he had put me to a scribe? Would I have to go and learn wisdom and be separated from Petronicus once again and so soon?

My wrestle with sleep must have disturbed Petronicus.

"What troubles you, child?" he asked. "Why doesn't sleep come to you?" I sat up and looked for his face in the darkness.

"Will I have to go away again, to leave you again?" He sat up with me and pulled our blanket around our shoulders.

"No, child. You cannot sit cross-legged on the floor and learn wisdom as you learned the letters."

I smiled into the darkness and settled down to sleep knowing that Petronicus would teach me wisdom. When he would start I didn't know.

We travelled far during those long moons and visited so many places that I cannot remember their names.

One night when the moon showed its full face with both Petronicus and me gazing into it, I asked him: "When will you teach me wisdom, Petronicus?"

He looked at me and said nothing for a while. I was about to repeat my question when he said: "Wisdom cannot be taught."

"Then how will I learn it?" I asked.

"Wisdom cannot be learned in the way you mean ... hush, child ... still your impatience."

"I am sorry Petronicus, I will be patient."

We set off next morning and headed towards the Land of the Large Stones. The summer was over and we felt the cooling breeze on our bodies. Petronicus now put his hand on my shoulder as we walked, not on my head and he said how tall I had grown in the year we had been apart.

One night we made camp after a long day. We had eaten our food and were sitting still to let the food become part of us. Petronicus pulled me close to him and we put our blankets around each other. It was a cold night and the wind was blowing from the mountains.

"Wisdom," he said at length, "cannot be taught or learned … but it can be found. Wisdom comes in its seeking."

Petronicus knew I did not understand so he did what he always did; he told me a tale: "There was once a man, a wise man who would sit on the temple steps and people would come from days around to ask his advice."

"What about?"

"About anything and everything. About things that puzzled them. Where the world came from and why the wind blows. Why some flowers grow tall and others remain small."

"Was he the wisest man in all the world? Did he know all manner of things?"

"Yes, child, he knew about all manner of things. But no, he wasn't the wisest man in all the world. There was a much wiser man living at that time. He was known as the Revered One. That is what we always call the wisest man in all the world. You have heard me speak to other healers about him often. But the man I am telling you about was also very wise and he was often to be seen in the House of Tablets in the town, that is where all the great thoughts of wise and learned men are written on clay tablets."

"Did they give him coins when he answered their questions?"

"Yes, that's how he earned his food. Now be patient as I tell you more. This wise man had two sons, one he favoured and one he did not."

"Why did he favour one and not the other?"

"Because he thought only one of them could become wise and the other could not. He told them he would send them both on a quest to find wisdom."

"Where did he send them? Was it to the Land of the Large Stones? Is that why we are going there now?"

"Hush, child, so many questions! He told them to travel across the great lake to the Land of the Whispering Rocks, then go through the Land of the Tall People and along the trail to the Far Country."

"And wisdom is in the Far Country?"

Petronicus did not answer but continued with the story. But when he did, I noticed his eyes became dulled with sadness and he looked beyond me. It was then that I realised that this was a true story.

"To each son he gave a small pouch and told them to open it when they had begun their journey. In it, he told them, was all they needed."

I remember pulling myself closer to Petronicus as I wondered what was in the pouches.

"When one son opened his pouch, he found some coins in it."

"And the other, what did he find in his pouch?" I asked.

"Stones, just small stones. The first son clasped his hands with delight and said: 'Oh, what joy, to be the favoured son'."

"It is surely wrong, Petronicus, to favour one son with coins and give the other stones."

"Why do you say that, child?"

"Because the favoured son could buy a donkey and perhaps leather for his feet and would reach the Far Country before the other and find wisdom and the other might never get there."

"Hmmm," said Petronicus, "it is sleep time now."

For days the puzzle lived in my mind. We journeyed far and Petronicus said little. I never asked him to explain more because I knew he was expecting me to answer my own questions.

And then one night as we sat together and ate our food, I looked up and saw the star of Petronicus twinkling in the night sky. He smiled at me as we waited a while before my own naming star began twinkling just by it.

"That is because it is further away, isn't it Petronicus? You once told me that."

"That is right, child. Always watch the stars and they may tell you things."

Sleep didn't come that night. It was cold and we kept the fire going as long as we had sticks and bracken. I put warm stones on the edges of his blanket to keep him warm. I lay down and looked up and began to think more deeply than I had ever done before. I thought of the journey Petronicus had made me undertake in order to find him. Those lonely wandering days.

The night blew over us and all became silent save the whistling of the wind through the grasses and the trees waving overhead. It was then that I realised why Petronicus had never told me where to find him; he wanted me to make a journey entirely alone.

I reached over and put my hand on his shoulder.

"Petronicus," I said softly. "Do you sleep?"

"No, child, not yet."

I spoke to him in a soft voice: "Petronicus, did you ever see your brother again?" I heard him turn over and saw him looking at me in the starlight.

"No," he said sadly. "We never found each other."

"Do you still keep the pouch your father gave you? Will you show it to me?" He sat up and told me to throw some leaves on the fire to make light.

"What is it you expect to see, child?"

"The stones he gave you."

His face lit up as the dry leaves sparkled in the fire. I could see him smiling proudly.

"Tell me more," he said. "How do you think we parted?"

"Your brother set off quickly to the Far Country to find wisdom and left you behind."

"How do you think I felt that day?"

"Confused, as I am, Petronicus, but joyful knowing that you were the favoured son." He pulled me close to him and said softly: "You are right, child. I have taught you well. My father knew that I would seek wisdom all my life whilst my brother thought he could travel swiftly and find it easily in one place."

"And that is why you made me journey all alone to find you. That is why you did not give me coins to make my journey easier. You only gave me enough to pay the scribe and the temple priest."

"Yes, child. And soon we start another journey." He turned and smiled in the firelight. "Tomorrow we set off and follow the evening sun towards the Mountain of the Year. I am going to present you to the priests of the temple as my novice."

That night I slept content.

Five

It was the year the world rumbled beneath our feet and, it was said, somewhere a huge hole opened like a mouth waiting to be fed. Petronicus was disturbed and said there was evil in the air. Shortly afterwards, a great plague of insects flew out of the Inner Lands and settled on the crops near the coast. There was much sickness that year and the priests said that the insects came out of the world's mouth to bring ruin to everyone.

I was sad because our journey to the Mountain of the Year was interrupted. We kept away from the towns and villages to avoid the sickness but we earned our living treating people we found on the trail. We would make camp at a crossroads and set up our medicine box and wait for travellers and traders to come along. Many had bad feet, which had blistered and become poisoned. Fevers from insect bites were very common and Petronicus and I earned our bread and meat quite easily. We also earned several good coins.

"They run from one bad place to another bad place," said Petronicus. "They should stay near their fields and plant next year's crop."

When the sickness faded away we travelled more rapidly. I had never known such a feeling of anticipation before in my life and as our journey brought us nearer to the Mountain of the Year my excitement became so great that I ran ahead jumping and cartwheeling in front of the donkey. Petronicus laughed and shared my joy.

When we arrived, there were other healers who greeted Petronicus as an old friend. They embraced each other and spoke rapidly about their travels since last they met. I was no longer expected just to stand behind Petronicus now that I was a scribe; I was allowed to sit with them and listen to their conversation. My one disappointment was that the Revered One was not at the Mountain. Petronicus explained that the Revered One was very old and travelled very little. Often, nobody knew where he was.

The day after our arrival we climbed the steps to the Temple of the Healers. It was the biggest temple I had ever seen and many trees and stones had been used in its building. Petronicus stood with his hand on my shoulder until the priests had assembled.

"This is the child I have taken as my son," he shouted. "He is known as Petronius, the son of Petronicus." The priests nodded their heads and the temple scribe wrote my name on the reeds. "He is my novice and will carry my knowledge when I return to the ground."

Petronicus gave the priest a coin and in return I received a novice's hood, which Petronicus placed on my head. I was to wear it proudly for many years. I now had two symbols of my new status: the cape of the scribe and the hood of a novice healer. There was no feasting or other ceremony but I was allowed to enter the temple unaccompanied at any time for the rest of my life.

We descended the steps and made ourselves comfortable in a glade amongst the trees.

"When will we climb the mountain Petronicus?" I asked. "Will it be soon?"

"No, not for a while yet. The snows are too low and you must enter the House of Humility first."

"But why is that? Surely I must learn all about the flowers and herbs."

"Patience, child. Young things want to do everything at once." I hung my head low and promised to be patient. Petronicus explained further: "But I am pleased you want to learn. And yes, you must learn about the flowers and herbs. But more importantly, a healer must know humility."

"Why is that, Petronicus, why must healers be humble?"

"Because they can give life and also take it away."

"I understand," I said.

"What do you understand?"

"Healers could become arrogant."

"Yes." He smiled at me and added: "You learned many new words with the scribe. But always remember, the coins you ask for must be no more than the sick person can pay. From a poor man you ask little, from a rich man you ask more. Do you understand, Petronius?"

"Yes," I said and smiled inwardly; Petronicus was addressing me by my given name more now and not just calling me *child*.

The House of Humility was made of many trees and a lot of straw had been used to make the roof. But it was a sad place; it was where people went to die.

"Sickness and death humble the greatest men," Petronicus said, "and the most courageous hunters."

Each day I had to work tending the sick and listening to the instructions of the presiding healer who sat on a large stone seat at the end of the House. Sometimes Petronicus sat on the large seat and all the novices and healers went to ask his advice. One day I was cleaning out the pus from a man's wound when Petronicus came and stood behind me.

He handed me a small blade and said: "Make a small cut on the palm of your hand and let a few drops of your blood drip into his wound."

I did as I was bid and then wrapped leaves around my cut. I knew it would heal up very quickly because I was young.

That night as Petronicus and I covered ourselves in our blankets around the large communal fire I asked: "Why did I give my blood to the sick man?"

"Because your blood is young and strong and sometimes your strength can enter his body."

"There is so much I must learn."

"Yes, there is and I am old and must teach you before I return to the ground. You must study; you must learn, and learn quickly or all my knowledge will be lost. And once you have learned you must practise constantly or your skill will fade away. Do you understand, Petronius?"

I did not answer but without knowing it I must have looked up towards the Mountain of the Year. I yearned to climb it with Petronicus. He understood my impatience and did what he always did; he told me a story:

"Once there lived a man whose house was by a river. Many times he tried to catch the fish but the river flowed too swiftly."

"Why didn't he use a pointed stick or make a net by weaving goat hairs ... the way we saw them do in the coastal towns?"

"Yes, he could have done that, but he had a better idea."

"He was a wise man then?"

"Yes, child, but be patient. I will tell you all." I nodded and held my eyes to the ground whilst he spoke further. "He built a weir to make a large pond where the fish could breed and make more fish."

"Truly, a wise man ... sorry, Petronicus, I will be patient."

He smiled and continued: "One day he watched a wolf catching fish in his pond. The wolf stood very still in the water until a fish swam nearby. As quick as a flash of lightning the wolf whisked the fish from the water onto the bank."

"Then he should study the wolf and learn from it."

"Correct, child, that is what he did. It took him a long time to learn the skill of the wolf and then he found he could catch fish himself."

"It is a wise man who learns from the animals," I said.

"Truly, it is a wise man who learns from everything. But he found that if he did not fish every day the skill began to leave him."

"He had to practise then?"

"Yes. But one day he drove his sheep up into the high pasture and when he returned he saw another man, a stranger, standing in his pond fishing."

"But the pond did not belong to him, he had not helped to build it."

"That is correct; the man was a thief. But he had caught only a small fish – he had not yet learned the skill. Maybe the thief came in the night to practise." I knew what Petronicus would say next. "What do you think the man should do?" Petronicus always did that: told me a story and made me think of how it would end. That was the clever way he taught me.

We settled down for the night around the communal fire below the temple. There were about twenty of us sitting around the large fire and some had their women with them. Petronicus told me that his wife had died many years ago. The healers were discussing why the wind blew from different directions. Novices were not allowed to take part in these wise discussions but we were allowed to sit and listen.

The days passed contentedly. I watched each morning as spring progressed to see if the snows had climbed up beyond the trees on the lower slopes. Each morning I would tell Petronicus. He always smiled at my impatience and then took me back into the House of Humility.

"Now, we will attend to our duties," he said. "Our enemy is pain and suffering so look away from the mountain and assist me here."

On the floor lay a man who had been bitten by a snake. His arm was very painful and the sickness was spreading through his body. I must have shown some guilt about my impatience and Petronicus smiled and said: "Young things want to walk so fast. But remember, a man who walks fast and looks only to the horizon does not see as much as he who walks slowly and looks towards the ground. There is often just as much to see on the ground as there is on the horizon."

I just smiled and knelt down by the sick man.

"He needs to have his mouth emptied of vomit; there is danger of him choking on it. But be careful. He is old but still has some teeth."

"You have teeth Petronicus and you are old."

"Yes," he said, "the gods have smiled on me."

"May they continue to do so, Petronicus."

"Thank you, Petronius. Shall we work now?"

We worked happily together and I scooped out the vomit and helped the old man to breathe more easily.

"Will we cure him?"

Petronicus shook his head and whispered: "No, we will only ease his pain. Soon he will be dead and we will leave him outside the House for his people to come for him and do what their beliefs tell them."

"Why do people have different beliefs? Do wise men tell them what to believe?"

"Wise men would never do that. Not if they were truly wise. That we leave to the priests." He paused for a moment and then added: "Wisdom and beliefs are different things."

It is amazing that I still remember things he told me after all these years. But that is what Petronicus did: plant thoughts in my mind that grew into understandings later. But all this was before the great cataclysm when our world nearly ended.

"Do people always believe what they are told?" I asked

"Sadly, yes." He looked at me benevolently knowing that I did not understand. "They find it easier to believe what everybody else believes; many feet make a smooth path."

"Like on the trail?" He smiled and looked away from me. We worked quietly together until the afternoon when the women brought food for the healers and the sick. Petronicus did not say very much to me except to teach me and explain what he was doing.

I sensed there was something troubling him but it was to be years before I discovered what it was.

"How high are the snows this morning?" he asked several days later. We had eaten our bread and drunk the goats' milk the women brought us.

I replied with enthusiasm: "Way beyond the tree line."

"Hmmm." He smiled and looked at me in his old familiar way. "Today we begin our preparations to climb the mountain." He put his hand on my shoulder and added: "It is time you learned the secret of the plants."

The donkey was laden with food, woollen blankets and furs. We climbed through the trees and emerged into a much colder region. We stopped frequently and knelt down to examine small plants and shrubs.

"Summer is shorter here and winter longer. Always remember, child, everything comes from the ground and everything returns to the ground. Now see here." He pointed to the ground where there was some dung from a boar and showed me how the plants grew more vigorously around it. "The boar ate the grass which gave the animal strength and what was not digested returned to the ground."

"To make more plants grow? Why do plants grow? Why does anything grow?" He smiled but did not answer. He showed me how to take just one leaf from each stem. "Take just what you need, never more, and then the plants will replace those leaves."

There were so many different plants and so many illnesses I had to remember that when we lay down to sleep that night amongst some rocks I began to worry that I would never master it all. Petronicus was tired and the donkey lay down close to us and kept the cold wind from us.

"What troubles you, child?"

"So much to learn," I said.

"What about the man who made the fish pond. Have you thought about that?"

I had to confess, I hadn't thought much about it with the excitement of climbing the mountain.

I said quickly: "He could fight him, the thief I mean."

Petronicus had that disapproving look on his face and simply said: "And risk injury? An injured man starves."

I was silent for a while as I tried to picture myself in the story. "Perhaps if he offered to trade fish for something the other man had?"

"Yes, he could do that."

Encouraged I added: "Each could practise a different skill. The other man could catch rabbits and bring birds from the sky with stones, the way the hunters we saw near the town of Klinbil do ... and then they could trade."

"Hmmm," said Petronicus. "You would trust a thief?" I smiled. This was how he taught me, with questions and answers.

Another day of steady climbing brought us to the snow line and Petronicus indicated that we should make a more permanent camp, as we would be here for several days.

"Higher up it is winter nearly all year round. We have climbed through spring, summer and autumn and now we are following winter as it climbs up the mountain and reveals yet another spring. It is here that we collect the rarest and most potent plants. Gather some rocks and long grasses to make a shelter. It will be very cold at night."

Petronicus became silent and did not even question me about the story. The next day he was up before me which was unusual and I saw him kneeling down a short distance away. I prepared our morning meal and melted some snow in a pot by the fire to make hot water to drink.

I took his food and water over to him and stood by him.

"Aren't they beautiful, these plants of early spring? Look how winter climbs up the mountain and leaves spring in its path," said

Petronicus. His manner was strange that morning. He was both sad and joyful and I watched him running his hands and fingers gently through the plants. I watched him silently. I had never seen him like this. He would hold a petal between his fingers and gaze at it lovingly. I knew that he did not want to talk to me just then.

After a short while he stopped and ate the food I had prepared. He beckoned that I should kneel beside him and then he spoke to the flowers and plants: "And this is Petronius who will take our name when I return to the ground. He will carry our knowledge and wisdom all his life."

And then he said to me: "From each plant take just a little and take care not to damage any other part of the plant. We call these The Gatherings; put them in here and keep them safe." He handed me a small pouch made from goatskin. "When we take a leaf we are taking part of the plant's strength. We must leave enough for it to live and prosper."

"And will you tell me what each plant is for?" I asked.

"Yes, in good time."

It was then that I noticed another healer some distance away doing exactly the same. He was kneeling gently by a small mound with his novice by his side. And then I realised!

"Petronicus, is this your master?" I asked. "Is your master buried here?"

"Yes," he said and leaned back on his haunches and looked at me sadly. "All his wisdom and all his knowledge is now in the plants. That is why the plants cure people's ills. From here the birds and insects spread his goodness all over the earth."

"I don't understand," I said inadequately.

"Everything comes from the ground. Even the light at the end of the day, even that returns to the ground and then rises again with the sun. We come from the ground because our food comes from the ground."

"Do you mean that when we die our wisdom grows again in the plants?"

"Yes," he said smiling joyfully. "All that is good in us returns up through the ground and out once again into the light. And all that is bad goes down into the dark caverns beneath the world. But sadly, it can seep up again to infect evil men."

"Do these plants have their roots in your master's body?"

"Yes, they send their roots down into the earth and mingle with him. He was a good man, a wise man and he gave me his name. You see, child, it is wisdom and thought that makes the world live – without it the world would die."

"Will you give me your name when you return to the ground?"

"Yes, child, one day you will call yourself Petronicus just like me and my master before me." He smiled warmly and put his hand on my shoulder. "And one day this will be your special place. The plants that grow where Petronicus lies are the strongest and are used to cure the very sick. Only healers are allowed to climb the Mountain of the Year and only you will be allowed to take plants from this grave."

I didn't speak for a while as I found it difficult to understand the enormity of what he had told me. Now I knew the secret of the plants and knew what made the world live!

We stayed in that place for several more days collecting petals, leaves and bark scratchings. Petronicus taught me all about the mosses and how to scrape tiny patches off the rocks.

When we began our preparations to return to the temple I felt very proud but I knew that Petronicus was watching me. On the morning we left he said: "There was once a healer who became so arrogant that nobody would consult him. He earned so few coins he had to beg in the streets. He became arrogant because he failed to distinguish between good fortune and achievement. Remember, it is our good fortune to have been taught. We did not achieve that ourselves."

On the first day of our descent we saw a young novice climbing up towards us. He was dragging a dead body wrapped in furs. It was the body of his master. Petronicus and I helped him lift the body over some difficult rocks and then asked the name of the man. The novice told him and Petronicus said: "An old friend. We travelled many trails together years ago. You are the healer now and will take his name. That will be entered on the scrolls in the temple."

We continued our journey down and that night we found shelter between some bushes. Our fire burned brightly and I felt content. Petronicus turned to me and said: "My place, Petronius, must be beside my master." I was silent. Life without Petronicus could not be imagined.

"And mine beside you," I said. He smiled but it was a sad smile and his eyes seemed far away so I tried to please him. "If I was the man who had built the pond I would offer to *give* the thief one fish every day."

"You would give to a thief? Why do that?"

"And then he would become idle and all his skill at fishing and hunting would leave him. And then I would stop giving him fish and he wouldn't be able to catch any himself. He would begin to starve and have to go and beg in the streets and leave me in peace. If you don't practise your skill every day you will lose it … you told me that."

Petronicus smiled but said nothing. I never knew if my answer was correct. Only many years later did I realise that wisdom lay not in finding answers but in finding the right questions to ask.

But I think I really pleased him later that night when I said just before sleep found us: "I would like to work in the House of Humility for some moons and then join you on the trail in the autumn when the leaves return to the ground."

Six

I was in my fifteenth year and thought of myself as a man full-grown but Petronicus did not say anything about it. However, looking back on it now my childhood had to end abruptly because that was the year the Great Cataclysm began.

Petronicus and I had journeyed to the Mountains that hold up the Sky, which was where the world ended. This was the longest journey we had undertaken together but I was older and stronger now and Petronicus was able to ride the donkey most of the time.

"One day soon," Petronicus told me, "we will have sufficient coins to buy another donkey and then we can both ride." I was excited because I knew only the greatest healers had two donkeys.

We had been away from the towns near the coast for over a year and had no notion of the great event that was taking place. I remember asking as we journeyed back: "How big is the world, Petronicus?"

"Well," he said, "nobody really knows. There is sea on three sides and it would take several moons to walk from the night side of the world to the morning side. And from furthest sea where our present journey started to the Mountains that hold up the Sky has taken us a year but we have been treating and healing the sick. I don't know how long it would take to walk straight there, but who would want to do that anyway?"

"So after this journey we will have walked right across the world?" Petronicus just smiled at me. I think he enjoyed my excitement as I saw things for the first time. Petronicus had tramped the world for many years. "But what is beyond the Mountains that hold up the Sky?" I asked.

Petronicus smiled again and said: "Nothing, child. That is where the world begins and ends. No man could ever go there."

One day we stopped at a crossroads and Petronicus dismounted to examine the small stones that told of the healers who had passed that way recently. It was the custom for scribes and healers to leave small messages for each other and avoid competing in a particular town. I had learned to read the stones and knew that the sign of Petronicus was five stones arranged in a unique pattern that only he was allowed to use.

"Ah, see here," said Petronicus. "Melonicus passed this way and look there – what does that sign tell us?"

"It tells of danger, I think."

"You are correct, child. But the nature of the danger is not clear." Petronicus stood up and rubbed his head. "I don't know, but the signs say there is much trouble ahead of us."

"Has Melonicus come away because of the danger? Will we take the other road away from the danger?"

"Patience, child, there is much to think about." He was silent for a while and then said: "The other road leads to Bedosa and there are too many unhappy memories for us there."

I did not say anything. Bedosa was where I was born and where Petronicus had rescued me as an infant from being exposed on the city wall to die when my father had been hanged as a thief. I waited for my master to make the decisions. "We shall continue our journey to the coast. If there is danger there the people might need our skills. Melonicus might also need our help. We will avoid Bedosa as we always have. Make our sign with five stones so other healers will know we have passed this way."

For most of that day we journeyed with great apprehension. We saw very few people and those we did see avoided us. Most of the houses had animal skins fastened across the doors and some had their doors boarded up with logs.

"Petronicus!" I said as we approached a small settlement. "Is it the Great Sickness? You have often told me about the Great

Sickness." There were about six houses but no people could be seen.

"No, I think not," said Petronicus. "There is something most strange here."

We continued our journey towards the coast hoping to arrive before nightfall. We saw more signs in the stones as we approached. Each warned of danger and said *Keep Away*.

And just as the sun reached the top of the sky we saw a youngish man running towards us. He wore the black cape of the scribe and the hood of the novice. He approached us and then stopped a short distance from us and looked at us with fear. And then he shouted: "Petronicus? Is that you Petronicus?"

"Yes it is I. But what troubles you?" He turned to me and whispered: "This is Melonius, the novice. His master is Melonicus." The youth approached cautiously. Petronicus demanded: "Where is your master? Where is Melonicus?"

Melonius threw himself at our feet. He took hold of Petronicus's cloak and held it close to him. He had much fear on his face but slowly he began to tell us his story.

He told us that Melonicus was alarmed and much troubled by what they had found on the coast and had gone to Bedosa to find out what was happening. Melonicus said that the new Ruler was a wicked man and all the priests were supporting him.

"The priests!" exclaimed Petronicus in alarm and that was the first inkling I had of the Great Cataclysm. "The priests!" repeated my master.

I also realised in that moment fraught with anxiety that Petronicus had not told me much about the priests. I knew they looked after the temples and performed the ceremonies. The prayers that healers gave to the sick were usually written by the priests and some priests tried to treat the sick just with prayers but Petronicus was against that. Petronicus always said that sick people needed both medicines and prayers. Petronicus always seemed to know more about the gods than the priests. But to continue the story Melonius told us that day …

Melonicus and his novice had arrived as the moon waned and they found a great commotion on the coast. The people had been running about in great fear. They were neglecting their animals and children. They were not tending their crops. And there were men armed with long blades. The blades were longer than anyone had ever seen … and the Ruler … Melonius stopped speaking at that point and just looked up at Petronicus who reached down and tried to raise him to his feet. But Melonius went limp and he was shaking from head to toe. Petronicus and I crouched down beside him and tried to comfort him. He kept looking back down the trail as if in great fear of pursuit.

After a short while Petronicus said: "Let us get off the trail, Melonius." He pointed to the trees a little way up the hill. "Let us go there and no one will see us. And then you can tell us more."

We both supported Melonius as he rose to his feet. He cast frequent glances back along the trail but we managed to coax him to walk and soon we reached the shelter of the trees.

We sat down amongst the undergrowth and Petronicus stroked the novice's head, the way he often did to me when I was frightened or very tired.

"Now then, Melonius," said Petronicus in a soft reassuring voice, "tell us all you know. Tell us what has happened."

Melonius looked up at Petronicus and stared at him for several moments and then he said in a fearful voice: "The gods have come!"

Many clouds passed overhead as Petronicus coaxed the story from Melonius, who told us that a great boat bigger than any boat ever seen before had been washed ashore. A merchant travelling to Bedosa found it and ran as quickly as he could, abandoning his donkeys, to bring the priests. The Ruler came as well and they waded out into the water to secure the boat. Then they knelt down by the boat and the priests said prayers. The gods were asleep in the boat and then they were carried to Bedosa.

"Truly, friend Melonius," said Petronicus, "you have seen many strange things. But tell me, did you and Melonicus actually see the gods?"

"No," said Melonius. "They had been taken away when we arrived. My master went off to Bedosa to see what happened."

Melonius was a little calmer now that Petronicus and I were with him. Petronicus questioned him further: "Do you know what the gods looked like? Have you met people on the coast who saw them?"

"Yes, and they had wondrous tales to tell. They say the gods were very tall and their hair was very long and reached behind them down to their hips."

"Were they bigger, do you think, than the Tall People whose lands you and Melonicus must have passed through many times?" asked Petronicus.

"Yes," said Melonius. "They wore robes of fine cloth and no animal skins on their bodies. They had helmets made of eagle feathers on their heads."

"Wondrous," I said and was told to keep quiet.

"And each had a huge blade as long as a man's arm!" said Melonius.

"And they were in a sleep, you say?"

"Yes and Melonicus told me that gods can sleep for a hundred moons and great calamities come and sickness comes and the crops fail and ..."

"Calm yourself," said Petronicus. He held Melonius's hand firmly and looked kindly into his eyes. "But tell me, Melonius, why didn't you go to Bedosa with your master?"

"I wanted to go with him ... I wanted to stay with him ... but he told me to go in search of the Revered One and tell him what had happened."

"Ah, I see," said Petronicus. "That was wise. Melonicus is wise; the Revered One must be told."

Petronicus gave the youth a coin to buy food on his journey. Melonius embraced each of us and set off down the trail on his quest to find the Revered One.

"Petronicus," I said.

"Yes, child, what is it?"

"Why is the Ruler of Bedosa wicked and why are the priests supporting him? I do not understand."

"Truly there is much neither you nor I understand. It is true that most Rulers are wicked but not all. In some towns the Ruler is simply a man the people appoint to govern them and they obey him. But," said Petronicus sadly, "they often appoint the wrong man."

"Why is that, Petronicus?"

"A man who appeals to the goodness in people, to their hopes and better nature is soon overthrown because the people quickly become disappointed and disillusioned. But one who appeals to their selfishness and fears is supported and flourishes. That is how it has always been in Bedosa." I nodded but Petronicus seemed to know I did not fully understand. "What else troubles you, child?" he asked.

"If the gods sleep, will great calamities come to the world as Melonius said? I do not understand all these things."

"There is much we do not understand. So what must we do, child?"

I was silent and fearful and then I said: "We must go to the coast and see for ourselves."

Petronicus smiled at me, the way he always did when he felt proud of me.

Seven

Petronicus was solemn as we started on our journey to the coast. We turned and watched Melonius disappear along the trail. He never looked back.

"Do you think he will find the Revered One, Petronicus?" I asked.

"I hope he does; we need all our wise men just now."

"I have never seen the Revered One, have I Petronicus?"

Petronicus looked down from the donkey at me and said: "Yes once, when we were travelling beyond the Whispering Rocks; we met him on the trail."

"I do not remember."

"No," said Petronicus smiling down at me. "You were so small I used to carry you in the folds of my blanket. But I remember he put his hands on your tiny head and said your head was a good shape and that you would live by your head and not your muscles. Always remember that, child."

We did not speak again for a while. I held the donkey's rope and led the way but I felt fearful and Petronicus often reached down and put his hand on my shoulder.

And then as we approached the coast we saw a large crowd of people standing near a very strange boat. It was a wondrous thing and the biggest boat I had ever seen in my whole life. I had seen boats before when we visited the coastal towns and I had watched the fishermen as they rowed out and cast their nets. They knew of course, as everyone knew that if they ventured too far out they would be burned alive in the great fires where the sun rested at night beyond the seas.

As we approached, a man recognised Petronicus and shouted to him: "Do not tarry here, Petronicus. Healers are no longer welcome near Bedosa. The priests have banished them."

We pushed our way through the crowd and then I just stood and gazed at the huge boat. The sight of it left me completely without words. It was like a sea monster that had been washed up on the shore. We saw the long oars and a strange large cloth attached to an upright pole in the centre. The boat was so big that a man could walk twenty paces from the front to the back of it. The gods themselves were indeed gone, as Melonius had told us, but Petronicus questioned the people about them. They told him that the gods were sleeping by their oars and that the gods had clothes of fine cloth and did not wear any furs of animals anywhere on their bodies. They told us about the hats of eagle feathers worn by the gods and of the long hair that came down to their hips. The gods were very broad across their chests and were even bigger than the Tall People to whose land Petronicus and I had travelled often. Several told of the long blades each god carried by his side, blades so big that one blow could kill three men.

"But where are these gods?" asked Petronicus. "I see nothing in the boat."

"They have been taken to Bedosa," said a man in the crowd. "The gods were taken at night because they were sleeping. We were not allowed to see them. The priests will build a new temple for them."

"Aye," said another, "and when the gods wake they will be pleased and send us good animals to hunt and fine crops to grow." Most of the people nodded their agreement but others seemed confused and afraid.

Petronicus was about to question the people further when there was a sudden commotion. Armed men were approaching. I saw the long knives they carried. The sun glinted on the blades and the men swung them about with great menace. They were different from the small iron blades I had seen. The men were from Bedosa and had two priests with them.

"You are not welcome here, Petronicus," said one of the priests. "Be away and take your novice with you. The former times are gone. You false healers have no place here any more."

Petronicus looked away from them and did not answer. Some of the people began to surround Petronicus and me and I saw one or two men picking up stones ready to throw at us. The priests were smiling in a very satisfied and cruel manner and I began to feel afraid. An elderly man poked his face close to Petronicus and said: "Go away, healer, we have no need of you. The priests will cure our ills. They have brought the gods to us."

Petronicus stepped back and held me close to him. He spoke to the old man: "You have boils on your face. It is not prayers you need but the powder from a leaf of the bindan tree."

The old man had a look of hatred on his face. He spat at Petronicus and the crowd began to shout insults at us. The priests looked on smiling.

Petronicus put his arm around my shoulders and whispered: "Come, child, let's be gone. Quickly now."

We hurried away and several people threw stones at us. One hit the donkey on the rump and another narrowly missed Petronicus. We were out of breath when we stopped on the side of a hill and looked back.

"Why do the people hate us, Petronicus?" I asked in desperation.

"They are doing it to impress the priests, child. I don't think they really hate us. Now, child, I need your young eyes; mine do not see far now that I am old. Look closely and tell me all you can see. I will remember all you say for I have a wise head and you have young eyes. Tell me about the long blades and everything they take from the boat."

I tried to do what Petronicus wanted but words ran about in my head like demented rabbits. My master held me close to him and all I wanted to do was hide my face in his robe.

"Petronicus, what is happening? Let us get away from here. We must run for the trees and hide ourselves." Petronicus stroked my head to comfort me and turned my head back towards the people and the boat of the gods.

"Yes, child, I know of your fears and I share them. But I need your young eyes now. Look, child, and tell me all you see." I felt a little more comforted holding onto Petronicus. He continued to stroke my head as I began to describe all I could see. "Everything, child. Tell me everything."

I watched and saw the blade men rounding up the people and making them tie ropes to the beached boat. The blade men were pushing and kicking the people to make them work harder. The priests looked on. The people were taking everything out of the boat in order to lighten it. All sorts of strange things came from the boat and were loaded into large leather bags slung onto donkeys.

Petronicus did not interrupt me but smiled encouragement as I tried to describe everything I saw: "I see the long blades. They are fearful weapons; only gods could make them," I said.

"Truly," said Petronicus. "They are wondrous things. Iron is made only by the most skilled of men and even they can make very little of it."

"Do the gods make coins? Maybe the gods make much more and are very rich."

Petronicus did not answer my question, which was unusual. He continued to look towards the boat whilst stroking his beard with one hand and holding me tightly with the other. He then moved me gently away from him and turned me fully round facing towards the boat. He put his hands on my shoulders and said: "How many blades can you see? How many armed men? Use your eyes again, child, and tell me everything you see. Do you hear me? What is happening now?"

I described everything I saw. I told him about the blades and the armed men. I told him about the priests and how they were ill-treating the people. I was shivering with excitement and fear. Petronicus held me close to him. I looked up and he was smiling down at me as he spoke. "Well done, child!"

I heard shouting from the boat so I looked back towards it. "The people are trying to pull the boat away! They are trying to pull it along the shore. I can see a large town in the far distance."

"Bedosa!" said Petronicus in anger. "What are they doing now?"

"They are bringing more donkeys to help. What are they doing, Petronicus?"

Petronicus spoke sadly, but I detected a note of anger in his voice.

"They are using the people as slaves to haul the boat away," he replied. "But the people are free people! Oh, there is such wickedness here."

"They are stealing the boat of the gods?" I asked in astonishment.

Petronicus nodded. He was both afraid and angry at all we had seen. He put his arm around me and said: "Now, child. You have seen all I need to know. Let us be away from here."

We moved further inland until the shouts of the people died away. We kept walking until we were safely in the forest.

Petronicus who had been deep in thought turned to me and said: "Now listen, Petronius, we must move quickly. I have a task for you which is dangerous and distasteful." I realised the importance of the task he was giving me because he addressed me as Petronius, which was my given name. Petronicus added: "But only you can do it. I must leave quickly."

"But Petronicus!" I said anxiously. "I don't understand. What's happening to the world? I mean, is it true, is it true what the people are saying about the gods coming?"

"Truth does not matter in this case," he said. "It's what people believe that matters."

We parted just as the sun was going to rest in the great fires beyond the seas. I travelled in the twilight and only slept a little during the dark hours. It was cold and I felt very alone and full of fear. I curled up for a while just before dawn by an arabak tree and that made me feel close to Petronicus.

As the sun rose on the far side of the world, I continued my journey towards the town of Bedosa. I kept repeating to myself the last words Petronicus had said to me as we parted: *'Be brave, Petronius, and use your eyes and ears. And if in danger be swift of foot and return to me. I will leave signs for you in the stones at all the crossroads and you will know where to find me.'*

Petronicus had told me not to approach Bedosa from the shore but to go across the hills and find the back trail and to enter the town from the rear. This would take most of a day but it would be safer. I often tried to imagine what the town of Bedosa would look like. Petronicus seldom mentioned it, which made me think it was a bad place. If the people of Bedosa supported a wicked Ruler then they themselves must be wicked. I never thought about my father being hanged as a thief, but I sometimes thought of myself as an infant left exposed on the city wall to die. In my fondest dreams I imagined Petronicus coming for me, bundling me up in his cloak and taking me with him on his journeys.

I spent another night alone watching Bedosa from some trees. I didn't sleep at all and I felt danger all around me. The next day I approached the back gateway into Bedosa. I hid my scribe's black cape and hood under my blanket so that I couldn't be identified as a healer's novice.

There were guards on the back gate who were stopping people from entering to demand coins from them. I had only two small coins that Petronicus had given me, which I would need to buy food. I began to pick my way through the bushes and around the town towards the main gate. And there I saw more people than I had ever seen in my whole life. I learned later that I got to the main gate, which is opposite the sea, just after the great boat of the gods had been hauled into the town. Many people were still on their knees with their heads bowed. That was how they showed respect to the Ruler in Bedosa. They must have knelt like that as the boat was brought in. There was also a subdued silence amongst the people having just witnessed one of the greatest events the world had ever known.

I remained outside the main gate for most of the morning. Traders set up some stalls around the gate so I bought the largest loaf of bread I could get for one of my small coins. I felt I should enter the town but I have to admit that I was afraid. After all, this was the town where my father had been hanged as a thief. Occasionally one or two men with sharpened sticks would come out and take coins off the traders and I actually saw one of them strike a merchant.

I did not admit it to myself at first but I returned to my hiding place for the night near the back gate of the town with some shame. '*Use your eyes and ears,*' Petronicus had said but I found the town of Bedosa too intimidating that day. I returned to the cover of the trees and curled up for the night with my loaf of bread and my blanket under the bushes.

The next morning I felt refreshed and more courageous. '*Dishonest men,*' Petronicus always used to say, '*give themselves away by being furtive and hiding their faces.*' I resolved that I would walk into the town that morning with my head high as if I had nothing to fear. I managed to slip in through the main gate without any one noticing me.

The centre of the town was crowded with the many stalls of the merchants and traders. I searched in vain for the stall of a healer who might know the whereabouts of Melonicus.

I asked a sick woman who was lying by the well and she said: "There are no healers any more, they have been banished. See the priests if you are sick. They will say a prayer for you ... if you have coins."

A man who had overhead our conversation said: "The healers are false; the priests have told us so. It is prayers to the gods that cure the sick, not filthy potions."

I did not say anything more as my instructions were to watch and listen.

I wandered around the market place for most of the morning. I had a full stomach, having eaten some of my bread, and the rest was tucked under my blanket for that night. The sun was half way up and burned very hot. I found shade in the shadows of the houses and positioned myself in a corner from where I could watch the comings and goings. Towards midday several learned men came into the market place calling for pupils. Some people shouted insults at them but others just looked away.

One of the learned men called out: "Come and sit with me beneath the kollen tree and I will teach you."

"And what will you teach?" asked a youth lounging by the town well. "You have nothing to teach us. The priests will tell us all we should know."

"Sit with me and you will learn all about the scrolls, the writings and memories of the wise men."

The youth laughed at him but the learned man's enthusiasm continued. "I will tell about the great events. I will tell of the men of wisdom and their thoughts."

Although he seemed to be gathering no pupils I could not help but notice the enthusiasm on his face. He walked with the aid of a stick, as one of his legs was very short and withered.

And then I noticed that other learned men had a priest with them as they called out for pupils: "Gather by the new temple as the sun sinks below the tower and hear about the great gods that have arrived from the sea. Come and you will be shown one of the great long knives of the gods."

As they walked around the market square they were gathering three or four youths each. The other learned man, who offered to teach about the Histories and Thoughts of Men, continued to shout for students but without success. He eventually left the market square with no pupils at all. I sat and ate some of my bread and waited and watched.

More time passed and my loneliness increased. I felt vulnerable and isolated sitting in a corner when everyone else seemed to have business to attend. Petronicus had told me to use my eyes and ears so I decided to spend my last small coin and listen to one of the learned men. But which? I really wanted to see the blades of the gods. Petronicus had small blades from time to time but if we were hungry especially during the winter he would have an ironer melt them down into coins for food. Only the most skilled could make iron knives but they were never longer than a man's finger because everyone knew that they would break if made longer. '*Better to use sharp stones,*' Petronicus always said, '*and have your pieces of iron made into coins by a skilled man.*'

But which learned man should I submit myself to? And then I remembered a tale Petronicus had told me one winter when we were in the town of Klinbil, which is particularly well known for men of wisdom and learning. Petronicus had given me a small coin and told me to spend an afternoon sitting listening to one of them.

I asked: 'But which learned man should I listen to?'

Petronicus just smiled in his usual way and said: 'Which learned man has the most pupils?'

I looked around the market place and noticed that one of them had several youths sitting at his feet whereas another who was waving his hands in great enthusiasm had only one.

'I will join the biggest group. Clearly he is discussing matters that the youths are interested in.'

Petronicus was silent for a moment and then said: 'Do not limit yourself to matters of interest to idle youth. The best lessons are not those that interest the pupils. No, the best lessons are those that interest the teacher. That is because he brings greater interest and enthusiasm to his lesson.'

And so I spent the afternoon hearing about why the stars move about the sky and why the moon gets bigger and then smaller. But the man taught with such enthusiasm that time fled, until I felt Petronicus's hand on my shoulder, to tell me it was nearly dark time.

I sat with the learned man under the kollen tree down an alleyway just off the market place. The wise and learned man's name was Mentis and he spoke with such enthusiasm that I sat ever closer to him – most pupils sit well away from the master in case he raps their heads with his knuckles for inattention. After a short while he stopped speaking and looked at me very intently. It was only then that he asked my name.

"My name is Petronius," I said and added proudly: "Son and novice of Petronicus."

"Of Petronicus!" he said with some alarm. "Tell me, is Petronicus in Bedosa?"

"No, but he is not far away," I said.

"Then I fear for him. Now listen, Petronius, tell him to keep away. It is too dangerous for him here."

Just then we heard a commotion from the other side of the market place. People were running about and shouting but we could just see what was happening through the narrow alleyways between the houses.

"Mercy on us," said Mentis as we watched. "It is the Ruler and the head priest. And look, men with long blades!"

We watched as the horror unfolded. I could see clearly the immense blades they carried and how they swirled them around themselves and nobody could ever get near to them.

"They have taken them from the gods in the boat. Oh, there is such evil here. They carry the weapons of the gods! Come we must go, quickly," said Mentis.

"No, wait, Mentis! Look!" The Ruler of Bedosa, a young man but very tall and muscular, approached a scribe who had been reading a prayer for an old woman. He held one of the great blades in his hand. He grabbed the scribe and pushed him to the ground. And then I witnessed the greatest horror I had ever seen. The Ruler brought his long sharp blade down and cut deeply into the scribe's leg. The people fell silent. I wanted to run to the scribe and push my clenched fist into his wound to stop the bleeding as Petronicus had taught me. But I felt the hand of Mentis on my shoulder restraining me. Nobody moved in the market place and then the people fell to their knees with their heads bowed before them.

Mentis whispered to me: "Come quickly, Petronius."

He held me by the arm and pushed me into a side alley between the houses. We moved quickly through alleyways and streets that Mentis was familiar with.

"Where are we going, Mentis? Where will we hide?"

"We go first to the House of the Tablets. I must give you something for Petronicus."

I knew about such places, as Petronicus had taken me into the House of the Tablets in Klinbil one summer. It is where the great events are written into clay tablets and then hardened in fire – that way they last forever.

Behind us we heard a roar from the crowd, and fearful shouts: "Death to the scribes! Death to the false healers!"

I followed Mentis, who although he limped could move quite fast, until we arrived at the House of the Tablets.

"Come quickly now, Petronius." We entered and Mentis sank to the ground in despair. There was chaos inside. Men had entered the House of the Tablets and smashed everything in sight. I watched as Mentis rummaged amongst the debris. He crawled about on the floor sifting through fragments of the tablets.

He spoke but it was more to himself than to me: "Everything destroyed. Everyone gone. All the writings … No, wait! … Perhaps not."

He picked up two small fragments, looked at them carefully and then pushed them into my pouch. "Go quickly and give these to Petronicus. Tell him what's happening here – tell him that all the records and histories are destroyed. And if you can't find Petronicus, take them to the House of Tablets in Klinbil."

We hurried out of the House of the Tablets and Mentis said: "Now, Petronius, you are young and swift. Go now and speak to nobody. Tell Petronicus he must find the Revered One and gather all the wise and learned men at the Mountain of the Year and decide what to do."

"But what about you? You must come with me!"

"No, child, I am lame and I tire very quickly. I know places to hide. I know what I must do. I pray that the gods will guide you and protect you."

I ran from the House of the Tablets as swiftly as I could. I kept my novice's hood and scribe's cape hidden beneath my body blanket. I turned into the Temple Square and stopped in my tracks. I was truly amazed by what I saw in front of me: the biggest temple I had ever seen being built. There were many large stones that people were bringing and a huge number of trees that had been brought for the building of it. I stood watching for a moment and then I remembered the words of Petronicus: *Use your eyes and ears – find out all you can.*

I walked slowly to avoid suspicion and entered the temple. I did not call out my name to the priests because that would have identified me as a scribe. What I saw inside left me speechless and without thought. The new part of the temple was made of whole trees, which had been recently brought into the town. In the centre was the huge boat of the gods with a tall pole in the centre. Hanging from the pole was a large blanket with a strange marking on it. Of the gods I could see nothing.

A man whispered to me: "The gods are sleeping in the main part of the temple. Only the priests are permitted to see them."

There were about twenty people kneeling around the boat with their heads bowed. I did the same. A priest was walking around and between the people looking sternly at them.

As he came up behind me I looked up to him and asked: "What is the strange blanket tied to the pole?"

I felt a harsh crack as he put his stick across my shoulders. He bent down towards me and shouted in my ear: "Do not question! It is not for you to question! What is your trade, what do you do?"

I thought quickly and lied: "I gather wood and sell it in the market place."

"How much wood do you give to the temple?"

I was unable to answer, as I didn't know the customs of the Temple of Bedosa. Another sharp crack came across my shoulders. The pain was intense and it was the first time anyone had ever hit me in my life. I was not a slave and Petronicus never struck me, he was always quiet and patient with me.

"From today," the priest shouted at me, "you will give half to the temple every day."

"Yes," I said. "Yes, every day."

He leaned further down and grabbed hold of my hands and looked at them closely. I was horrified in case he noticed that I was not used to rough work and that I chew I my nails to keep them short which is something all scribes do. And had he noticed the remains of black ink on my fingertips? He moved away and I breathed more easily but my shoulders were on fire. Quietly I slipped away and got out of the temple.

I turned a corner and ran straight into a crowd. They were shouting and falling over each other to escape the Ruler's men. I was dazed and confused and suddenly a tall fierce man appeared in front of me. I saw him raise his long blade and then I went down into a mass of bodies all fighting and lashing out at each other. The light in my eyes went out just like it does at night when I sleep.

Eight

When the light returned to my eyes I was struggling for breath. There was silence all around. I felt a huge weight pressing down on me and I could move only with great effort. My skin felt sticky and I realised that I was covered in drying blood. I lay still, listening for any sounds of fighting. I turned my head and could see the face of a dead man next to me. His face was rigid and his mouth was open for his last scream. All around was the smell of death and sweat.

I remained there for some time until I sensed the danger had passed. I felt no pain. At first I thought I must be dead and that the gods would come for me and take me to the Land of Wisdom, a land where only good men live. Petronicus had told me about it but I didn't know where it was! I began to move a little and managed to slide out from beneath the dead bodies that were piled on top of me. The light I could see was from the torches in the alleys between the houses; it was nighttime and no sounds came from the town.

I crawled away and realised that I was unhurt. I was also very hungry and thirsty, which Petronicus always said was a good sign. I leaned against the wall of a house to steady myself. My head ached and when I looked at the bodies in the firelight I was horrified. Many of them had been cut with the long blades of the gods and others had been crushed with the clubs that the Ruler's men always carried. I knew I must get away from Bedosa as soon as I could and go and find Petronicus.

I moved slowly and silently through the darkened alleyways of the town. Petronicus had taught me years ago that the essence of stealth was patience. I did not allow my sense of fear to tempt me into a run but I planned each step before I took it. I was trying to get as near to the main gate as I could before dawn. I turned a corner into a small opening just as the moon emerged from behind the clouds. And then I saw it: a sight that has haunted me for many a year. I saw the body of a man hanging from the scaffold. Instantly I thought of my own father who suffered the same fate at the hands of the Ruler of Bedosa so many years ago. I stepped back quickly into the shadows and looked at the body. It hung loosely in the wind, blowing to and fro as the wind played with it. I knew immediately who it was when I saw that his healer's cloak had been dirtied and torn, deliberately mocking him in death. I knew I was looking at the corpse of old Melonicus who had come to Bedosa just like myself to find out what was happening. I moved down the alley towards the town gate. I intended hide until it opened at first light.

I found a dark corner and I waited, huddled against a wall, just beyond the Taxing House where guards took coins from traders and merchants passing in and out of the town. It was cold where I sat and I felt very lonely. The only times I had spent my nights without the company of Petronicus was when I was learning to be a scribe and that now seemed many years ago. I began to imagine that Petronicus was lying there beside me, and that I could talk to him ask him questions. And then something that had been lurking behind my mind came starkly before my eyes. Why had the priests and the Ruler of Bedosa destroyed the tablets? A sudden panic came over me and I reached into my pouch and to my relief I found the two fragments Mentis had given me. They were safe. I wrestled with the problem and that helped to keep me awake. I needed to remain alive to what was going on around me in case the Night Watch came and questioned me. I remembered something Petronicus had said the night he sent me on this quest. He had said: *'Truth does not matter in this case; it's what people believe that matters.'*

What people believe? I wasn't sure of his meaning but there had been no time to question him further. And then as I let my thoughts wander a little amongst the stars above, something Petronicus had told me years ago came back to me. It was just after I had become a scribe when he said: '*Words are the most important things we have. They tell of remembered thoughts – thoughts that all men can share. If we have words we can hold onto thoughts; without words the thoughts would be lost.*'

Suddenly, I sat upright against the wall as an immense realisation flooded through my mind: the priests were destroying the words. The words that had been pressed into the tablets by generations of scribes and baked in the fires were being destroyed. But why? Why should they do that? I could find no answer in my head. I realised once again how desperate I was to find Petronicus. And then it came to me! The pain across my shoulders from the beating I had received from the priest gave me the answer. '*Do not question,*' he had said and then he hit me again. I could not imagine a world without questions. That would mean a world without wisdom, a world without wise men and a world without men like Petronicus.

My impatience with the slow return of daylight gnawed at my spirit until at last I saw the guard come out of his hut and open the gate. I watched as he went back inside to sleep. I knew he would remain inside until traders and people began to come and go. I ran out as silently as I could and headed for the trail. I was very hungry and stopped by a stream to search for some roots to eat and to wash the blood from my body and clothes.

Towards nightfall I came to an inn and I thought I would be safe enough to seek rest and shelter. I decided to use my last coin to buy food. It was the coin I had intended to give to Mentis for teaching me. I could have a long journey ahead of me because I didn't know how long it would take me to find Petronicus.

It was warm inside the inn and several travellers were already preparing to sleep on the raised platforms around the fire. There was an old man whose task was to keep the fire burning all day and night. He nodded to me and said: "We have bread and we have meat. Do you have something to trade, or a coin?"

I said that I did and asked to see the food first. It was poor food but I was so hungry I exchanged the coin for it and ate quickly and then I lay down to sleep by the fire. The old man put some hot stones around me to keep me warm. I had hardly closed my eyes and ears when I sensed there was a man standing over me.

I looked up and saw that he had a large stick in his hand as he spoke: "Wake, boy, and stand up."

Before I could obey he picked me up, dragged me off the sleeping platform and pulled me towards the fire. He looked closely into my face. He pulled my blanket off me and saw my scribe's cape and novice's hood.

"He is a scribe and a healer's novice!" shouted the man, and immediately other men came in to look at me. "He must have escaped the massacre in Bedosa."

"The Ruler will give coins for him. Take him. Tie his hands," said another.

I was handled very roughly. I wriggled free for a moment and jumped like a frog between one man's legs onto the sleeping platform. I trampled on several people who shouted obscenities at me. And then I had nowhere to run and I let them grab me knowing they meant me no immediate harm. They would hardly kill me if they could get coins from the Ruler for me.

I was being dragged towards the door when a woman's voice rang out sharply: "Unhand him, unhand that child I say!"

Suddenly I was allowed to fall to the ground.

"Bring him," said the woman. I was pushed into another part of the inn. The woman sat on a wooden bench that was covered with furs and blankets. She was old and looked at me intensely and said: "Your name, child?"

"Petronius."

She continued to stare into my face and then she said: "Come here, child. Come closer."

I approached with apprehension.

She touched my face: "You are a scribe and novice to a healer?"

I nodded.

"Your master, who is he?"

"Petronicus," I said defiantly. "The greatest of healers."

She was silent for a moment and then asked in a quiet voice: "How many years have you seen?"

"I am in my fifteenth year."

She remained silent whilst she looked at me closely. And then she asked: "And were you a child of summer or winter?"

"The summer, I think."

"Sit with me, child, but you must be on your way at first light. There is danger for you here. Those men out there would sell you to the Bedosians for the smallest coin." She gave me food and goat's blood mixed with milk to drink. "Petronicus," she said quietly. "Yes, I know of him. He has been to Bedosa before, I think."

"Yes, but that was many years ago."

The woman smiled and said: "Get under my blankets, child, and I will have fire and food brought in."

When I awoke the next morning, the woman was gone and only the old man remained in the inn.

He brought food for me and said: "You must go now and do not stop for anybody. The Ruler's men are searching for healers and scribes to kill them. They have killed many already. They say the gods have come to the world and the former times have passed away. I do not understand. I am not a wise man. But be gone, child, and I hope you find your master."

I ate the food, which was much better than the night before. There was clean milk in a pot and my cloak had been washed. As I left the inn the old man stopped me and said: "Here, child, the mistress left you these." He gave me a stout stick with a small blade bound to the end. "I fear you will need to defend yourself. These are dangerous times. And the mistress left this for you. Now be gone, child, and leave no tracks behind you."

He handed me a small leather pouch.

I ran from the inn and joined the trail as fast as I could. There were no travellers that I could see so I stopped, opened the pouch and found several well made coins.

As the sun rose to the middle of the sky I began to feel better. My head no longer ached but there was a large lump just above my forehead. My stomach was full of good food and the land had plenty of berries and roots that Petronicus had taught me were safe to eat. The coins would buy food for Petronicus and me for several moons and above all, I had a stout stick with a blade tied to the end to defend myself.

My feelings of wellbeing, however, soon came to an end when I came to the place where the trails crossed. I looked in vain for the five stones making the sign of Petronicus. There were footprints in the dust and it was clear to me that any signs in the stones had been deliberately kicked away. I did not know where Petronicus was.

I travelled the trail for the rest of the day hoping to find some sign of Petronicus at each crossroads. At dark time I searched for an arabak tree so that I could embrace it and perhaps know that Petronicus was safe. If the Bedosians had caught him he would be dead now and I would be completely alone in the world. The panic set in quickly and I had little time to think about my experiences at the inn. I began to run about looking for an arabak tree. *'Quick thoughts,'* Petronicus used to say, *'are false thoughts.'* So I slowed my pace and began to search more thoroughly. When I found an arabak tree I sat down and looked up and searched the sky in vain for my naming star or the star of Petronicus. Dark clouds came over and I could see nothing. I sat down and cried and that was the last time I cried; well, almost the last time. But I realised that night that I could no longer be a child.

The night passed over me and as the moon went home and the sun began its slow climb far away on the other side of the world I woke suddenly. There was silence all around me. I reached out instinctively to touch Petronicus but all my hand found was the stout stick with a sharp blade bound to it. I had kept my blade stick close by whilst I slept and my hand never far from its handle.

I sat up and sucked a little dew from the leaves of the arabak tree. I faced another day of uncertainty as to what I should do next and I thought I heard the voice of my master from deep inside my mind: *'Think, child, think. Ask yourself what you know for certain and what you are not sure of.'* That's what he always taught me and then he would say: *'And then do only what you know for certain.'*

I moved from my sleeping place and felt my body begin to warm. Petronicus said that blood ran all though the body to make it warm at night but not all healers agreed with him. I set off on the trail.

About mid morning, just as the sun was climbing the steepest part of the day, I arrived at a crossroads where several trails met. And there I saw it: the body of a youth hanging from the branch of a tree. His scribe's cape and novice's hood lay torn on the ground below his feet. I approached and saw the body swing lightly in the wind. The victim's face was distorted in the agonies of death but I recognised Melonius, the young novice of the hanged Meloncus whom we had met only five days before. I climbed the tree and crawled along the branch and cut the rope with my blade. Melonius's body felt limply to the ground and I carefully placed his scribe's cape and novice's hood on his chest and asked the gods to take him to the Land of Wisdom where only good men live.

I hurried away and found a sheltered place to sit just off the trail. I needed some quiet time to collect my thoughts and suppress my fears. I asked myself, as Petronicus had always said I should: *'Just what do I know for certain?'* Well firstly, Melonius had not found the Revered One to tell of all that had happened on the coast. Of Petronicus, I wasn't sure. And then the words of Mentis of Bedosa back came to me: *'Go and find Petronicus and tell him all the tablets have been destroyed. Tell him he must find the Revered One and summon all the men of wisdom to the Mountain of the Year and decide what to do.'*

But I wasn't sure if Petronicus was still alive. A thought so horrible spread over me like a damp fog: supposing the priests of Bedosa had read the signs Petronicus had left for me at the crossroads and knew where to find him. What if the Bedosians had caught up with him and hanged him as they had Melonius and Melonicus? I felt so fearful knowing that the Ruler of Bedosa had killed honest and good men and that it would enrage the gods. The full horror of what had happened descended upon me. Melonius and Melonicus both killed and all their knowledge and skills lost; truly I was living through a great cataclysm.

I did not let myself think too much about Petronicus at that moment because I felt that tears would not be far away. I looked back to the crossroads. One trail led to Klynos. But that was a long and tortuous route, which avoided the Land of the Towering Rocks. Petronicus and I always called it the Happy Trail to Klynos because we had spent many happy times there. And I shall always remember it had been on the Klynos trail that I had caught up with Petronicus when I had finished my studies as a scribe. Perhaps I would find him there again? Yes, that would be possible. The gods might make that possible but it would take a whole moon because I would have to hide and avoid seeing people who might recognise me as a novice healer and scribe. I stood up to walk back to the crossroads when I began to imagine the disapproving face of Petronicus saying: *'Do what you are certain of – always do what you are certain of.'* I stopped, looked up to where his face would be if he was standing beside me and nodded.

The other trail led to Klinbil, a town known for men of wisdom and learning and where they also kept a House of Tablets. I remembered the way Mentis had rummaged amongst the destroyed tablets and found two small fragments. He had put them into my pouch and told me to give them to Petronicus. And there was such desperation in his voice. I brought them out from my pouch and looked at them closely. There were several words inscribed on them and baked in the fire. But the words were unknown to me, words the scribe I had studied under had never told me and words Petronicus had never used. Mentis had said that if I couldn't find Petronicus I should take them to the Keeper of the House of Tablets in Klinbil. Maybe he would know what they said. And what of the Revered One? Surely he would go to Klinbil to be with other learned men. But would they listen to me and all travel to the Mountain of the Year to decide what to do?

Petronicus could have persuaded them – not I, not a mere novice. But one day I would be a wise man if I remembered all that Petronicus had taught me. *'Remember,'* he used to say, *'wisdom cannot be found – it is in the seeking.'* And that is how I would spend my life: in an endless search for wisdom just like my master had done. The gods had decided my mind. I would take the trail to Klinbil.

Nine

I set off for Klinbil with a heavy heart. I was alone, full of fear at having to make all my own decisions. It would be a long and weary trek and I knew that the sun would rise and sink many times before I could reach the town. To occupy my mind I tried to recall as a many details of Klinbil as I could. Petronicus had taken me there on several occasions but all the towns looked the same in my memory. Except Klynos of course. That was a happy place and I remembered it well.

There was little food to be had on the trail. Some fruit still hung on the trees but the ground was hard and rocky and I found very few roots in the earth. Water was plentiful as many lively rivers and streams flowed through that country.

Petronicus always said that bobbing about riding the donkey or walking made the brain work. In the days that followed many thoughts and pictures raced through my mind as I trekked along the trail to Klinbil that I found I wasn't looking at the things around me. Petronicus would have been concerned had he seen me walking with my face down and just looking at my feet. Another horrible thought began stabbing into my mind. If Petronicus was still alive he would be searching for me. Our paths might never cross and I remembered the tale he told me about his brother: they lost contact and never met each other again. Memories of the panic and fear that I felt when I had to search for Petronicus after I left the House of the Scribe years ago came back to haunt me.

After several days on the trail I was getting very hungry and depressed. One night I was very sad because I could not find an arabak tree to curl under and I would not feel close to Petronicus.

The stars also hid their faces from me so I could not gaze at our naming stars.

It was cold and I had no flint to strike a spark and even if I had I could not have used it because I needed remain hidden in case the men and priests of Bedosa were near. I did not look around for fires of other travellers for fear of being identified as a scribe and a novice to a healer.

I huddled down into my blanket and pulled leaves and small branches over me to keep warm. I settled down for a cold night.

I cannot remember a time when so many bad thoughts stabbed through my head. How I wished that Petronicus were with me to smooth them out and explain everything. It would take many days before I really accepted that I was facing the world alone.

Sleep found me at last and I drifted away cold and lonely into the land of dreams.

Petronicus asked: 'What troubles you child?' I said I didn't know and Petronicus just smiled and said: 'Something troubles you but you cannot name it, is that right?'

I nodded and said: 'Sometimes there is a sad thought deep within me and I do not know what it is.'

'Then you must smother the thought with good things. Try asking yourself some important questions. Come here, child, and do exactly as I say.'

I watched as Petronicus picked up a small stone. He showed it to me and then threw it about ten paces and said: 'Go and pick it up, child, and bring it back to me.'

I did as I was bid and brought it back and handed it to Petronicus.

'Now come and sit with me,' he said. We sat close together beneath an arabak tree and he asked: 'How did you know what I wanted you to do?'

I smiled thinking this was a trick: 'I heard you,' I said.

'And how did you know where the stone went?'

'I watched it.' I was now smiling broadly.

'And then you went after it and picked it up. Am I right?'

Laughing, I said: 'I reached down and picked it up. This is funny, Petronicus.' I continued to laugh and Petronicus joined in with me.

'And then what did you do?'

I rolled over onto the ground laughing at his silly questions. In between bouts of laugher I said: 'I walked back to you and handed it to you. Just like you asked.'

Petronicus paused for a moment and then said: 'Walk with me for a while.' He put his hand on my shoulder as we walked amongst the trees. 'Enjoy walking, enjoy breathing, enjoy the good health of your body. Enjoy the freshness all about you. You can hear, you can see, you can reach down and you can walk. And yet you say you are troubled! How can that be when the gods have given you so much?'

We set off and walked together in the sunlight towards the next town. Our donkey walked with us and he kept pushing me with his head playfully. We looked and marvelled at all the things we saw. We sang with the birds and I ran with the small creatures that scurried away when we passed. Petronicus smiled and all the world smiled with us. When we reached the next town we earned some coins and a large loaf of bread.

Petronicus said to me: 'Now go and give to those on whom the gods have not smiled as they have on you, and as you do, thank the gods for what you have.'

I went first to a blind man who was begging in the market place. Next I found a deaf beggar and then I found one who could not walk. For each I pulled off a large wedge of bread and handed it to them.

Light was finding me behind my closed eyes. The cold of the morning came up through the ground and chilled my bones. I stirred and was about to stretch myself into the new day when I sensed a tall figure standing over me. I knew without thinking that I was in danger and I reached for my knife stick: it was not there. I looked up and saw a priest. He was holding my knife stick in his hand pointing it at me.

"Get up, boy."

I began to rise keeping my eyes on the priest and the blade. I knew that my only chance was to be *swift of foot,* as Petronicus always said. As I rose I took into my mind the lie of the land. There were bushes in front of me, and the ground rose steeply towards a hill. I judged I would be fitter than the priest and could outrun him.

I stood to my full height but before I could run I felt myself being grabbed from behind. My arms were being pulled painfully behind me and I was unable to move. I heard some voices over my shoulder but in my fear I could not hear their words clearly.

The priest came menacingly close to me and said: "Who are you? Where are you from?"

I did not answer and felt my arms being pulled tighter. The pain across my shoulders was becoming unbearable and I knew I would shout out very soon. The priest then grabbed my scribe's cape and pulled it close to him to examine it. He then pulled my novice's hood from my head and held it to my face.

"These yours? Or have you stolen them?"

I felt anger rising within me. Defiantly, I said: "They are mine."

The priest continued to examine my hood and cape and I felt the pressure on my arms easing slightly. I did not know how many men were behind me.

He spoke again holding the novice's hood close to my face: "Who is your master? Where is he?"

Anger swelled up inside and blotted out my fears. I now committed myself to make a break for it and try to get to the high ground. I relaxed my shoulders and arms, which were still held behind me and then I tensed myself and leapt at the priest and pushed him aside. I grabbed my knife stick and hood from him and then ran like no antelope has ever run and headed straight for the rising ground. It was very steep and I felt I was straining my chest and legs to maintain my running pace. After a short while I realised my captors were no longer pursuing me. I had outrun them I thought. After all I was young and the priest was not. I did not stop until I had put a great distance between us.

I dared not stop to gather food until the sun was going to rest in the great fires at the end of the world. The moon was hiding behind thick clouds and I could see little of the trail in front of me. Soon I would have to stop and find somewhere to stay for the night; if I should trip and fall I might injure myself or strain my legs and I would then be lost.

To my great joy I found an arabak tree just off the trail. It grew amidst some bushes which contained berries I knew were safe to eat. There was a clear passage into the centre of the bushes where the arabak tree grew. It was a trail made by the sheep that graze in these hills. I crawled into it, collecting berries as I went and then I positioned my knife stick so that it was pointing outward and would wound anybody trying to come in after me. I felt secure for the night.

How I longed for a fire that night and how I longed for the company of Petronicus. I don't think that I had ever known real fear before these days since Petronicus and I first heard about the arrival of the gods from Melonius. I lay down huddled in my blanket, a blanket Petronicus had bought for me many moons ago. I chewed on the berries, which were sour but would give me strength for the coming day.

'*Our thoughts,*' Petronicus always said, '*come from nowhere.*' I remember asking him to explain that one day but he said that no man knew where thoughts came from. Maybe from the gods, but he wasn't sure. It was like that with my next thought. But it was a thought so stark and alarming that I sat upright immediately and looked to see if the stars were showing themselves. I parted the bushes above me and to my great joy I could see the moon was small like a bent finger and I could see the star of Petronicus shining brightly. Very soon now my own star would twinkle into life just above that of Petronicus and then I would embrace the arabak tree the way we both used to do when I was studying to be a scribe and we were apart.

The thought came to me from the tree. Petronicus must have thought I was dead before the priests and soldiers of Bedosa had caught up with him. He would have heard about the massacre in Bedosa and thought that I had died with all the other scribes, healers and men who denied the gods. I felt so sad knowing that Petronicus may have died in loneliness.

I called out in the darkness to the star of Petronicus to watch over me and protect me on my quest.

Ten

I was now so afraid of people and towns that I approached Klinbil with great caution. I found a place on a small hill above the town where I could hide and watch. The town seemed to be quite peaceful with people entering and leaving through the main gate. There was a small wall around the town to keep wild animals out and to keep sheep and goats that belonged to the townspeople from straying. And then I noticed some men were building the wall higher with logs and branches of trees. As I watched, several stone throwers came up onto the wall and started practising. They had small sticks positioned outside the wall at various distances and I watched with admiration as the stone throwers could hit any stick they chose. They had their sons with them and they were teaching them their skills. The stone throwers of Klinbil were famous, Petronicus once told me. They hunted in the hills behind the town and I remembered Petronicus saying they could down a bird with just one stone.

I also noticed that the guards on the main gate were not stopping people from entering or leaving. I watched some merchants come down the trail and approach the main gate. They had several donkeys fully laden with trade goods and tied nose to tail in the usual way.

I watched as they entered the gate without hindrance. It was strange, I thought, that no coins were demanded of them as would have happened in Bedosa. I thought that perhaps they paid coins inside. I was desperately hungry and longed to enter the town and earn some bread or a coin by writing for people or reading prayers for them. I would use the coins I had in my pouch only as a last resort as I wanted to keep them to see me through the winter.

When the sun had reached half way down the sky on its way to rest in the great fires, I was so hungry that my caution began to weaken. I stood up and walked slowly down the hill towards the trail that led to the gate. And then I saw it, a sight that delighted my eyes and filled me with hope. I saw a scribe come out of the gate and set up his stall to catch any passing trade. He wore his scribe's cape openly and had quills to write with and reeds to write on. He began to shout for custom.

I approached him gingerly. He was older than I was and I said: "May your pen write true and your words be honest," which is the traditional greeting of a scribe to a comrade scribe. He looked up and nodded.

"Greetings, my friend, but I fear you will have no trade here. The people of Klinbil are well supplied with scribes."

"I do not seek employment," I lied. "I seek the House of the Tablets."

"It is in the market place but you can wear your scribe's cape without fear in this town."

"The men from Bedosa? Have they been here?" I asked.

"No, but we know of the horrors that took place there. I fancy it is too far for them but if they do come I don't know what we shall do. Healers and scribes will have to get away to wherever they will. Some men say they will defend the town against them but that is for our wise men to decide. Enter, my friend, and enter in peace."

Inside the town there was much preparation for defence. Large collections of smooth round stones were being placed on the inside of the wall. More branches and logs were being piled up ready to strengthen the wall and I saw packs of hunting dogs tethered.

I crossed the market place to the House of the Tablets. Inside there was good order and tidiness, unlike the wrecked House of Tablets in Bedosa.

"Who are you, friend?" asked the Keeper. "And what is your business here?"

"I come from Bedosa. Mentis of Bedosa said I should come here."

"Mentis? Mercy on us! Come here, child."

I learned that the Keeper's name was Kelcit. He rushed over to me and beckoned me further inside. There were rows and rows of clay tablets and a tablet of soft clay on the floor that Kelcit was using to write on.

"I am recording the horrors of our time," he said and pointed outside through the door. "What is happening to the world, child? Do you know?"

"The gods have come to Bedosa," I said. "And the priests and the Ruler are building the biggest temple that man has ever seen."

"And the gods? Where are they?" asked Kelcit anxiously.

"They sleep and some say they will sleep for a hundred moons and great calamities will come to the world."

"Yes, yes I know what is said. It is in the tablets. And is it true they came in a huge boat and have you seen this boat?"

"Yes, the boat is wondrously great and could hold many gods."

"Mercy on us!" exclaimed Kelcit. He was then silent and I could see that frightening thoughts were racing through his head. "You say you came from Mentis. I know Mentis well. We studied together before we were scribes. We sat at the feet of the Revered One and learned our letters and wisdom from him."

I then began to tell him about the massacre of Bedosa and of all the evils I had seen. I told him about the gods and the new temple. I told him about the blades the priests had taken from the gods and I told him about the clothes the gods wore. I waited until he had taken all the knowledge into his head and then I told him that Mentis might already be dead. That almost brought tears to Kelcit's eyes, and then a look of horror clouded his face when I described how Melonicus had been hanged near the market square of Bedosa just because he was a healer. Kelcit sat down on a stone and held his head in his hands. I paused and waited for him to calm himself and then I told him that the novice Melonius had also been hanged where the road from Bedosa crossed the road to Klinbil.

Kelcit remained silent as he took into his mind all the horrors I told him.

He looked at his soft clay tablet on the floor and said: "I fear I will need many tablets for all you have told me."

"What about Klinbil? I saw a scribe working at the gate. Is he not afraid?"

"No, not yet. The priests have left."

"How many priests do you have in Klinbil?"

"Four," said Kelcit. "Three left for Bedosa when we heard of the strange events and one walks the trails stopping travellers and asking for news."

I told Kelcit that I had met a priest on the trail but had escaped from him.

"You were wise," he said. "Do not trust the priests until the wise men have decided what is true and what is not."

I smiled at him because he sounded just like Petronicus. "And now my friend, what did Mentis say to you?"

I took out the two fragments of clay tablets from my pouch and said: "I do not know the words. Mentis did not know them either."

Kelcit looked at them then rubbed his head in puzzlement. He took them over to the door where there was more light and continued to shake his head. "No, I do not know these words. You have young eyes, what do you see in them?"

I looked carefully and moved my finger over the letters. There were about ten of them, some very small and very worn with age. I had tried to read them before but now I tried to say some of them out loud.

"I read *fidik* … *gilbid* … and *kandis*. And these are not words I know."

"*Fidik? Gilbid? Kandis?* No, they mean nothing to me. The tablet is very old, very old indeed and could even be as old as the world." I felt my eyes grow bigger in wonderment and Kelcit added: "Yes they could be of the time when the world came out of the great hole at the top of the Mountain of the Year." Kelcit began to move around the room taking short nervous steps. He looked about on the shelves of tablets and kept repeating: "I don't know. I just don't know." And then he turned to me and said: "Why did Mentis tell you to come to me?"

"He told me to take the bits of clay to my master ..." I hesitated and my words choked in my throat. "But I fear my master is dead. Mentis told me to bring them to the House of the Tablets in Klinbil if I could not find my master."

"What is your name, child?"

"I am Petronius, son and novice of ..."

"Of Petronicus? Petronicus! He is the wisest of men. Mercy on us. If the Bedosians are killing men like Petronicus we are surely doomed. The gods must be sleeping and we will suffer for a hundred moons."

I asked Kelcit for food and water. He gave me some and we then sat in the House of the Tablets silently together.

At length he said: "I remember Petronicus very well. His first son died you know ... and his wife ... in the great sickness."

"I did not know that; Petronicus never told me."

"Yes it was in the town of Kelemos in the Far Country. The child was born there and the sickness was also there. After that Petronicus always said that towns are bad places."

"Petronicus doesn't like towns. We work in them but we always prefer to sleep in the open by our own fire. Was Petronicus very sad?" I asked.

"Oh yes, I remember him well; we were friends."

I was silent for a while wondering why Petronicus had never told me. Perhaps he was too sad to tell me. Perhaps he wanted to forget about it. But I felt I had to ask: "Was his son named?"

"No, he was too small to have a naming day. But that is the way of it. More children die than live." Kelcit broke off another large wedge of bread, dipped it in some milk and gave it to me.

And then he asked: "What of Melonius, the novice of Melonicus? What did he tell you?"

"He said that his master had gone to Bedosa to see what was happening and that Melonius was to find the Revered One and tell him all that had happened."

"Ah, yes, the Revered One, yes, he will guide us."

"And Mentis said that if I could find Petronicus, I must tell him to assemble all the men of wisdom at the Mountain of the Year and decide what to do."

"You have done well, my young friend. Eat your fill and tonight we will sit at the town fire and listen to the travellers."

Eleven

Unlike most towns in the world, Klinbil always had a fire in the centre of the market place where travellers and those who had no shelter in the town could sit, prepare their meals and sleep. Some towns expelled strangers at night and they had to camp outside the stockade, but Klinbil was a free place governed by men of wisdom and learning.

Kelcit and I went to the market place just as the sun settled down to rest in the great fires beyond the sea. It was the custom of the town for newcomers to announce themselves as they sat down. Petronicus always used to say that honest men need never fear to shout out their names around any man's fire.

I watched as a man and his family approached the fire and made room for themselves in the circle: "I am Kenos, merchant and trader from the Land of the Tumbling Waters." The man and his wife and children sat down and warmed themselves. Many people greeted them and welcomed them to the fire, which as everyone knows is the gift of the gods. There was an elderly man and a boy whose job it was to keep the fire going all night to warm the travellers. They sat near a pile of sticks and logs ready to wake the fire up if it tried to sleep.

Kelcit whispered to me: "Announce yourself, child, and let them see your cape and hood; there is nothing to hide here."

I stood up and shouted: "I am Petronius. I am of the trail." I received the usual greetings but nobody took much notice of a boy. I sat as close to the fire as I could and pulled my blanket around me for there was a cold wind coming in off the mountains behind the town. At first there was little talk as everybody was concerned with the preparation of meals and then when all had eaten their fill the discussions began.

"The news from Bedosa is terrifying," said a traveller, who said his trade was in animal skins. "If the gods sleep we must help the Ruler of Bedosa and his priests to prepare a temple for them. And then when the gods awake the calamities will stop."

It was difficult to see who was speaking in the firelight. A woman called on the old man to feed the fire: "The fire is hungry," she said. "It gives us no light."

"What calamities?" shouted another. "I see no calamities. The animals feed and give meat and milk. The sheep give wool and our crops grow. What calamities do you speak of?"

"The Ruler of Bedosa and his priests say …" At that moment an angry voice boomed out from the doorway of the temple:

"His priests? *His* priests?" It was the Elder of the Scribes of Klinbil. I looked at him closely in the firelight. He used a long staff to support himself because he was very old. He was even older than Petronicus! The people listened respectfully. "The priests belong to the gods and the people, not the Ruler of Bedosa."

There were mutterings from the crowd. Many agreed with him but there were others who did not.

"We must obey the priests," said a woman. "Or great calamities will come that will last forever." And then a stone thrower stood up and spoke. He still wore the small sack for stones around his waist but it was empty.

"I have heard that the Ruler of Bedosa is taxing the people. All towns within two days' walk of Bedosa must give half of their coins and food to the new temple."

Many people recoiled with horror and there were mutterings: "What shall we live on?" "How will we get through the winter?"

The stone thrower spoke again: "The priests and the Ruler of Bedosa will grow rich on our labour whilst our people starve."

An old man whose face in the firelight showed the wrinkles of many hard years said: "They may come and take our young men to work on the temple. They have long blades I hear, longer than a man's arm."

Sounds of fear wafted through the people and then they were hushed. People looked at each other in horror.

Another face in the crowd spoke fearfully and said: "But if the gods sleep what else can we do? We must obey the gods and priests."

"We must wait until our own priests return from Bedosa. They will tell us what to do," said another.

Kelcit whispered to me: "See how fearful and confused they all are. What the world needs now is a Council of Wisdom."

"What is a Council of Wisdom?"

Kelcit leaned closer to me and explained into my ear: "There has only been one Council of Wisdom in my lifetime and I was too young to attend. But in ancient times when great calamities came, the people held Councils of Wisdom. It is recorded in the tablets."

"Where?" I asked. "At the Mountain of the Year? Was that what Mentis meant? Is that what he wanted me to tell Petronicus?"

"Yes, I think it was," said Kelcit.

"But the wise men of the world will not listen to me. Not to a novice."

Some of the voices had become angry whilst Kelcit and I had been whispering together. Some younger men even stood up to shout at those around the fire who disagreed with them.

And then the stone thrower stood up once again. "Listen, friends," he said. "Let all who wish to speak do so. We will solve nothing by anger. But we must decide for ourselves. I say we must prepare to defend the town."

"Against blades longer than a man's arm? This is foolish talk."

"Aye," said another. "Their blades are the blades of the gods. Everyone knows that iron will break if it is longer than a man's finger. But, I've heard it said, the blades of the gods never break."

I turned to Kelcit and said: "Shall I speak? Shall I tell them about the killings and how the Bedosians hunted down the scribes and healers?"

"No," said Kelcit. "You are too young to speak. It is for the young to listen, not to speak in the counsels of their elders." I nodded and remembered Petronicus saying to me: '*Spend the first half of your life in the accumulation of wisdom and the second half sharing it with others*'. Secretly I was pleased because to speak before that crowd would be terrifying. I would rather face the wolves than that!

It was now dark and the fire grew tired and burned more slowly. The sun was sleeping peacefully in the great fires and the travellers and people around the town fire gradually became silent as they settled down for the night. I wrapped myself into my blanket and moved as close to the fire as I could. I gazed into the night sky and tried to find my naming star but dark clouds hid everything from me. I felt lonely even amongst the travellers of Klinbil. Kelcit lay nearby but when I later turned over to look he was gone.

Petronicus always used to say that a man lives in two worlds. One is the harsh world that we all know and the other is the world of his dreams where there is no pain. I had hardly begun to live in the world of dreams when I heard the soft voice of Kelcit whispering in my ear. He shook my shoulder gently and said: "Petronius. Wake up, child; you are wanted."

I pulled my blanket around me and stood up. There was silence all around and only the old man remained awake, sitting by the pile of logs. He would tend the fire all night to keep the sleepers warm and then hope for a small coin or some food next morning.

"Come, Petronius and be silent," whispered Kelcit. I let him lead me away from the fire. I was consumed with curiosity and a little bit afraid.

"Where are we going? Who wants me?"

Kelcit did not answer but he led me through the dark alleyways of Klinbil to a house hard against the far wall. There were several donkeys tethered outside and I could see firelight through the windows.

Kelcit stopped at the doorway and called out: "It is Kelcit and I bring Petronius, who brought the news from Bedosa."

We went in and I looked across the fire in the centre of the house at a very old man who sat on skins and blankets against the wall. There were two healers sitting alongside him but I did not recognise them. They also had novices who were preparing food in another part of the house. The Elder Scribe of Klinbil was also there. I looked at the man in the centre and somehow I knew that he was the Revered One.

"Come closer, child," said the Revered One, "and sit by the fire so I can see you." He looked like the oldest man in the world. His blanket showed the shape of his bony shoulders and his feet were hard as leather. "So your name is Petronius, which means the son of Petronicus; is that right?" I nodded, too nervous to speak.

"I did not know Petronicus had a son," said one of the healers who sat next to the Revered One.

"I am not … He took me as his son. I am also his novice."

"And what of Petronicus? When did you last see him?" I held up the fingers of my hands but could not bring myself to say the words. The more days that passed without news of Petronicus meant that he was certainly dead.

"We have heard nothing of him," said the Revered One. "But we have heard of wickedness. You must prepare yourself because I fear you are masterless now."

The Elder Scribe of Klinbil spoke next: "The Bedosians have killed all the scribes, healers and men of wisdom they can find. Anyone within three days' trek of Bedosa, I fear is lost. The Bedosians followed the messages left on the crossroads and hunted them down."

I held my head down and said: "Yes, I know."

"Come my child," said the Revered One, "and sit with me. And now everyone listen. Bring the novices in from their cooking and let me tell you what must be done."

I shall remember until I die, that I Petronius, son of Petronicus, sat next to the Revered One when the great plan was made.

Everyone sat up expectantly as the Revered One began to speak: "These strange words in the tablets that Petronius showed to Kelcit are unknown to us. We do not know why Mentis sent them here. Did Mentis of Bedosa know their meaning? We don't know. That is right is it not Petronius?"

"Yes, and as Petronicus always said: '*if we lose the word we lose the thought*'."

"Petronicus was indeed wise," said the Revered One. "And so was Mentis. He was correct and so is Kelcit; we must hold a Council of Wisdom at the Mountain of the Year."

Whenever I have told this story in the years that have passed I have always emphasised how the Revered One took a commanding role and gave us his instructions. There was no more time for debate and argument; at that moment the world needed a leader. And I was sitting next to him.

"Young scribes must remain here in Klinbil and examine the tablets," the Revered One continued. "They must try to find traces of these words and their meanings because Mentis believed they were important. That task will need young scribes because old eyes grow tired and cannot see clearly. As for the rest of us, I know the season is advanced but we must leave for Klynos immediately. We shall winter there and then all assemble at the Mountain of the Year in spring."

There were murmurings of assent from all present. I felt relieved that at last we were all getting together to plan for the world and prevent the wickedness spreading. And then the Revered One turned to me and said: "In spring at the Mountain of the Year it would be appropriate for you to take the name of Petronicus and be known as a healer. We know the Bedosians have killed many of our learned men of wisdom. So many of them are gone and their wisdom is lost to us. I hope your master taught you well, Petronius. You are welcome to travel with us to Klynos or remain here and read the tablets."

"He should remain and read the tablets," said the Elder of the Scribes of Klinbil. "His eyes are young and need less light than old eyes."

"Yes, you are right, my friend. But first I ask you this, Petronius. Apart from the killings you have seen, what disturbs you the most about the happenings at Bedosa?"

I thought hard for a moment. There was silence all around me as these great men of letters, healing and wisdom awaited my answer. I stiffened myself and said: "It was in the temple at Bedosa when the priest hit me across the shoulders and told me I must not question. That I must never question, but I must believe what I am told. Revered One, how can there be a world without questions?"

"You have the beginnings of wisdom, my young friend. If we do not question searchingly we will live with wrong answers because wicked men will give us the answers they want us to have."

He reached forward and held my head in his hands. He followed the shape of my head with his fingers and looked closely into my eyes. Then he turned to his friends, nodded in a very knowing way and said something I could not hear, then added: "So, will you travel with us, Petronius?"

"No," I said. "There is something I must do."

The Revered One, who always seemed to know what I was going to say, smiled benignly and nodded as I continued: "I will return to where I last saw Petronicus and follow the trails until I find his body and then I will carry it myself to the Mountain of the Year and lay it down beside his own master, no matter how many moons it takes. And then, and only then, will I take the name Petronicus."

They all nodded their approval because the loyalty of a novice to his master was a virtue of the highest order amongst them. The Revered One patted me on the head and said: "Tell all learned and wise men you meet on the trail to meet at the Mountain of the Year in spring."

Twelve

I shall always remember my lonely wanderings after I left Klinbil. I spent the next two moons searching the trails near Bedosa for signs of Petronicus, but with no result. I moved along animals' paths whenever possible and lived off the country. There was little food and my belly ached with hunger. I was too afraid to go to an inn and use my coins in case I should be questioned and betrayed.

One day I met a woman who was taking her cow to pasture on higher ground. She had a festering sore on her lower arm and I treated it with maggots that I found in the rotting corpse of a wolf. She was grateful but had no coins to give me. Instead she offered me a night's shelter in her hut and shared what little food she had. She told me tales of unbelievable horror. The Bedosians had taken her only son to work on the temple. She was now alone and had to fend for herself with the cow and a small patch of land that she cultivated. When her son was not returned to her she went to beg the Ruler of Bedosa to release him. Her voice became low in sadness and anger when she said that her son was now a slave of the temple. I told her nothing about the Council of Wisdom because that news must not reach the ears of the Ruler. The Revered One, however, thought that the Mountain of the Year was much too far away from Bedosa for them to come and interrupt the Council; the Revered One was always right but I took no chances.

All the land within two or three days' trek of Bedosa seemed to groan in poverty. The people were going hungry because the armed men and priests of the temple took half of whatever they had. Each night I huddled down by an arabak tree and covered myself with leaves. It was autumn and there were many dried leaves which helped to keep me warm. I always tried to enter the land of dreams before I got too cold and hungry. The only comfort I had was a picture in my mind of all the men of wisdom and learning making their way through the winter moons to Klynos. There they would recover from their winter travels and come together in one great assembly at the Mountain of the Year. I dreamed of being able to take the body of Petronicus to the mountain at the time of the Council and then he would *be there* in a way. That was the only comforting thought I had. I even considered stealing a donkey to make it easier to transport the body of Petronicus to the mountain but that was such a low and vile thought that I kept it in the dark area of my mind. Often I imagined the face of Petronicus looking down at me with disapproval when I thought of it.

One night when the moon had all but disappeared and was like a bent finger once again, I decided to extend my search for Petronicus further afield. I planned to collect what fruit I could from the trees and bushes and then trek away from the Bedosian territory and head for the Land of the Towering Rocks. Petronicus and I had wintered there several times. There were deep caves and most people were afraid to go there because the rocks that towered high above kept the sunlight away and made strange frightening noises when the wind blew between the rocks. Petronicus had explained it to me and I remembered as a child the two of us making whistling noises as we blew into shells and jagged stones. Other people thought it was the land of evil spirits so few ventured there. The trail was also difficult to follow because it was not well worn by travellers. After the Land of the Towering Rocks I intended to pass through the Land of the Tumbling Waters where food for the winter would be plentiful. I would then pass into the Land of the Tall People just as the warming winds of spring began to blow. There would then be new growth on the trees and bushes and small animals to catch and I would be within a few days' trek of Klynos.

I passed the crossroads where I had found the body of Melonius, which was still there rotting and had been gnawed by wild animals. I took what was left of his blanket and his cape and hood as I had greater need of them. The winter would indeed be cold in the Land of the Towering Rocks and Melonius was now beyond the cold. I knew that a good novice and scribe like Melonius would now be in the Land of Wisdom where only good men live.

I had difficulty finding the trail that ran into the Land of the Towering Rocks because so few people passed that way. The road to Klinbil went off towards the place where the sun began its journey across the sky each day. My trail went towards the huge rocks that stuck out of the ground like the stiff arms of dead men. It was then that I smelt the smoke from a fire. I approached very cautiously, and as I peered around some rocks I saw that blocking my trail was a man with a long blade, and a priest. There were also two young men who tended to the donkeys and a woman who prepared their food. I had no alternative but to wait until nightfall and try and get round them.

Night came with a grudging slowness. The Bedosians did not seem to be going anywhere; maybe they were just blocking the trail to prevent the escape of scribes and healers. I grasped my knife stick firmly and waited for darkness.

As I waited I imagined the face of Petronicus looking down at me: *'Why do you carry a knife stick, child?'* asked Petronicus in my inner mind. *'What do you propose to do, fight the man, the priest and the youths?'* I did not answer because I knew what he was going to say next. *'A man who has a weapon comes to rely on a weapon and he will prevail only if his weapon is greater than that of his enemies and he is well practised in its use.'*

I was thoughtful and then said to him in my mind: *'But it comforts me, Petronicus. I am alone now and have no friend to hand.'*

Petronicus smiled in his loveable way and said: '*I understand, Petronius. But you should live by your head, as the Revered One once said of you. Use your mind and thoughts and you will avoid the need for a weapon.*'

As I lay gazing up at the darkening sky behind a clump of rocks I noticed that the clouds were driving fast across the skies. As everyone knew, they were going to waft the great fires beyond the sea to make them hot enough for the sun to rest in. I smiled up at Petronicus and could imagine him smiling back. And then just as the last light was leaving the far sky the wind began to howl through the Towering Rocks. The sound of wailing could be heard and it was like the slow choking screams of dying men. I knew what it was because Petronicus had told me long ago. I looked over the rocks and to my relief the enemy were loading their belongings onto the donkeys and preparing to leave. I watched them pulling their cloaks over their heads and looking fearfully at the rocks. They departed towards the trail for Bedosa in great fear; they were not men of thought and reason. My way was now open.

I did not travel quickly through the Land of the Towering Rocks because I was enjoying the feeling of comparative safety. There were no signs of other travellers and only occasionally did I see old signs of donkey droppings on the trail. Small bushes with berries of various colours grew amongst the rocks and Petronicus had taught me which colours I could eat. The food did not give me much protection against the cold but kept me alive as winter approached. Water was plentiful as small streams rippled down the rocks towards the great river, which ran into the Land of the Tumbling Waters.

I also slept more soundly because I felt more secure and had the blanket and cape I had taken from the body of Melonius. I thanked him in my mind and wished him well in the Land of Wisdom where only good men live. He would be reunited with his master Melonicus and I imagined them travelling the eternal trail together as I hoped Petronicus and I would do one day.

I had been in the Land of the Towering Rocks for about three days when I ventured down towards the river. As I approached I was suddenly halted in my steps by a strange sound several paces behind me. I stopped to listen and the sound also stopped. And then when I walked on the sound followed me. It was not the sound of the wind but of some living thing and it was very close.

I grasped my knife stick firmly and hurried my pace. The sound kept up with me as I moved more quickly, so who or whatever was following me did the same. A horrific picture came into my mind: the Bedosians had returned and were following me. I knew I had been careless walking through soft ground and spitting out the stones from the berries. I thought I was safe and alone in that strange land.

And then my mind ceased to control my actions and my instinct to run came to the fore. I ran along the trail increasing my pace as fast as I could. I was no longer thinking straight and the extra blanket I had taken from Melonius impeded my flight. I kept glancing behind me to see my pursuers. That was my undoing! An exposed root from a tree caught my foot and I fell forward violently and for the smallest moment my mind closed. When it opened again I saw a giant figure standing over me. His legs were astride my fallen body and I could see the thick leather wrappings he had on his feet. Before I could move I felt a huge hand grasping me around the waist and picking me up. He held me against his chest with his immense arm and I saw the wicked long blade he held in his other hand. My mind faltered and I was swimming in a twilight world. In the dark light and just for an instant I looked into the face of the god!

My last vision before all life went from my body and my mind closed was of a huge face with a helmet of eagle feathers. And then before my ears finally closed to this world I heard the loud call of the god; it was like a roar from the deepest chambers in the earth and it thundered round my imagination. Darkness closed all around me as I was lifted from this life.

Thirteen

I seemed to be swimming frantically in the emptiness of my mind. I had nothing to hold on to and felt like a leaf in the wind trying to find the ground. There were strange sounds all around me and then a swirling confusion of terrifying pictures came to grapple with me. Something was trying to draw me ever inwards, holding my arms and stopping my puny attempts to surface into consciousness. My body was limp and lifeless and my thoughts were not my own. There was a vague red light in the distance pulling me towards it. It was trying to force open my tightly closed eyes and deliver me to the horrors that awaited me.

There was a hollow sound calling me from somewhere but I could not see where. I was trying to swim towards it because it was familiar.

Gradually it took human form: "Come awake, child … come back, child … open your eyes."

I called out: "Petronicus … is that you, Petronicus?"

"I am here, child … I am here … try and open your eyes."

Slowly my eyes opened to admit the red light. The face of Petronicus slowly filled my vision. His face was crimson and the firelight made his wrinkles look deep and old. "I am here, child." I threw myself into his face and grabbed his shoulders.

"Petronicus! Hold me. Hold me. Are we in the Land of Wisdom where only good men live?"

"No, child. Sadly we are not. We are still in the world of pain and wickedness."

How long I clung to Petronicus I do not know. He let me burrow my face into his beard the way I did when I was a small child, and neither of us spoke for a while.

"But, Petronicus …" I said fearfully at last "… I saw the face of the god."

"No, Petronius … you saw the face of a man … a man like you and me."

I felt myself gripping Petronicus more tightly and I tried to stammer that I did not understand.

"And if you turn your head, Petronius, you will see the face of Zilk. A man like us."

Zilk was behind me, away from the fire. Slowly I turned but held Petronicus in a clinging grip. I was afraid to let myself turn fully round so I just made a quick glance to take in the horror. I wanted to look away again quickly but I couldn't.

The face of Zilk broke into a broad smile. He no longer wore his helmet of eagle feathers and his huge blade was standing against the wall of the cave.

"Now," said Petronicus. "I want you to hold your hands together and reach towards him. He will then grasp your two hands between his. That is the way they greet friends where he comes from."

Slowly I released Petronicus and turned fully round and did as I was told. I held my hands together as if I was rubbing a leaf between them. I was terrified because I still thought of him as a god. Zilk slowly put my hands between his and rubbed them warmly. The smile on his face became even bigger, but I don't think I smiled back just then.

Petronicus broke the tension between us and said: "Time to eat now. All three of us, together."

That night was the first time since Petronicus and I had parted near to Bedosa that I felt truly safe. I was able to banish all the horrors I had experienced to the dark part of my mind as we all settled down to sleep. Zilk wanted to rub hands before we slept and when we awoke he did it again with a big smile on his face. I soon got used to his customs. But that night I was happy as I snuggled down in my blankets with Petronicus on one side of me and Zilk on the other. Our donkey slept at the mouth of the cave and although still hopelessly confused I sensed that all was well with us. The fire died down and I felt Petronicus putting warm stones around me. Sleep came and I went into the land of dreams where everything was warm and peaceful.

Slowly, during the next two moons, Petronicus explained all about Zilk to me. That knowledge is now known all over the world but to me at that moment it was unbelievable. From the very beginning I knew I was witnessing the greatest event that the world had ever seen. Petronicus had already learned much about Zilk and gradually whilst the winter moons waxed and waned I too discovered much. The order in which I learned about him is now confused in my memory. But as each day progressed we became closer in understanding.

But there was one question I had to ask and this was probably the first morning we were all together. Zilk had gone down the hill towards the stream where he ran the water through his long hair every morning. Petronicus and I were alone and I asked: "How did you find him? What happened when I left you?"

"I will tell you very quickly before he returns. After that we must never speak about Zilk unless he is sitting beside us. We must never let him think we are talking behind his back because he is still afraid and understands very few of our words."

"I understand."

"Well, you remember when we first saw the boat and we went and sat on the hill nearby?" I nodded. "I asked you to describe everything you saw. You remember, I said your eyes were young and could see further than mine."

"Yes, but I don't …"

"Don't interrupt, child. Listen because he will be back soon." I held my head down towards the ground for an instant in submission. "You counted the long blades they had and you counted ten."

"That was because there were ten armed men from Bedosa."

"Yes, child. That is correct. The Ruler was not with his men but he would have kept one for himself. So if each man had a blade and the Ruler had a blade, how many was that?" I held up the fingers of both hands and then added one more.

"Eleven," I said. "But I still don't underst..."

"Be patient, child. Young things want to know everything at once. Be patient and I will explain. Well, if there were eleven blades there were eleven men in the boat. Am I right?"

"Yes, that would be sense."

"Wrong, Petronius, use your eyes. How many seats and oars were there?"

"I did not count them." I said.

"No, but I did, just before we left. There were twelve seats so there were twelve men in the boat. Where was the other long blade?"

"But ..."

"And if they were all dead, who steered the boat to the shore? The boat would just drift in the sea until it sank or was sucked into the great fires."

"Where the sun sleeps at night?" I asked with astonishment.

"Yes. I realised that one of them still lived." Petronicus paused whilst I took all that he had said into my mind.

"And I thought you were afraid to enter Bedosa because you would be recognised. But you already knew one of the gods lived."

"Yes," said Petronicus. "I was fairly sure of that."

"You are truly wise, Petronicus," I said in admiration.

"No, child, observant. I kept well away from the trails as I searched for him because that is what a man would do if he were escaping in a strange land. I travelled inland after you left for Bedosa and early the next morning I found him. He was only a breath away from death. His belly was empty and I did not think he would last the night. He was unable to digest any food I gave him. I tried chewing it myself before giving it to him but he could keep nothing down."

"You thought he was dying?"

"Yes, I did. I was sure of it."

"But what did you do?" I asked.

"I made a space for us inside some thick bushes and fed him on tiny pieces of fish and rabbit. I mixed rabbit blood with water and gradually he was able to keep something inside him."

"You saved his life, Petronicus."

"Yes but I really wished you had been there to help. I had to keep right away from the trail because I saw armed men from Bedosa rushing about from place to place. We stayed many days until Zilk was strong enough to take proper food. I went down to the crossroads to see what was happening and met a merchant who told me about the massacre in Bedosa." Petronicus held me tight and there was great sadness in his eyes. "The merchant said you would surely be dead. Nobody escaped, he said. That is why I didn't leave a message for you."

"You didn't?" I gasped. "Oh, Petronicus, the gods smiled upon you indeed. The priests were reading the healers' signs and sending men after them to kill them. Many died not only in Bedosa but also on the trails. Oh, Petronicus, we are indeed fortunate."

Petronicus was silent for a while. He still held me close as his sadness turned to anger.

"The priests!" he said. "The priests have betrayed us. I knew this would happen one day."

"Then what did you do?"

"When Zilk was strong enough we came here."

"To the Land of the Towering Rocks? You have been here all the time?" Petronicus then hugged me very tight, his eyes dampened and he whispered: "I thought you were dead and had gone to the Land of Wisdom where only good men live."

I was confused in the early days because I couldn't understand why Zilk could not speak with us. His words were different! One evening Zilk was sitting by us and seemed content to listen to us talking although he could understand few of our words. Petronicus had taught him the names of things we had with us. Zilk learned the words cave, fire, animals and several other common words. He knew the words for sleeping and eating and also our names. Petronicus had also learned words from Zilk and between them they could speak fairly well together but only about everyday matters.

I remember, and it must have been about the second or third day we were all together, Zilk pointed to Petronicus and said: "Peetranicus," and smiled. Then he pointed to me and said: "Peetronus," and smiled again. Finally he pointed to himself and said: "Zilk," and we all smiled.

He enjoyed it even more when I pointed to him and said: "Zilk." Then he wanted to rub hands with me.

One day I asked Petronicus: "Why are his words different?"

Petronicus did not answer immediately. He looked very thoughtful so I asked: "Where do words come from?"

"From the gods, probably," Petronicus said. "When the world first came out of the Mountain of the Year and the people came … perhaps …"

"But where did the people come from?"

"Too many questions, child. Too many questions." That meant he didn't know. We both smiled.

I well remember another evening during that long winter in the Land of the Towering Rocks. We were sitting just inside the cave mouth. Zilk was sleeping inside and Petronicus and I were just sitting quietly together. We had been silent for quite some time when Petronicus said: "What troubles you, child?"

We had been out hunting all day and although Zilk came with us he could do very little because he was still very weak. He had not recovered from his ordeal in the boat. Zilk could lie down and fall asleep immediately after we had eaten our food, whereas Petronicus and I liked to talk together before we entered the world of dreams. I looked over to Zilk and saw he was sound asleep.

"I am not troubled, Petronicus, I am confused. We have learned a lot about Zilk."

"And he of us."

"Yes," I said. "But the thing we have not learned is perhaps the biggest question of all."

"You are right, and I think I have the same confusion. Say what you mean, child."

I looked over at Zilk. He always slept on his back with his face uppermost. His great blade was never far from his hand and his helmet of eagle feathers nearby. He looked peaceful and by now quite familiar.

"But, Petronicus. Where did he come from?"

My master was silent for a long time. I thought he was in the land of dreams until his face began to twist in puzzlement. At length he looked at me straight in the eyes and said: "I have always taught you to ask questions because therein lies the path to wisdom."

"Yes," I answered. "The Revered One also said that."

"Petronius, I think you and I share a knowledge that nobody else in the word has."

"Not even the Revered One?" I asked in astonishment.

"Correct. Not even the Revered One." He went silent again which I knew meant he was thinking very deeply. Perhaps his thoughts were so deep that they were amongst the gods. After a while he looked at me and said: "Those of us who ask questions must never be afraid of the answers. Nor must we be impatient for the answers. Now listen, Petronius, do you think it possible that there is another world in the sea?"

I would have laughed out loud if I had been talking to any man but Petronicus. I did not laugh but I felt my eyes bulging with astonishment.

118

"How can that be? They would be burned alive in the great fires where the sun rests each night ... you have told me that often."

"Yes, I know I have. But maybe we are wrong. Maybe the great fires are further away than we think. Perhaps our world is not the only one."

The idea sounded unbelievable. Perhaps there are questions that should never be asked, I thought. And then I remembered something I had said to the Revered One. I remembered how he asked me what disturbed me most about the cataclysm that had come to the world. I said being forbidden to question troubled me the most. I had told him about the priest in Bedosa hitting me when I asked a question about the boat of the gods. And now I was with Petronicus, the wisest of men, asking ourselves the biggest question of all.

The question was so immense that I began to feel cold and afraid.

On the morning after the shortest day of the twelfth moon we made our greatest discovery. The snow was piled high outside the mouth of our cave but we had some fish we had smoked days earlier for our food. Zilk was particularly skilful at catching fish. He would lie by the bank with his hand under the water waiting for a fish to come along. He was able to remain absolutely still like a tree without the wind for long periods and then he would whip the fish out of the water and onto the bank; we never went short of fish whilst Zilk was with us.

Petronicus and I sat by the fire whilst Zilk rested from his fishing. Petronicus and I were discussing once again my experiences in Bedosa and in particular what happened to Melonicus and Mentis.

"Mentis was very old," said Petronicus. "And he often flew about in his own mind. His thoughts were often confused."

"But why did he tell me to take the tablets to you?"

"Well, there you are, you see. If he could not read them himself and he was the Keeper of the House of Tablets in Bedosa, why did he think that I could?"

"I do not know. Kelcit couldn't read them either," I said

"Nor could the Elder Scribe of Klinbil, you said."

"Or the Revered One. Perhaps," I said smiling cheekily, "they all know you are the wisest of men."

Petronicus smiled indulgently but did not respond.

I reached into my pouch and took out the tablets Mentis had given to me in Bedosa. We had often looked at them and moved our fingers over the markings that made the words. I must have disturbed Zilk because he turned towards me and smiled.

"Hmm," Petronicus mused looking at them closely. "They are strange words indeed."

"Yes," I said. "Strange words … *fidik* … *gilbid*."

Zilk sat up from the floor and pushed his blanket away. He reached forward and grabbed hold of his long blade pointing to it saying: "*Fidik … fidik*." Petronicus stood up and went towards him. He knelt down by him and touched the long blade and said: "*Fidik? Fidik?*"

Zilk smiled broadly and wanted to rub hands in excitement. I brought the tablet over to him and showed it to him but the markings meant nothing to him.

"*Gilbid?*" I asked and looked at him excitedly. "*Gilbid? … Gilbid?*" Zilk reached over and picked up his helmet of eagle fathers and said: "*Gilbid. Gilbid.*"

What an exciting day that was for all three of us. However, we were wrong about *gilbid*. It did not mean helmet, it meant eagle, but that didn't matter. We were also wrong about his understanding of our word hunger; he thought it meant stomach. His word for hunger we learned later was *sunka*. The next day we were eating fish that Zilk had caught the day before. He held up a piece of smoked fish and said: "*Kandis*." That was another word on the tablets. We enjoyed our *kandis* that day and Zilk caught some more *kandis* in the days that followed.

Fourteen

I have often wondered what would have happened to the world if Petronicus had not found Zilk. Supposing he had been killed by the priests and soldiers of Bedosa or even worse used by them to prove they were the only ones with power through the gods? As the years have passed I have come to realise that Petronicus saved the world and I have always been proud to have played a part, however small, in that wonderful event.

Petronicus had questioned me in great detail about my time in Bedosa and on the trail to Klinbil. Every detail of my conversations with Mentis, Kelcit and the Revered One had to be repeated over and over again as Petronicus used his great mind to understand the strange events that later became known as the Great Cataclysm.

"Going over the details many times helps us to understand," said Petronicus.

As the winter snows began to melt Petronicus decided that we should leave the Land of the Towering Rocks and head for the Land of the Tumbling Waters. There we could catch the early fish, or *kandis* as we now called them. It pleased Zilk to hear us using his words.

It took Petronicus and me many days to explain to Zilk why we should move. We could not explain about the forthcoming Council of Wisdom at the Mountain of the Year in spring nor could we explain that we needed to meet the Revered One in Klynos, because we did not have the words Zilk could follow.

However, our departure from the cave was delayed when Zilk developed a painful rash on his legs. Petronicus said that children travelling in some lands often scratched themselves on small bushes and this caused the rash. Grown people, he said, had got used to it, were stronger anyway and it did not affect them. Zilk of course was not used to our bushes and he suffered greatly.

Zilk allowed Petronicus to examine his leg. It was red raw and looked to be very painful.

We knelt down to look at his leg and Petronicus said: "You know, child, I don't think they understand healing where Zilk comes from. I think they just make sick people comfortable and hope they get better. There is much we can teach his people."

"And much he can teach us. Have you looked at his long blade? Their ironers must be very skilled." Petronicus nodded but did not speak because the one thing that worried him about Zilk was his huge blade and how he never let it out of his sight.

Zilk began to say the word 'rash' whilst we were looking at his leg. He smiled whenever he learned a new word. As Petronicus was examining his rash I noticed that Zilk looked at him in admiration and affection.

"Now," said Petronicus to me, "go down the hillside amongst the trees and bushes and bring back some leaves from a kollen tree, some bark from the arabak and some yellow moss from under the rocks near the stream. And don't forget the berries."

I did as I was told but found it difficult to get the leaves. The kollen shed its leaves in autumn and I had to rummage on the ground to find them.

Petronicus knew that I had made this skin preparation many times so he let me do it when I returned to the cave. Zilk watched with admiration as I crushed the berries to make a greasy base for the preparation and then shredded the bark with my teeth. I daubed it on the leaves and let it stand for a short time. And then when Petronicus agreed that it was ready I put the leaves on Zilk's legs and fastened them down with strips of moss. The pain stopped after two days and he felt strong enough to walk down the hill to the stream with me to put his hair into the water.

On our way back to the cave we found a large dead bird that had been attacked by a wolf or a fox. Zilk picked up the remains of the creature and began to pluck its feathers. These he took back to the cave and by that night he had made a helmet of feathers for me. He was full of smiles when he put it on my head and we rubbed hands. It was then Petronicus and I realised that Zilk's helmet of feathers was not to make him look fierce but simply to keep him warm.

We decided to move when the moon had grown fully once more so that we would have more light at night. Several nights before we left Petronicus and I were sitting by the mouth of the cave. Zilk was sound asleep inside whilst the donkey chewed small pieces of moss that I had brought for him from down the hill.

"Petronicus," I said in the still of the evening. This was the time we often talked together.

"Yes, child. What troubles you?"

"I am not troubled, Petronicus, I am curious."

He smiled and said: "Then what are you curious about?"

"Kelcit of Klinbil told me there had been a Council of Wisdom when you were very young." Petronicus nodded confirming what Kelcit had said. "Kelcit said he was too young to attend but you were allowed to sit behind the wise men and listen."

"That is correct. Kelcit remembered it well. My master was alive then but sadly he died within ten moons of that. I think he was broken hearted by what was said at the Council. After that I travelled the trails with the Revered One for most of the next twelve moons and we discussed it over many fires. But he was not known as the Revered One then; his name was Conicus."

I did not know that Petronicus and the Revered One had travelled the trails together so many years ago.

"But what troubled your master so much that he died?" Petronicus looked away into the night sky deep in thought and then he said: "Well, you may remember that when you were small I told you that part of the gods live in all good men."

"Yes, but not wicked men. When they are wicked, you told me that sometimes the gods leave bad people and then when they get sick …"

"Yes, yes, child, you remember well, but do not interrupt. Well, the priests decided amongst themselves that we were all wrong. They said that the gods did not live in people but in what they called the Separation."

"I don't understand," I said.

"I know. And many of us did not understand either. But from then onwards the priests kept much to themselves and did not join in discussions with wise men. We became divided: healers, scribes and men of wisdom on one hand and the priests on the other. We did not become enemies and there are some good priests who think as we do … but most of them …" Petronicus did not finish his words but tightened his face without saying anything further.

"But what about ordinary people? What did they think?" I asked.

"Oh, I don't know. They do not have the years of learning that we have. They do not question anything. They just believe what they are told."

We remained silent for a while as a thought so great began to take shape within me. I felt my belly tighten as the thought rose up until it had to come from my mouth.

"But, Petronicus, is that why the priests are against us now? Is that why they destroyed all the tablets that Mentis cared for in the House of Tablets in Bedosa?"

"Yes, child, sadly I think it is. You see, Petronius, if you want to control people, you first control their beliefs and that is what the Ruler and priests of Bedosa are doing. But first they had to destroy the histories and thoughts of wise men."

The statement Petronicus made that night about controlling people through controlling their beliefs remained with me all my days and has been my guiding principle.

The next day Zilk and I went down to the valley floor to collect berries and roots for our journey. Zilk put his head into the water of the stream and let his long hair flow with the water to clean it. When it had dried in the wind he pushed it down inside his robe and that kept his back warm in the winter. I wondered if he cut it in the hot moons but I did not have the words to ask him.

We stood together watching the watery sun begin its climb towards the top of the day, when Zilk suddenly put his hand on my shoulder as a sign of danger. I could see or hear nothing, but Zilk was sniffing the wind and holding his finger to his lips to tell me to remain silent. Zilk was older than I was and very tall. Slowly he removed his long blade, which he carried across his shoulders and held it in front of him. And then I heard it myself: the snorting and movements of a large animal. Zilk indicated that I should stand behind him as we faced the oncoming beast. It was a large black boar with fearsome face and huge teeth. I wanted to run and try and climb into the rocks but Zilk kept me behind him. As the animal prepared to attack us, Zilk just held his long blade in front of him. The beast ran towards us and impaled itself on the point of the blade. Badly wounded, it shrieked in pain and tried to rub its injured mouth in the ground. Zilk just went towards it and brought his blade down into its neck.

It was after the feast of roast boar we had that night that Petronicus, in a sombre thinking mood, said to me: "You know, child, perhaps we were wrong about the long blade. Perhaps it is not a weapon to be used against other people at all. Maybe it is just for hunting."

We slept well that night with full bellies and the next morning we began to make our preparations to leave. We smoked as much meat as we could over our fire and wrapped it up in the spare blanket I had taken from Melonius. Zilk smiled at us as he watched and then indicated to me that I should go to the river with him.

This time he washed himself very quickly and waded into the reed beds in the swamp. The reeds were nearly as high as me but

Zilk towered over them. Once again he took out his long blade and swirled it in front of him. The reeds fell like magic and in less time than it takes to tell he had collected an arm full of good stout reeds. These he began to weave into baskets on the stream bank.

That night in the cave Petronicus asked Zilk if he could hold the long blade. Zilk was pleased to hand it to him and Petronicus indicated his admiration.

"Yes, child, perhaps we were wrong about the long blade." I smiled because I had told him all about it when we returned from the stream. "And what about your weapon, child? What about your knife stick, do you intend to keep it?" I did not answer immediately because I was preparing myself to counter what I knew he would say next. "A man who has a weapon …" Petronicus began.

"'Comes to rely on that weapon'," I interrupted. We both smiled. "And as the Revered One once said …"

"… 'You should use your head.' Yes, you are very sharp tonight, Petronius. A good feast, eh?"

"Yes, a good feast," I said and rubbed my belly. Zilk did the same and we all smiled.

"Tell me again," said Petronicus. "Just how did you come by the knife stick and the coins you have?"

I went through the story once again. I told him about the trail from Bedosa and how I had stayed at the inn where bad men tried to capture me and sell me to the priests. I had not thought very deeply about my time at the inn; there had been so many other frightening things to think about.

Petronicus listened, nodded and then said: "But I do think, Petronius, that the stick would be better put on the fire to keep us warm. Unlike Zilk you are not skilled in its use."

I smiled in a submissive way. Petronicus was right as always.

"I will remove the blade and keep it to cut our food and the stick will go on the fire as you say, Petronicus." I removed the blade and wiped it clean on my blanket and carefully put it inside my pouch. I looked at Petronicus and saw a strange but benevolent look on his face. A knowing smile passed between us. And for the first time in our lives together it was not a smile between master and novice, man and boy, but a knowing smile between two men.

And even after all these years, I still have the blade my mother gave me.

Fifteen

After several days of preparation the three of us set off on the trail towards the Land of the Tumbling Waters. I think Zilk was sad to leave the safety of our cave. He had fully recovered from his ordeal in the boat but he still mourned the death of his companions. I had been alone and unprotected in the world myself in recent moons so I could understand how terrified he must have been before Petronicus found him.

Our donkey was laden with the reed bags Zilk had made. We had the spare clothes I had taken from Melonius and the smoked meat from the boar Zilk had killed. I had collected moss and small pieces of dry wood to make fires when we stopped for the night. I also collected leaves from the kollen and bark from the arabak in case Zilk's leg hurt him again during the long trek ahead of us. We were well provided for. We had the coins I had been given at the inn and the boar skin could be traded in any town. But although all seemed well with us as we set off, I had strange feelings within me, feelings that I did not want to put into words.

Petronicus led the way as we left the cave because he knew the trail through the Land of the Towering Rocks which was difficult to follow in places. Zilk had his long blade, or his *fidik* as we all now called it, across his shoulders and I had my mother's precious blade in my belt. I had much to think about as we set off on the trail. I knew great events would take place in Klynos and at the Council of Wisdom and I would be there to see it all.

Petronicus had often said to me as I grew up that '*walking makes the brain work*'. We had not gone far before the thought, which had been lurking deep within me came into my mind. Petronicus was walking in front, I was behind with the donkey and

Zilk followed behind me. I was confused until I realised that all my life with Petronicus there had only been the two of us. And the donkey, of course, the donkey was always with us. But now there were three and I found it very strange. I also think I was a little disturbed by the thought that I might have to share Petronicus with Zilk for a long time to come. On the other hand, I told myself, Zilk was big and strong and possessed of a great blade and could protect us if we met the men from Bedosa.

On several occasions I noticed that Petronicus stumbled a little and seemed unsure of his feet. On each occasion Zilk rushed forward to help steady him and seemed to want to support him. There was no doubt he had grown very fond of Petronicus.

Just before the sun reached the top of the day, Petronicus suddenly stopped and held up his hand. Zilk came forward and began to sniff the wind. He indicated that we should walk slowly and quietly for a few paces. And then we saw it: the huddled body of a man on the trail in front of us. His cloak blew in the wind and it was clear before we reached him that he was dead.

I gave the donkey's rope to Petronicus and ran forward with Zilk and turned the body over so I could see his face.

"It is Mentis," I shouted back to Petronicus, who now hurried to catch us up. He knelt down to look at the body and said: "His neck is broken and I think he has been dead for some days."

"Was he attacked?" I asked.

"No, child, thankfully he was not. He has not been robbed. See, his clothes are untouched and his pouch is still around his waist. No, I think he must have fallen and hit his head on the rock."

Both Zilk and I watched as Petronicus examined the body very thoroughly. "His belly is empty; he has had very little to eat. Is there any food in his pouch?"

I opened it and felt inside. "No, no food."

"Hmmm. Take the leathers off his feet, Petronius."

I did as I was told and we saw that the leathers had worn through and his feet were cut and blistered.

"It must have been very painful for him," I said sadly. "And one of his legs is withered. What a cruel journey for him."

"Yes, but an urgent one, it seems," said Petronicus.

"I think he was trying to get to the Mountain of the Year," I said and Petronicus agreed.

"Any coins in his pouch?" I shook my head and looked down sadly at the body.

"Come closer, child, and see here, look at his fingers and finger nails." I picked up Mentis's stiff hand and I could see how the nails were broken and his hand covered in tiny cuts. Under his nails were traces of red clay.

"The tablets," I said. "He's been searching through the tablets in Bedosa. He must have gone back there."

"Yes, you are right, Petronius. Gather up his pouch and we will take it with us. And his clothes. We have more need of his clothes than he does."

I nodded and said: "Goodbye, Mentis." I turned to Petronicus and asked: "Will he be in the Land of Wisdom where only good men live?"

"Yes," said Petronicus. "A good man like Mentis is sure to be."

Zilk and I carried his body away from the trail and placed it in a small clearing amongst some rocks. We removed his clothes and piled stones over his body so that wild animals could not come and disturb him.

Not long after the sun began to slide down the day towards the great fires, Petronicus said we should make camp for the night. We were nearing the end of the Land of the Towering Rocks and would soon enter the Land of the Tumbling Waters where we would encounter more people. The Tall People often hunted in the area and Petronicus was still pondering the problem of Zilk. He did not want people to see him dressed all in fine woven cloth, carrying a huge blade and wearing his helmet of eagle feathers. The news about the arrival of the 'gods' had probably reached the area although we did not expect the men of Bedosa had raided that far.

"If the news has carried this far," said Petronicus, "it is probably about huge giants with the wings of eagles coming out of their heads and blades as big as a man that could kill ten with one blow." I smiled and Petronicus added: "Many a tale grows with the telling."

Petronicus led us off the trail and we prepared a camp for ourselves where a lively steam entered a small lake. I busied myself preparing moss and wood to start a fire for the night, and clearing the sleeping ground of small stones and scrub. Zilk went to the lake and began to fish. I watched him and saw another peaceful use of his great blade. Zilk would stand absolutely still in the water with his feet apart letting the point of his blade dangle downwards towards the water. He wrapped small twigs and grass around his ankles to attract the fish. As I watched, a large fish swam towards his feet. Zilk remained absolutely motionless until the fish was directly under his blade. He then just dropped it straight into the water and speared the fish.

Petronicus was resting, propped up against a rock. He called me over to him and said: "Empty the pouch we took from Mentis and let us see if we can find out why he was hurrying to the Mountain of the Year."

As expected, I found several small fragments of clay tablets. They looked to be very old.

"Kelcit told me they could be as old as the world, from the time when the world came out of the mountain."

"Hmm," mused Petronicus. "They are certainly ancient, older than the memories of all the learned men."

Zilk had now returned with his fish, which he laid on the ground, and smiled. He sat by Petronicus and watched the old man fingering the tablets. "Come, child, bring your young eyes and read the words."

"*Aroo*, I think, but the marks are so worn it is difficult. *Aroo*, yes, maybe."

Zilk stood up in much excitement: "*Aroo* … *aroo* … yes. Please to come. Come please."

I jumped up and followed him towards the small lake. Petronicus roused himself from his resting position and followed. I watched as Zilk reached down to the ground and searched for a suitable piece of wood. He picked up one or two and discarded them and continued until he found one he wanted. It was a small fairly flat piece of wood, which he smoothed with a small blade. I then watched as he held it up to me and said: "*Aroo*."

I smiled and pointed at his piece of wood and said: "*Aroo*. For fire?"

He shook his head because he knew our word for fire. He took me by the hand and led me to the water's edge. He placed the wood carefully on the water and repeated the word as he gently pushed it half an arm's length into the water. He then made rowing movements with his arms saying: "*Aroo*," over and over again.

"So," said Petronicus, "*aroo* means boat." Zilk was now beaming all over his face. His long hair was blowing in the wind as he reached down and picked the boat out of the water. I watched in fascination as he poked a small twig into the centre and then picked a large leaf from a bush and threaded the twig through it. He placed the boat in the water and pointed to it as the wind gently acted on a sail and moved the *aroo* into the lake.

We now know all about sails on boats, but it must be remembered that we had never seen one before. Our fishermen's boats were very small with only two men on them and were only rowed a short way out because they were afraid of being blown out to sea and into the great fires. Zilk waded out into the lake and picked up his boat and brought it back to me. I pointed at the sail and then pointed towards his mouth. Zilk looked at me and pointed to the leaf and said: "*Midit*."

I noticed that night beside the fire that Petronicus looked happier than I had seen him for several moons. Zilk was cutting up what remained of the large fishes he had caught ready to smoke and take with us the next day. The word *midit* was important, I realised that, so I looked once again at the clay tablets I had been given by Mentis. I found it, but I had to rub away much dust and dirt with spit before I could see it. It was very scratched and worn as if countless scribes had handled it since the world began.

"Well," said Petronicus, "we now know that the wind blew the 'gods' here. What a tale … what a tale." I smiled and reminded him of the great piece of woven cloth that I had seen on the boat in the Temple of Bedosa. "But you know," said Petronicus, indicating that I should sit closer to him, "the mystery is now clear to me. Is it clear to you, Petronius?" I said I was not sure because I wanted to hear his reasoning.

"It means this whole thing, the 'gods' coming from the sea, blown by the magical wind, has happened before." I was stunned and did not speak. Petronicus continued, but I think he was speaking aloud to himself more than me. "If the ancient scribes recorded Zilk's words for boat, long blades, feather helmets and other things, words that we have never used, it must mean that Zilk's people have been here before." Petronicus was silent again.

"But, Petronicus," I said, "if Zilk's people came in ancient times, where are they now? Are they here in our world? What happened to them?"

"These are things we do not know. Maybe we will find out later if we keep on questioning." He smiled and drew me closer to him. Zilk sensed that we were happy together and looked up from his work and smiled broadly at us. "You know, child," Petronicus continued, "I have always taught you the importance of words and the thoughts they tell of. Now just think, where would we be now if some scribe in ancient times had not taken the trouble to learn the sounds of these strange words and inscribe them on clay tablets? It must have been a time so long ago, just as the world

began. Just think on that. Because of that we know the truth."
Petronicus paused and smiled broadly and looked more contented
than I could remember. "And then," he went on, "think of Mentis.
If he had not found these tablets and perhaps understood their
importance … and supposing the priests of Bedosa had destroyed
them … you see the importance of the word. The word is the
thought and the thought is truth."

We felt inwardly content after our meal of fish and sweet
leaves. We sat back listening to the friendly crackle of the fire.

It was just before we rolled ourselves in our blankets that
Petronicus said: "With the words and truths we now have,
Petronius, we can stop the Ruler of Bedosa from ruling the whole
world … we can stop the priests of Bedosa destroying all the truth
and wisdom of the world. But sleep well tonight, child, for I have a
mission for you tomorrow."

Sixteen

It was a sad parting the next morning. We divided the coins between us and Zilk wrapped some smoked fish in a small reed basket for me. He tied it on my back with a length of plaited spruce. I had my blade on my belt and I carried the cloak we had taken from Mentis over my shoulder because it was still very cold in the Land of the Tumbling Waters.

Petronicus held me close just before I left and whispered in my ear: "Be careful every step, and use your head and your swiftness to protect yourself. And remember, Petronius, speak only to the Revered One; tell our tale to nobody else."

Zilk also embraced me and I saw great regret at our parting in his eyes. It was with sadness and some fear that I set off alone for Klynos through the Land of the Tumbling Waters.

On my second day on the trail I found the weather getting warmer as the spring winds blew from the great fires beyond the sea to bring new life to the world. I had seen nobody on the trail except a hunting party of the Tall People in the distance. The Tall People, Petronicus often told me, do not welcome strangers but have great respect for healers. I kept my novice's hood under my robe ready to reveal it if I met any of them.

Towards nightfall on the second day I heard somebody calling from some rocks near the trail. I stopped and listened and realised that it was a call for help. Without thinking, I put my hand on my blade, ignoring the disapproving image of Petronicus I had in my mind.

"Who is there?" I called but no one answered me. I waited and again I heard a moan of pain from just off the trail. I revealed my novice's cape and climbed up the hill. "Who calls? Where are you?"

"Please … please help me …" I heard. I approached cautiously and found a man, one of the Tall People lying on the ground groaning in considerable pain. His mind was not his own and he was mumbling: "Please … please … *sunka … sunka*."

I knelt down and spoke loudly to him: "Where are you hurt, friend?" I learned later that his name was Combanius and he was a hunter whose task it was to run far ahead of the main hunting party and locate the animals. He opened his eyes and gave me a painful smile. He pointed to his leg, which I examined, and I found a huge swelling just above his knee. It was red raw and appeared to be extremely painful. I touched it gently but he grimaced in pain.

I took his hand and said: "I am Petronius, son and novice of Petronicus the healer. Your leg is badly inflamed and the poison must be removed or you will die."

"Please to do what needs be done," said Combanius faintly. How long he had been lying there I could not tell but the pain must have been unbearable. I could see a small puncture in his skin where a snake had bitten him. "Two days ago," he managed to say.

I made him as comfortable as I could and went in search of some evergreen leaves. I also needed soft moist moss to place on the wound when I had drained it. I searched amongst several small rocks until I found the tiny lichen I knew would ease his pain. I returned to Combanius and he tried very hard to smile at me.

"Now, friend, chew on this. Get as much juice out of it as you can before you swallow. And when that has gone I have more."

I took my blade and cleaned it on the grass before squeezing the poisoned skin of his leg between my fingers. Slowly and carefully I made a small cut in the blistering skin and eased the poison out. It came out quite easily and I did not have to make a bigger cut, which was a blessing.

"Keep chewing the lichen," I said to Combanius. "And get as much juice out of it as you can. It will ease your pain."

I continued to drain the wound and then soothed it with damp leaves before putting a binding of soft moss on it. His pain subsided slightly but I urged him to continue to chew more lichen that I gave him.

It was clear that I could not leave Combanius alone and uncared for. I felt an urgent desire to continue my mission to Klynos but the sight of Combanius lying on the ground in pain greatly disturbed me. I was a healer and my first duty was to Combanius. '*True freedom,*' Petronicus always said, '*does not come from avoiding obligations but from fulfilling them.*' I knew I could not leave Combanius. I would either have to help him along the trail or go and find his people. If I could find them they would have to come for him whilst I continued my mission to Klynos.

We sat together in the late afternoon sun and I noticed that Combanius's face was returning to its natural colour. The poison had all seeped out of the wound and I knew it would heal up quite quickly in a day or two. Combanius was a young and healthy man probably of no more than twenty summers. He carried a long knife stick, such as the Tall People use for hunting. He smiled at me and thanked me for cleaning and draining his wound and then he said something that excited me greatly.

He looked at me pathetically and said: "I am very hungry."

I gave him the smoked fish Zilk had given me, which he ate ravenously. I sat back and watched him devour it. And then in that moment of rest a momentous thought grew within me. The word *sunka*, the word he had used in his delirium, was the same word that Zilk used when he indicated his belly as he anticipated food. The thought stirred deep inside me. It excited my stomach and made my chest feel tight as it emerged into my brain: '*The Tall People!*' I looked at Combanius closely but I could not estimate how tall he was, certainly not as tall as Zilk but taller than most of us. I wanted to run back and tell Petronicus of my discovery and ask him to explain it to me, but I knew my duty was to get to Klynos and speak to the Revered One.

I stayed with Combanius that night. He had a flint in his pouch so we were able to light a fire and keep warm. He did not say very much and went into sleep quite early. I put the extra blanket I had taken from Mentis over him and placed warm stones around it. It was a clear frosty night and the naming star of Petronicus twinkled into life. I waited and, as the night grew darker, my own naming star which, Petronicus had told me was much further away, probably more than a day's walk away, joined it and they both twinkled together. I knew that Petronicus was also watching with Zilk somewhere back along the trail towards the Land of the Towering Rocks. Sadly, there were no arabak trees near us that I could touch and feel closer to my master.

The next day I examined Combanius's leg and replaced the moss bindings. He said he felt stronger and was anxious to return to his people. We left just as the sun began its long climb up the day but I very quickly realised that Combanius was still too weak. We rested and after a while I asked: "Do you know where your people are now?"

"They are not far. I think I can smell their smoke." He propped himself up against a tree trunk and pointed towards some small hills in the near distance. "It is probably one of our hunting parties but they are a long way ahead of us and I do not think I have the strength today."

"Then we will prepare a place for you and I will go on ahead and bring your people to you."

I left Combanius as comfortable as I could and set off towards the small hills. I covered the ground quite quickly but approached their fire cautiously. Always in the dark part of my mind was a fear that it might be the men and priests from Bedosa. There were about ten men and several women around the fire. They were preparing the animals they had hunted: skinning them and cutting the meat up into small pieces ready to carry them back to their settlements. I put on my novice's hood and scribe's cape and approached slowly.

"I am Petronius, son and novice of Petronicus the healer."

"Welcome, healer. Welcome to our fire."

Several of them gathered around me and offered me food as I told them about Combanius and offered to lead them back to him. They organised themselves immediately into a rescue party. They broke two branches off a tree to make carrying poles and stretched a blanket between them so that Combanius could lie on it. They also sent out runners to recall other groups of men who were out looking for Combanius.

The Tall People invited me to stay the night at their fire. They were so grateful to me for saving Combanius and were concerned about me travelling alone on the trail. It would have been insulting to refuse fire at night so I agreed. Just as I was about to examine Combanius's leg once again there was a commotion as a large hunting party entered their camp. A very tall man who clearly had authority over the others came right over to us and embraced Combanius.

He turned to me and said: "I am Combanicus and this is my son."

I realised immediately that Combanicus was the leader of the Tall People, and that night when we had feasted well on the meat they had hunted he stood up and announced: "Let it be known that Petronius, son and novice of the great healer Petronicus, is called friend by Combanicus. Let him always travel safely in our land."

There was much cheering and they began to put small choice pieces of meat on my blanket for me. It was a pleasant and above all a very safe night.

Seventeen

I enjoyed a feeling of wellbeing and safety when I continued my journey the next morning. I had been well fed by the Tall People and I was under their protection as I journeyed through their lands on my way to Klynos. I estimated it would only take me three more days before I reached the town. I saw several hunting parties of the Tall People and although they did not approach me I knew they were watching over me. At the crossroads, where the Klynos trail from Klinbil met the trail from the Land of the Tumbling Waters, I had another pleasant surprise. I noticed that several healers had left their signs in the small stones and this indicated that the Bedosians had not penetrated this far in search for healers and scribes. The stones also told me that men of wisdom and learning were answering the call of the Revered One and travelling to Klynos ready for the Council of Wisdom at the Mountain of the Year in spring.

The gate into Klynos was open as usual and many people were thronging the streets. There was a party of the Tall People come to trade their furs and animal bones, and trains of donkeys belonging to itinerant merchants were snaking through the main gate. I wore my hood and cape quite openly as I entered the town.

There was a lively trade going on in the market place with merchants, healers and scribes all vying with each other for business. The temple doors were open and people seemed to be going in and out as usual. I looked round for a healer who might know the whereabouts of the Revered One.

"You were the novice of Petronicus, you say?" asked a healer called Venicus who we had met on the trail some years earlier.

"He is dead I hear. Killed by the priests of Bedosa and all his knowledge and wisdom lost. Such wickedness is beyond belief."

"Is the Revered One in Klynos?" I asked.

"Yes," said Venicus. "You will find him in the House of Scribes behind the market place."

The House of Scribes at Klynos was world famous for teaching letters and words to novices. There were several young men and boys milling around but they seemed to be tending to the donkeys and cutting wood rather than learning their letters. As I approached the House I saw several healers and other learned men sitting around in the early spring sunshine in front of the house. There was a general bustle and it seemed to be a place of great anticipation and activity.

I approached the door and asked a man: "May I speak to the Revered One? I have urgent business with him."

He looked at me with some suspicion. "You are very young to have business with the Revered One. Where is your master?"

"I am here on my master's affairs. Please tell the Revered One that Petronius is here and needs to speak urgently with him."

I was told to wait at the door. One of the healers must have heard me announcing myself. He approached me. "Petronius? Then you are the son of Petronicus?" I nodded. "I am Yeminicus. Your master and I were friends of many years. Please allow me to say how sorry I am to hear of his death at the hands of those wicked Bedosians. If I can help you please say. You are welcome to travel the trails with my son and me."

I thanked him but told him nothing of our remarkable story. Just then an elderly scribe came to the door. Two young novices accompanied him. The scribe looked at me with some suspicion.

"I see you wear the cape of a scribe and the hood of a novice but you are without your master. Why do you want to speak with the Revered One?"

"I am sorry but I do not withhold my respect for you when I say my business is urgent and it is with the Revered One only. Please tell him that Petronius is here and needs to speak with him."

He looked at me closely. "The Revered One sleeps. He has had a long and difficult journey from Klinbil and he is old and needs rest. Wait here with the other men who wish to see him. Perhaps when he wakes … who knows?"

It was nearly nightfall and I was still waiting outside the House of Scribes. The fire lighter of Klynos was preparing the great night fire in the market place where travellers and those without shelter in the town could sleep. I had wasted too much time already and could imagine Petronicus scolding me for idleness. Just then a young scribe appeared, carrying food from the cooking fire in the back of the house towards another room where I thought the Revered One would be.

"Friend," I said, "please let me speak to you. I will take little of your time. I will not ask you for food."

"What is it, friend? Be quick or I will be scolded if the food is cold."

"Is it for the Revered One?" The scribe nodded and I said in a whisper: "Tell the Revered One that Petronius is here and he has a message from Petronicus." The scribe nodded and hurried away. Almost immediately he returned and told me to follow him into the room where the Revered One sat.

"Petronius, I greet you. I am told you have a message from Petronicus. How can that be? We have heard nothing of Petronicus this winter and believe him dead."

"Revered One, Petronicus is alive and well and sent me to speak to you … to you … and no one else."

"Then he must have good reason. Come, child, and sit with me and give me your message." The Revered One asked his companions to leave us.

I cannot estimate how long it took me to tell our tale. The Revered One sat very still and listened to every word. I was amazed at how involved the story was. I told how Petronicus reasoned that one of the 'gods' had survived and how he found Zilk starving and very sick. The idea that Zilk came from another world beyond the sea where they spoke different words astonished the Revered One. He listened to me telling of the words of Zilk with great interest and frequently stroked his beard in puzzlement. He asked me to tell again the story of my time in Bedosa.

"My memory is like a rotting apple that has lost its juice," he said. "Tell me once again."

Horror disfigured his old face as I retold him the story of the massacre of scribes and those who would not accept the new beliefs in Bedosa. He nearly came to tears when I described seeing the body of Melonicus hanging by the town gate.

Our time together seemed to pass very quickly and it became darker and darker outside. We could see the lights dancing on the wall of the house from the town fire in the market place and heard the people talking and arguing with each other. Food was brought in twice for the Revered One and he shared with me. It is a tale I still tell to young novices and scribes: how I shared fire and food with the Revered One.

At length my tale was told and the old man looked out of the window at the people around the fire.

"Come here, Petronius, and see." I went over to him and he put his hand on my shoulder, more to steady himself than to indicate friendship, I think. "There, you see the people? They all wait for us men of wisdom to tell them what to think. They depend on us, people like Petronicus and Melonicus and all the healers and men of wisdom, to guide them through this world."

"You are indeed the wisest of men," I said. "Petronicus needs your wisdom. He is alone with Zilk and needs your counsel."

"Where is he now?"

"He will be in the cave by the Giant Rock near the sea in the Land of the Tumbling Waters. He said that I should meet him there when I have your thoughts."

"Tomorrow you will guide me to Petronicus. We have donkeys so we will travel faster than on my old legs. I must see Zilk and Petronicus before the Council of Wisdom. Tell nobody else of this. But listen carefully, Petronius." He indicated that we should return to the fire and sit closely together. "I am old, Petronius, very old and I have been sick. If I should die on the journey, say this to Petronicus. Tell him, although I think he already knows, that if the gods are not within men, then we are no more than the animals. If that is so, where do our thoughts and words come from, if not from the gods? Animals do not have these things. How will our medicines cure us when we are sick if the gods are not within us? To kill good men is to kill the gods inside us. It is wickedness beyond our understanding. Please give Petronicus my words." He paused and looked deeply into my eyes and there was determination in his voice when he said: "The Bedosians must be stopped; the old beliefs and certainties must prevail. Tell that to Petronicus."

That night I slept in one of the outer rooms with other novices and scribes. They all treated me with great respect, knowing that I had spent more time alone with the Revered One than any of them could remember. The next morning, the Revered One got ready to make the journey to the cave by the Giant Rock with me. Three donkeys were made ready, two for us to ride and one to carry food, blankets and furs because the old man felt the cold all the time.

Before we left the Revered One explained to his companions: "I must go with Petronius to consult with Petronicus who I now know to be alive and well. I will meet you at the Mountain of the Year at the next small moon. And if I should not return, I wish it to be known that I revere Petronicus above all other men."

I realised the full meaning of those last words immediately. If the Revered One should die on the trail, Petronius was to call the Council of Wisdom himself.

I set off, leading the Revered One's donkey towards the Giant Rock in the Land of the Tumbling Waters.

Eighteen

The story of my journey with the Revered One has been told and retold many times around many fires by many travellers. I have often smiled at their embellishments and, as Petronicus often said: '*Tales grow in the telling.*' I will now relate it as accurately as I can.

Petronicus had told me to meet him at the Giant Rock, which is in the Land of the Tumbling Waters. The first day on the trail from Klynos the Revered One and I saw two groups of the Tall People out hunting but they did not approach us. The Revered One found riding the donkey quite painful. His journey the previous moons from Klinbil had fatigued him and made him ill; it was a long journey of much pain and discomfort for a man so advanced in years. I frequently had to stop and help him down from the donkey and massage his legs to stop them becoming numb.

"My blood has lost its fire," he often said. "And my bones are like broken twigs in winter."

Towards the end of the second day we could smell the fires of the Tall People along the trail. We were made very welcome because they knew I was a friend of Combanicus and of course they all greatly respected the Revered One.

They had horrific tales to tell. Some of their people had traded beyond the Land of the Towering Rocks towards Bedosa. They heard that the country was paying half their produce and coins to the Ruler of Bedosa who was melting down the coins to make knife sticks. The land groaned with poverty and despair as the Bedosians were extending their rule far and wide. The Tall People, however, were confident that they would not attack through the Land of the Towering Rocks because they were afraid of the spirits

146

and demons that lived there. The Revered One looked at me knowingly as they mentioned the demons and spirits because men of wisdom like us knew they did not exist. I smiled back at him but we did not say anything.

Combanius sat with us as we ate that night. His wound was healing very well and many Tall People commented on my skill as a healer.

They fed us well that night and even in the morning before we set off for the Giant Rock they gave us bread and goat's milk. They offered to escort us out of their lands but I felt it was unnecessary so far away from the Bedosians. The Revered One was impressed that I stood so well with the Tall People and was called friend by Combanicus their leader.

Our journey the next day was slow and painful. The trail was very broken and in places quite muddy. This was the season of floods in the Land of the Tumbling Waters and I remembered that Petronicus and I had sheltered years ago in the caves of the Giant Rock when the rivers covered the land in deep water.

Towards the middle of the day we stopped so that the old man could climb down from the donkey and stretch himself out on the grass. He became very cold almost immediately so I covered him with blankets and fetched water for him to drink.

"You are a good man, Petronius. Petronicus must be proud of you."

I smiled with embarrassment and said something like: "I hope he is. Petronicus is my master."

When the Revered One felt rested we set off again along the trail. After a while I could see the Giant Rock that reared up like a huge arm pointing to the sky in the distance. The Revered One was relieved that his tortuous journey might soon end. He leaned over to me and said: "Petronius, are you sure Petronicus will be there?"

"Yes," I said. "He will be there if he said he would. And he will be there with Zilk. Please remember to smile at Zilk and rub hands the way I showed you, because he will be very frightened."

"I understand, Petronius. You have taught me well."

The final part of our journey took longer than I had expected. The old man needed to get off his donkey and rest frequently and we covered the distance very slowly. And then, thankfully, we were at the bottom of the hill and faced the stony track up to the cave. Petronicus had told me that the Giant Rock had been vomited out of the Mountain of the Year just after the world began. Many rocks had come with it and formed the caves at the base of the huge pointed rock.

We started up the stony track and then I suggested that the Revered One sit down and rest while I went ahead and warned Petronicus and Zilk that we were approaching. The old man agreed readily as he was in need of rest, and faced the prospect of the climb with much apprehension. I tethered the three donkeys to a tree and made the Revered One as comfortable as I could.

"Do not concern yourself with me, Petronius. I will still be here when you return."

I ran off upwards and there to my delight was our own donkey contentedly munching away at the grasses that grew amongst the rocks.

"Petronicus! Zilk!" I shouted as I approached. The donkey trotted down to me and rubbed his head against my chest and then I saw Petronicus coming out of the cave. He ran down and embraced me, with Zilk just behind waiting to rub hands.

"Petronicus," I said excitedly. "I have such a tale to tell. But first I have to tell you that the Revered One is with me and he waits down the rocky path. He is old and finds travelling difficult and painful."

"Then you have done well," said Petronicus. Zilk then rubbed hands with me and embraced me because he had seen how Petronicus had greeted me. "Go now and tell the Revered One not to hurry," said my master. "I need some time to explain to Zilk who our visitor is and that he is a friend."

I ran back and found the Revered One much rested and ready to continue. I helped him mount the donkey and we set off. He looked up towards the Giant Rock frequently and I suspect he was a little afraid of meeting Zilk. After much effort we could see the mouth of the cave and our donkey. We stopped for a moment to let the old man take breath and as we looked up Petronicus appeared. Beside him stood the huge figure of Zilk dressed all in his bright woven cloth with his helmet of eagle feathers on his head and his great blade in his hand. Both held up their hands in greeting. The Revered One stopped and looked at Zilk in astonishment. Petronicus and Zilk began to walk down towards us. I helped the Revered One dismount and the two old men embraced. Petronicus put his arm around the waist of the Revered One and helped him to face Zilk. They paused and looked at each other. The Revered One recovered his surprise first and held out his hands to Zilk. They both rubbed hands and smiled broadly. Petronicus and I smiled and we rubbed hands all round.

The tales told around the fires on many trails were accurate on at least one point. The first dramatic sight the Revered One had of Zilk gave him the notion of how we could save the world from bloodshed and death … but all that came later.

Later that day Zilk and I went to catch fish in the river at the bottom of the hill whilst Petronicus and the Revered One remained in the cave discussing the situation that faced the world. When we returned I realised that the two men were very old friends and were so pleased to be together. Zilk and I prepared our food and lit a fire, and we settled down together in the cave.

When we had eaten, Petronicus touched Zilk's hand and indicated towards the Revered One. Zilk looked nervously at Petronicus and hesitated. Petronicus touched his hand again to encourage him to speak. Petronicus had spent much time and effort teaching Zilk our words and we had learned some of Zilk's words ourselves. But the speech Zilk now made to the Revered One astonished me.

"I am a man. You am a man," said Zilk. He looked again at Petronicus who nodded and smiled encouragement. "My world is in the sea. Your world is in the sea. My world is in where the sun begins to climb the day and to us your world is in where the sun sinks into the great fires." Zilk stopped at that moment and seemed to be searching his mind for the words. I moved closer to him and held his hand. "Your world is by the great fires of the sun and we am afraid to be blown by big waves here." The Revered One realised that not only was Zilk struggling to use our words but also he was relating a painful disaster that had befallen his people. The old man reached over to rub hands with Zilk, smiled at him and waited for him to continue. "The moon went big and big again before we came to your shores. I was the childest and they gave me the food and water so I could live as they died." Zilk stopped and there were tears in his eyes and I realised perhaps for the first time that the other men in the boat must have been friends and perhaps even his family.

What a speech that was. Of course many travellers, including wise men who should know better, have told it and retold it many times until very few of Zilk's words actually remained. But that is the way of things. Men and women sitting around shared fires at night tell tales which grow as the trees with the passing years.

Nineteen

I have been asked many times to recall what happened during the next few days in the cave by the Giant Rock. Many have wondered how the Revered One talked to Zilk and what they said to each other. These matters have been discussed endlessly by people around night fires all over the world. At first Zilk was a little afraid of the Revered One. When he saw how Petronicus and I respected him he thought the Revered One was the leader of the world and very powerful. Zilk would always sit close to Petronicus or myself and only gradually did he begin to feel at ease with the Revered One. I sensed there were so many things the Revered One wanted to ask Zilk but they could only talk with the small number of words Zilk had learned. Petronicus often helped because he had been with Zilk the longest and knew more of his words.

The Revered One wanted us to remain in the cave for as long as possible in order to learn as much about Zilk as he could. However, he was anxious that we should leave for the Mountain of the Year in time for the Council of Wisdom. He had announced to all the wise ones before we left Klynos that they must meet together when next the moon was small. Already the moon was growing fat and time was running short.

One of the most curious things I remember from those days was something the Revered One and I discovered about Zilk. We noticed that when the clouds did not cover the night sky Zilk would sit at the mouth of the cave looking up at the moon and stars. I watched him several times smoothing the ground in front of him in the shape of a half moon. He then placed a large shiny stone and surrounded it with many other smaller stones. At first I did not take much notice, thinking that Zilk was just amusing himself

151

because he could not take part in the prolonged discussions between Petronicus and the Revered One. I also felt a bit shut out and lonely, but it would not have been appropriate for one so young to take part in their deliberations. I suppose I just wanted to sit close to Petronicus as I had always done for as long as I could remember. Petronicus, who always knew of my thoughts and feelings would often take me to one side and try to explain the thoughts that passed between them, but I did feel a little out of things at times.

One night as I sat near Zilk watching as he played with his small stones, the Revered One came and stood behind me and whispered in my ear: "Have you noticed, Petronius, how he moves the large shining stone along a slightly different trail on the ground each night? And how he moves the small stones but always in the same pattern?" I shook my head and looked up to him for an explanation. "It seems," said the wise old man, "that he is following the trails in the sky. The trails of the moon and stars, I think."

One morning when Zilk had gone down to the river to catch fish, the Revered One beckoned me to join him and Petronicus at the entrance to the cave. We sat on small rocks so we could see down towards the river and watch that Zilk came to no harm.

"Now then, child," said Petronicus. "Tell us again about the strange word that Combanius of the Tall People spoke. *Sunka*, wasn't it?" I had already told them several times but they made me go over it yet again.

"It is indeed strange," said the Revered One, "that the Tall People have a word belonging to the world of Zilk. How do you think that is, Petronius?"

I felt a hot flush in my face as both my master and the wisest man in all the world waited for my answer. I found my words came in fits and starts and my mind whirled around like a leaf in the wind.

"They are tall and Zilk is tall," I said hurriedly. "But they are not as tall as Zilk." The two of them smiled at me and nodded to each other.

Petronicus then said: "And you discovered only one word that you knew Zilk had used? Do you think the Tall People may have more?"

I shook my head. "They may have more. But I did not hear any other."

"A good answer," said the Revered One. "A good answer because it is based on just what you know and without wild guessing."

He then went inside the cave and Petronicus took me to one side and said: "That discovery you made in the Land of the Tall People is very important. You see, Petronius, both the Revered One and I think that people from Zilk's world who we know must have been here before …"

"When the world began?" I asked.

"Yes, child. Please do not interrupt. But we …"

"I am sorry, Petronicus, I will be patient."

He smiled at me and continued: "We know they have been here in ancient times because of the tablets and words Mentis discovered. But we did not know what had happened to them. Were they dead? Did they return to their own world? Or did some of them survive and …"

"And mix with our own world people … and …" I stopped speaking and looked guiltily at Petronicus. "Forgive me Petronicus, but I interrupt again."

"That is all right, child, you are forgiven. But your thinking is correct. You see, both the Revered One and I think that the Tall People could be the descendants of Zilk's people who came here when the world began."

My face must have frozen in wonderment as Petronicus smiled in a very fatherly way at me. He patted me on the shoulder and said: "Remember, always question and question again and then the truth will come to us. And with truth we can prevail against those who would do us wrong."

"The Bedosians?"

"Yes, child. The Bedosians."

For several days before we left the Giant Rock, Petronicus and I spent much time with Zilk trying to explain to him that he must come with us on another journey to meet lots of very wise men. Zilk was apprehensive at first, but he thought that the Revered One was the leader of our world and he felt that he would be safe with him.

The great day arrived and we set off with our donkeys and a lot of fish that Zilk and I had caught. We had smoked it over our fire so we could eat it later. I was tremendously excited and hoped I would be allowed to sit behind my master at the Great Council.

We could see the Mountain of the Year in the distance almost as soon as we left the cave of the Giant Rock but it was still several days away. We travelled quite slowly because the Revered One tired very quickly. Often we made camp long before the day's end for that reason.

One day when we were very close to the mountain, Petronicus said to me: "Now, Petronius, I have yet another task for you."

"I must leave you again? Please Petronicus," I pleaded, "don't make me leave you and Zilk again."

"I know you will be brave, and we will be separated only for a few days. You will not miss any of the great events that are to come. But only you can prepare the men of wisdom for what is going to happen. You are the only man who can do it." I smiled inwardly to myself and danced in the sunlit part of my mind, as this was the first time Petronicus ever called me a *man*. "You must go to the Mountain of the Year and tell all the wise men to assemble when the sun rises on the first day after the new moon. Tell them the Revered One and I will meet them. Tell them to have scribes ready to write down the words that will be spoken. Tell them nothing about Zilk but tell them the Revered One will speak to them in the Great Council of Wisdom."

"And tell them also," said the Revered One who now joined us, "that whatever happens, whoever we bring with us, there is nothing to fear. Tell them they have my word on that."

Twenty

I felt a great sense of excitement as I neared the Mountain of the Year, but it was an excitement mixed with apprehension. There was nobody by the path that led to the mountain but this was not unusual. Only healers and their novices were allowed to be at the base of the mountain by the House of Humility or below the steps leading to the great Temple of Healers that stood on a small hill nearby. It was forbidden for any one, even healers, to approach the foot of the mountain if they were not going to tend the sick in the House of Humility or to climb the mountain to collect rare plants for their medicines.

I remembered the pride I felt when Petronicus first brought me here. He took me to the top of the steps and into the Temple of the Healers. There he announced that I was to be his novice. Oh, the pride I felt on that day! And then joy upon joy when we climbed the mountain together and he explained what made the world live.

I ran swiftly up the steps to the great wooden temple on the hill, expecting to be greeted by the temple priests but all I found was an old man sitting in the shade of a dead tree. He asked me my business. He had earned his meat and bread in happier times cleaning the temple and chasing away the animals that came to rummage for scraps of food. I told him that I was a novice healer and entitled to enter the temple.

"There is no one in the temple, novice," he said. "The priests have gone."

"Gone! You mean, even the priests of the healers have gone?"

"Yes," he said. He spat on the ground and looked away from me. "There is nothing but calamity for us now."

"Where have they gone?" I demanded.

"Bedosa, where do you think? They have gone to join the evil ones."

I entered the temple sadly and announced my name and that of my master although there was no one there to hear. The place was indeed deserted, with dust and leaves everywhere. The scrolls on which the names of healers and their novices were written were still on shelves but there was no fire in the centre and no priests to greet me.

I left the temple and stood at the door looking up at the Mountain of the Year where Petronicus's own master was buried and where I would one day take Petronicus when he returned to the ground. And then I looked down at the place of assembly where Councils of Wisdom were held in ancient times. But there had not been a Council for longer than any one could remember, except perhaps the Revered One, but he was so old that he was long past the time when he should be in the ground. I walked sadly down the steps towards the House of Humility.

There were many sick people inside and the place smelt of illness and death. The presiding healer was Liminicus and he had two novices working with him. I had been very small when Petronicus and I met Liminicus on the trail so he did not recognise me. He saw my novice's hood and asked me if I was here to work.

"Yes, Liminicus, I will return tonight and help if I can. But first I must find the wise ones who have come for the Council of Wisdom."

"You will find them in the valley beyond the Pointed Rocks. Many have been here for days and more are expected tonight. The Revered One is not amongst them and many worry about his safety." Liminicus looked away and towards the long lines of sick people lying on the floor. "I fear the Revered One will not attend the Council and all will be lost."

I left the House of Humility and ran through the woods towards the Pointed Rocks. Petronicus and I had camped amongst the rocks on previous occasions so I knew the trail. The sun was just nearing the top of the day when I reached the rocks and could look down at the encampment.

I could see a huge communal fire with small groups of elderly men gathered around it talking together. Some had brought their women and children with them and the young ones were running about shouting and playing with sticks and small dogs. There were many cooking fires still smouldering from the previous night. Donkeys were grazing and travellers had brought sheep and goats for food and these were tethered to trees and large boulders. The whole scene was one of bustle and activity.

As I approached the encampment I tried to count how many people there were gathered in the valley. I could see healers with their novices, scribes and their pupils and men of wisdom who had their students and followers with them. I could not count them all but it was like a small town with well over a hundred people all waiting expectantly for the Council of Wisdom to begin the next day.

Petronicus had given me no advice about how I should go about my task or whom I should approach first. I had great misgivings about my ability to speak to such learned men, as I was only a mere novice. However, I need not have concerned myself because just as I approached along the trail I saw The Elder Scribe of Klinbil talking to a group of very old men. He saw me and immediately detached himself and ran as fast as his old legs could carry him towards me. Several other elderly men and their novices followed him.

"Petronius!" he called out in alarm. "Where is the Revered One, where is Petronicus?"

"Greetings, Elder Scribe, and my respects to you. I have a message from the Revered One. It is a message that must be given to all the men of wisdom who will attend the Council."

"What is it, child? Tell me quickly – is the Revered One safe?" I looked over towards the great fire and saw a large number of men and women with their novices and students approaching me. I felt nervous and did not think I could deliver my message with so many of them gathered around me.

I turned to the Elder Scribe and said: "Both the Revered One and Petronicus are safe but I think I should speak to you alone and then you can tell the other learned ones yourself … you could do it much better than I."

The Elder Scribe nodded and we went to the great fire to warm ourselves, as it was still cold in that early spring day. We kept apart from the other people but one of the women came and offered me some meat on a stick. I took it and thanked her. It seems everyone knew who I was. Not just that I was the son and novice of the great healer Petronicus, but that I was the youth who had gone off so mysteriously with the Revered One in the previous moon. The Elder Scribe guided me to a space near the fire where we could be alone. He motioned me to speak …

"The Revered One wants to speak to the Great Council of Wisdom when the sun rises tomorrow. He will wait for you in the meeting place beneath the Temple of the Healers. He says there is nothing for you to fear. He brings good news. Another man will also come to the Council and he is a man none of you know. The Revered One says that whatever you may think about the other man when you first see him there is nothing to fear, for he is a friend."

"But who is this man?" demanded the Elder Scribe of Klinbil. "And what right does he have to attend the Council?"

"I greatly respect you, Elder, but I do not know the thoughts of the Revered One in this matter. I only deliver his message."

"And Petronicus? What of Petronicus? Will he be with the Revered One?"

"Yes, he will. The Revered One is safe and well. He will speak to the Council tomorrow at the rise of the day."

I could see that the Elder was confused. He was not used to being told what to do by one so young. He was the Elder Scribe of Klinbil and more accustomed to instructing novices and rapping their heads with his knuckles for inattention than taking instructions from them. He was glancing anxiously towards the other wise men who had formed a group just out of hearing, anxiously awaiting news. They looked to be quite a formidable group of men; the finest brains in all the world and I began to think about how fearful the first meeting would be for Zilk. And then I had an idea, an idea that I knew Petronicus would be proud of.

"The stranger who comes with the Revered One and Petronicus has a strange custom. When he greets other men for the first time he rubs hands with them as a sign of friendship." I showed the Elder how it was to be done. I think he was both puzzled and slightly amused, but he did it several times with me. "Perhaps you would consider showing the other wise ones attending the Council what to do," I added.

The Elder Scribe of Klinbil left me and went to confer with the men of wisdom at the other side of the fire. They were arguing about which of them should be admitted to the Council and who should be left out. I felt that everyone was looking at me and I knew that they would try to engage me in conversation to find out about Petronicus, and where the Revered One had been since we left Klynos together. But my instruction from Petronicus was to tell them nothing so I moved around as much as I could. More people offered me food and goat's milk to drink but I kept very much to myself. I did, however, listen to their conversations whenever I could.

I smiled to myself as I remembered what Petronicus always said about tales being told and retold and how they grow like trees in the telling. The people in the encampment had heard horrific stories that were exaggerated beyond belief. The 'gods' had flown in a great boat of the sky. They had blades bigger than a man that could cut down twenty men with one blow. They had wings coming out of their heads and they slept for many moons at a time. I heard tell that the Ruler of Bedosa had become a god himself and all the world must say prayers to him and give him food and coins.

The first born of families were to spend several years as slaves of the huge new temple they were building at Bedosa. In fact, all sort of nonsense was being spoken around the encampment.

Before nightfall I left the encampment and returned to the House of Humility. Liminicus welcomed me and offered me food.

"I wonder, Petronius, if you would go and clean the feet of a man just brought in by two young scribes. I have sent the scribes back to the encampment because they are not sick, nor are they healers. The man's feet are badly bruised and cut from the trail. He is from Klinbil and his name is Kelcit."

"Kelcit?" I said in some alarm. "He is the Keeper of the House of Tablets in Klinbil." I went immediately down the line of sick people until I found him. I took a quick look at his feet. They were badly cut and blistered and he must have been in tremendous pain.

"Is that you, Petronius? I heard you were here. Where is the Revered One? I must speak to him."

"Then speak as I bathe your feet, because I will see the Revered One when all men sleep and the night has darkened the world. I will tell him what you say."

Kelcit tried to sit up to indicate the urgency and importance of his message. I gently pushed him back onto the straw and began to unwrap the cloth and animal skins he had tied around his feet. He cried out when I pulled the wrappings away. The scabs and dried blood came away very painfully for him. I was as gentle as I could be and then I began to soothe them with water and the large leaves of the shisklit plant. "Now speak, Kelcit. I can listen as I work."

"Tell the Revered One that Klinbil has fallen."

"Fallen! What? Klinbil has fallen to the Bedosians? But they said they would defend the town."

"You have the impatience of youth, Petronius. Do not judge us too harshly. We are a town of free men, we have no Rulers and our thoughts are free. But the Bedosians have destroyed my House of Tablets and all our wisdom is lost."

"Forgive my impatience, Kelcit, but why should freedom prevent you from defending yourselves? I remember that the stone throwers of the town were determined to defend it. Surely defending your freedom is …"

"Yes, I know what you are going to say, Petronius, but we have no leaders to direct us and we could not agree amongst ourselves. Some said it was wrong to kill other men even if they were wicked men."

"But, surely …"

"Yes, I know, I know … but we argued amongst ourselves in town meetings throughout the winter. Some said that even wicked men still have something of the gods within them and must not be harmed."

I did not answer him immediately because I understood his problem. Petronicus would know what was right and he would be here before dawn.

"The Revered One will be here soon with Petronicus; they will know what to do."

"Yes," said Kelcit. "We need the Revered One and all the men of wisdom just now."

I continued to treat his injured feet but a thought so horrific came into my mind: if Klinbil had fallen then the road was open to Klynos and thence to the Mountain of the Year!

I left the House of Humility in the darkest part of the night and headed for the trail to meet the Revered One, Petronicus and Zilk. They wanted to enter the meeting place before any of the other wise men arrived. Kelcit was sleeping quite peacefully as I left. I had given him some lichen to chew that dulled his senses and took his pain far away from him. Liminicus was also dozing on his seat with his novices curled up by the fire in the centre of the House of Humility.

I headed up the trail and sat by the crossroads waiting for them. I had not been there long before I heard the sound of the donkeys approaching. I ran forward in the darkness and was warmly greeted by Petronicus who climbed down from his donkey and embraced me. The Revered One remained seated but held his hand down to grasp mine warmly. Zilk dismounted with one youthful leap and we rubbed hands.

We arrived at the meeting place long before the first streaks of dawn appeared in the distant sky. Petronicus and Zilk went off alone so they would be out of sight when the meeting opened and the Revered One and I sat on the large stone facing the meeting place.

"I have much to tell you," I said to the Revered One when I had made him comfortable with an extra blanket and warmed his feet by rubbing them with my hands. I told him all about the encampment on the other side of the Pointed Rocks. I told him about the Elder Scribe of Klinbil and how he seemed to be trying to organise things. And then I told him about Kelcit and the horrific news he had brought from Klinbil.

The Revered One was silent for some time when I had finished speaking. He rubbed his old head to warm his thoughts.

"You are right when you say that after Klinbil the Bedosians will turn on Klynos. What the Bedosians are doing is destroying our thoughts and histories. They want all our records of wisdom to be lost and then only their thoughts will prevail. However, do not fear too much, Petronius. When dawn comes all the wise men of the world will be here and we shall decide what to do."

"Revered One," I said, "how will the Elder Scribe of Klinbil know who are the wisest men, who can be permitted to attend the Council?"

I could only just see his face in the starlight. He looked at me benevolently and said: "If there is doubt they will be guided by age."

"But does wisdom come with age?" I asked.

The old man looked up at me and smiled. "Well," he said. "If it does not come with age it does not come at all." I was silent as I thought about what he had said. The old man looked up at me again and said: "If you ask a man if he is wise, and he answers: '*Yes,*' then I doubt if he is. But if you ask a man if he is wise and he asks: '*What is wisdom?*' then he probably is wise, or if not he will be one day."

"I understand ... I think."

The old man smiled at me and said: "I do not think you do. But I think that one day you will."

I looked up towards the Pointed Rocks and could see tiny specks of light from the torches. The men of wisdom were approaching.

Twenty one

Immediately after the meeting, the Elder Scribe of Klinbil wrote down the words spoken by the Revered One to the Great Council of Wisdom. Those great thoughts and words are still with us, and I have even heard tell that scribes now perform his speech and pretend to be the Revered One for the amusement and enlightenment of whoever cares to listen. We all know about drama and oratory now but in those days we did not. This was how it all began and many scribes now earn extra coins 'performing' the great speech and the events that followed at Klynos. I will now tell it as it really happened because I was standing immediately behind the Revered One when all the men of worthy thoughts assembled and the great speech was made.

There were about thirty men of wisdom who descended the trail from the Pointed Rocks to the meeting place. Their torches bobbed about in the early light and I could see many other torches that remained high up amongst the rocks. They were the men whom the Elder Scribe of Klinbil and others had decided were not wise enough to attend. Many scribes have since described it as a ghostly scene as the mist of early dawn swirled around the meeting place. The Revered One remained seated until they had all found places to sit. I stood behind the Revered One.

"I may need your young shoulder to lean on, Petronius," said the Revered One. "My legs are not too steady at such an early time."

When all the wise ones had settled down, a respectful silence descended on the meeting place as the Revered One rose to speak. He stepped forward slightly and addressed them in a clear voice.

He began by reminding everyone of the last Great Council: "It was so long ago that even my body was clothed in the newness of youth, my blood was warm and my limbs enjoyed the suppleness of the new growths of spring. The priests of the time left our Councils and followed their own thoughts. They believed that the gods were separate from men and did not live within us."

There were expressions of disgust from many wise men in the assembly. They looked at each other for reassurance and did not like being reminded of the great schism that had blighted all their lives.

The Revered One continued: "And so we asked them; are we no better than the donkeys we ride on? Are we no greater than the beasts of the forest, or the sheep whose meat we eat and whose skins we put on our backs?"

There were murmurs of agreement from the assembly. Several called out loudly, supporting what had been said. The Revered One nodded and continued: "We have words! We have thoughts and memory. We have rules of civilised conduct. Would we have these things if the gods did not live within us?"

Several men stood up and shouted: "No! No!"

The Revered One warmed to his task: "The gods will not be at peace within us if we are wicked. But I think surely a little of the gods remain, even within wicked men. A child separates from the mother but something of the mother must remain."

The Revered One paused for a moment to let the assembled wise ones take his words into themselves. "And the Bedosians have killed good men, men in whom the gods dwelt. Our dear friend Melonicus the healer. His novice Melonius. Both dead! They brought about the death of Mentis and destroyed the House of Tablets in Bedosa. Many more died in the great massacre of Bedosa from which only my young friend Petronius escaped."

I felt my chest grow with pride as my name was used in that great speech.

"And along the trails we hear stories of killing and enslavement. Aye, and taking food and coins from the people. And now, my wise ones, they have taken Klinbil and destroyed the House of Tablets there. The gods are so outraged they may abandon us for a hundred moons or more."

The Revered One paused to let the assembly digest his words and their implications. Several began animated discussions with each other until the silence returned and they looked again towards the Revered One.

He continued: "And so, my wise friends, the gods will be so angry that they may even abandon us forever." His voice dropped and he spoke in sadness, but it was a sadness tinged with menace. "And man will be no better than the savage animals that roam the forests. Our healers will lose their skills and our wise men their thoughts and we will walk naked in the world like our ancestors did when the world first came from the great crater in the Mountain of the Year."

There was a spontaneous outburst of anger and fear from the assembly. Several rose to their feet and waved their arms about in frustration and disgust.

"And after Klinbil," the Revered One said in a raised voice, "they will attack Klynos." He then lowered his voice to a menacing tone, paused for a moment and said: "And after Klynos? The Mountain of the Year."

The Revered One was tiring very quickly. I could see he was feeling the cold of that early dawn so I put another cloak around his shoulders. It was the cloak I had taken from Mentis. The Revered One sat down for a few breaths whilst the assembly was so agitated. He waited until their alarm died down a little, stood up and continued: "And how have the Bedosians done this? It was not their weapons that conquered. No! The people were defeated by their own fears. Fears of false gods!"

The Revered One paused and there was silence in the Council as his listeners digested the implications of his words. He took a small step forward and turned slowly to his side and looked up to the top of the steps that led to the Temple of the Healers. All eyes followed his. There were gasps of amazement and fear when they saw Zilk standing at the top by the door of the temple. He was dressed in his finely woven cloth. He had his great helmet of eagle feathers on his head and the early morning sun glinted on the smooth iron of his great blade. Petronicus emerged and stood a full pace behind Zilk, which made him look even bigger. I turned and looked at the assembled wise ones. They were stunned into silence. Some shielded their eyes from the sight of Zilk, whilst others dropped to their knees in the manner of the Bedosians. Others tried to hide behind trees and stones.

They watched as if under a spell as Zilk began to walk slowly down the steps. Petronicus now walked several steps below him, which made Zilk look taller still. I could tell by looking into the face of Zilk just how nervous he was. I wanted to run and meet him, to rub hands with him, but the Revered One whispered to me: "No, Petronius. I understand your desires, but remain still."

Zilk entered the circle and walked towards the Revered One. As he approached, the old man held out his hands and they rubbed hands together. Zilk turned to me, embraced me the way he had seen Petronicus do so often and we rubbed hands warmly.

Zilk then turned towards the assembly. The Revered One stood on one side of him and Petronicus on the other.

He addressed the assembly in a faltering voice: "I am man. You all am man. My world is in the sea. Your world is in the sea. My people died in the boat. We are the same."

The silence in the Council of Wisdom was stunning and after far longer than it takes to tell, some slowly began to recover their wits and they looked at each other in wonderment. Some nodded their heads. Some shook their heads in confusion. And then I saw the Elder Scribe of Klinbil detach himself from the others, walk slowly and hesitantly across the meeting place and look into the face of Zilk. Slowly, he held out his hands in the manner I had shown him and they rubbed hands together.

I knew at that moment that the world would be saved and I knew how the Revered One would do it.

Twenty two

After the great speech by the Revered One and the appearance of Zilk at the Council of Wisdom, events happened quickly. Runners, mostly young scribes, were sent off to Klynos telling the inhabitants to prepare to defend the town against the Bedosians.

"Tell them we are coming," said the Revered One as the young runners set off. "Tell them we are coming. Tell them all the world is coming."

Arrangements were made to get all the wise ones to Klynos in order to confront the enemy when they attacked.

Towards nightfall a young novice who had escaped from Klinbil entered the encampment. He was hungry, tired and suffering from a beating he had received at the hands of the Bedosians. He had got out of the town in the late hours and travelled non-stop for the Mountain of the Year. His master had been hanged from the town gate. He told the Revered One that the Bedosians had taken complete control of the people of Klinbil and were preparing to move on Klynos. There was now great urgency in the encampment as people began to leave for the town. The Revered One was so old that many doubted if he could be there in time. His journeys during the previous moons from Klinbil to Klynos and then to the Land of the Towering Rocks with me and then to the Mountain of the Year had really fatigued the old man. A litter was made for him out of two stout poles with animals' skins slung across them. This was to be carried by young men in turn, with the Revered One lying on it covered with blankets and skins to keep him warm. He also had a donkey he could ride if he felt strong enough.

The wise ones would not travel in a procession but would arrive in Klynos in small groups. They would arrive as families, sometimes as a master and novice or as individuals. This way the people of Klynos would be encouraged by constant arrival of determined people who would help prepare for to the great event that would soon occur in their town. Zilk was going to travel with Petronicus and the Revered One.

Many people were afraid to approach Zilk at first but gradually during the evening of the Council and the following day more came to look at him and some tried speaking to him. Many people rubbed hands with Zilk and that pleased him greatly. I was able to show people that the great blade he carried was for hunting and fishing and not for killing, which many of them had feared.

At the height of all the excitement and preparations, Petronicus saddened me when he said he had another lone task for me that would take me away from my friends once again.

"The Revered One," said Petronicus the morning after the Great Council, "does not think that killing will be necessary. He thinks that once the people see that Zilk is not a god and does not threaten our beliefs they will realise how wicked and false the Bedosians are."

"I know you are right, Petronicus, as you are in all things. Killing is wrong even if the gods have left the Bedosians."

"Yes, your thinking is correct. But consider this, child, what would be the greater evil? To kill wicked men or let them destroy all the good thoughts we believe in?"

"I will think about what you say until we meet again. What is the task you have for me?"

"Both the Revered One and I think it would be helpful if you were to go in search of the Tall People. Find your friend Combanicus and ask him to bring his hunters and their dogs to Klynos. Tell them to harass the Bedosians on the trail and delay their arrival at Klynos."

I accepted the task with reluctance because I did not want to be separated from my friends again, but I could see the need for it.

The Revered One also came to say goodbye and said: "Tell Combanicus that you have my blessing for all you say to him."

They both embraced me before I left, and Zilk came to rub hands. As they walked away from me I heard the Revered One whisper to Petronicus: "Do you think Petronius is old enough for this task? He is very young. It is difficult country and there is much danger."

I felt inwardly strong and proud when I heard Petronicus reply: "Oh yes. Know the boy, know the man."

Once again I sadly left Petronicus. I really wanted to be part of the great event, to travel to Klynos with the Revered One, with Petronicus, with Zilk and all the great wise men of the world but sadly it was not to be.

Before I left, I returned to the House of Humility to say goodbye to Kelcit. I found him up off the straw, limping about with a stout pole in each hand. His feet were firmly bound up with animal skins and stout leather and he seemed determined not to be left behind.

"We found no more strange words in our House of Tablets at Klinbil," he said. "And now we will never know because the Bedosians pulled it down and destroyed everything."

"Such wickedness," I said. "But maybe there will be fragments in the rubble. Mentis found some in Bedosa."

"Aye, maybe, Petronius. Goodbye, my young friend. I will travel with the Revered One and Petronicus because I could not keep pace with the others."

It wasn't difficult to find the Tall People. It would be more accurate to say that they found me. The moment I entered their land they knew of my presence. The Tall People had always kept very much to themselves and avoided contact with other people.

They were not actually hostile but preferred to avoid strangers. They traded widely but seldom spent the night in towns, preferring always to leave before nightfall or to camp outside town walls. Healers and men of wisdom, however, were always welcome.

I had hardly left the Mountain of the Year when I saw a small group of the Tall People on a nearby hill. They were watching me and seemed to travel in the same direction but always keeping a distance between us.

Travellers and traders had told me before I left the encampment that the main settlement of the Tall People was by the Dark Lake in the Land of the Small Trees. I came near the lake just before sunset and was approached by their lookouts.

I stood still on the trail and shouted: "I am Petronius ..."

I was about to add my master's name but they interrupted and said: "Yes, we know who you are, Petronius. We have been protecting you since you entered our lands. You are called friend by Combanicus. Tonight you will share our fire and food."

During the time we spent around their huge communal fire by the Dark Lake, I tried to use some of the words we had learned from Zilk. *Sunka* was known to most of them, especially their children. When the women handed me food they would rub their stomachs and say: "*Sunka*," and smile broadly.

I tried other words but they did not know any of them. I had a long talk with Combanicus and his son, Combanius. We discussed the wickedness of the Bedosians but I did not say anything about the possibility that the Tall People might be descended from Zilk's people. That was something, Petronicus had said, that they might realise for themselves in the future.

Combanicus was a man of many summers but he was still at the height of his strength. He was also a good leader and gave clear commands to his hunting parties. Each party usually had six people in it; five men and women who killed the animals and a sixth, usually a youth fleet of foot, who would range far and wide to find the prey. Two hunting parties were sent out to harass the

Bedosians on the road from Klinbil to Klynos. The Tall People would watch the Bedosians from behind trees and from rocks high above the trail. The Tall People were also expert stone throwers and would shower the Bedosians with stones to prevent them foraging for food and to make them keep close together. Whenever the Bedosians attempted to fight back, the Tall People would melt away into the background for fear that they would be cut down by the large blades which the Bedosians carried. I stayed with Combanicus and the main party. We headed for the town of Klynos.

Klynos was built on a hill facing the path of the sun. It enjoyed the first warmth of the rising sun each day, watched the sun's trail across the skies and remained well lit in the evening as the sun descended into the great fires. There were small hills all around, but most of the wood had been cut down over many years to feed the cooking fires of the town. Petronicus and I always enjoyed coming to Klynos; the people were so friendly and they greatly admired healers.

When the Tall People and I arrived at the town, the Bedosians had only just made their camp outside the stockade. We positioned ourselves on a hill opposite the main gate. The stout wooden gates were firmly closed and the men and women of Klynos were standing on the walls facing their enemies. I was unable to count the defenders because there were so many of them. Clearly a great number of people had arrived from the Mountain of the Year.

One of the wise men of Klynos was standing on the platform above the town gate shouting to the Bedosians: "Go back to Bedosa and leave us in peace."

His voice was met with insults from the blade men and several of them threw animal dung and stones at him.

"That is Kelkos," said Combanicus. "A man of great wisdom and thoughts."

The Tall People numbered about twenty and were well armed with pouches filled with small stones, and their hunting dogs were straining on their ropes.

"Yes, I remember him," I said. "Petronicus greatly admires him."

We listened as the Ruler of Bedosa approached the gate and shouted: "You still have false healers within; send them out and we will not harm you."

"We are a free town," replied Kelkos. "We have no Rulers here, we are free men and have free thoughts."

"Then die!"

The Ruler of Bedosa returned to his men. The ten Bedosians who had the large blades they had taken from the ship of the 'gods' began to swirl them around at shoulder height. They looked menacing and I noticed the people on the town walls looking at each other with fear. The Ruler of Bedosa also had one of the blades, which he held above his head. There were about thirty other Bedosians who had very long knife sticks made by melting down the coins they took from the people.

The Bedosians had a large group of priests with them and they were calling on the gods to curse Klynos and all the people in it. "The gods will desert you. They will abandon you and there will be plague and hunger for a hundred moons."

The blade men also began shouting insults and telling what evil things they would do when they entered the town.

"The moment they attack the gate," said Combanicus, "we will send the dogs at them."

I watched how the Tall People began to wrap small pieces of meat in thick green leaves and secure them with twine. They let the dogs sniff the meat and made ready to throw it amongst the Bedosians and release the ropes on the dogs. Other men of the Tall People prepared to throw their stones amongst the Bedosians. The Tall People were renowned for their accuracy as stone throwers and many said that they equalled the skills of the stone throwers of Klinbil.

The Bedosians began to move in tight ranks towards the gates of Klynos. They continued to shout threats and insults but the men and women on the walls remained steady.

It was the next moment that saved the world, and I have always thought that the gods entered all our minds together.

All eyes, as if on a signal from the gods, turned to the platform above the town gate. The Bedosians were about fifty paces from the gates when the whole world stood in a hushed stillness. All eyes looked towards the platform as Zilk slowly appeared. He looked magnificent in his robe of finely woven cloth. His great helmet of eagle feathers made him look even bigger than he was. And his great blade, his *fidik*, glinted in the bright sun. He held it with both hands high above his head. And then the Revered One and Petronicus appeared and stood one each side of him.

The Bedosian priests reacted first. They hesitated in their advance and began to shake their heads. They looked terrified and broke ranks. Some of the blade men immediately knelt down in the manner of the Bedosians and bowed. The priests of Bedosa began to run about like startled rabbits shouting to each other in fear. Some of the men who carried the great blades let them drop to their sides.

At that moment the people on the walls of the town began to pelt the Bedosians with stones. The gates of Klynos were flung open and a group of stone throwers and slingers, who had escaped from Klinbil, loosed their stones into the enemy who were now running about in total confusion and fear.

Combanicus turned to his people and said: "Loose the dogs."

The Tall People threw the pieces of meat wrapped in stout leaves into the midst of the Bedosians, and released their dogs. Panic set in immediately. Zilk, the Revered One and Petronicus came down from the platform and out through the gates. They were followed by all the wise men of the world.

The Bedosians fled in total disarray back the way they had come.

Twenty three

It was the year that the people smiled again, and those enslaved by the Bedosians eased their aching backs. All over the world people returned to the old thinking and for a time all priests were shunned and not allowed to enter the towns. It was also the year the Revered One called on the people of Klynos and other nearby towns and settlements to construct a proper meeting circle at the Mountain of the Year. He had decided that a Council of Wisdom should be held every ten years to prevent the Bedosian madness ever returning to plague the world.

Nobody died in the battle of Klynos, although I did hear that the dogs of the Tall People savaged several blade men and priests. The stone throwers also injured some of the enemy as they ran away down the trail abandoning their bags and baggage. The Bedosians were harried all the way back to their own land. Hunting parties of the Tall People followed them to the limits of their territory to make sure they did not return. The Revered One sent runners in all directions to announce the defeat of the Bedosian wickedness and to tell them the truth about Zilk and the 'gods'. In towns far and near the people rose up and turned out the priests who were in error.

The men of Bedosa staggered back towards their own land tired, hungry and bleeding from their feet. They had killed several people during their retreat and stolen food and animals from anybody they found on the trail. Farms were raided and coins and possessions stolen. When the Ruler with his blade men and renegade priests arrived back at Bedosa the people shut them out. The people barricaded themselves in the town and pelted the ruler and his men with stones from the stockade. The young men who had been taken as slaves of the new temple had a particular hatred of the priests and the Ruler. They were too afraid to fight them openly but they ransacked the Ruler's house and destroyed all his possessions. Rumours circulated for many years that the temple slaves killed the Ruler's wife and children, but I do not know the truth of that.

The Ruler and his men were starving and could get no food from the town. Several of them were sick with infected feet and very weak from the want of food. Nobody would give or sell them anything and the people of the surrounding area took to the hills with their sheep and cattle whenever the Bedosians approached to steal from them.

We knew little just then about the fate of the Ruler and his men but I had a feeling deep down inside me that we had not heard the last of them. Most people believed they had fled to the Land of the Bubbling Mud. The great blades that the Ruler had taken from Zilk's people disappeared with them, and nobody knew what happened to them. The Revered One was thankful that the great blades had vanished from our world and could never again threaten the people. Only Zilk had a great blade, but I knew that was used for hunting and fishing.

Little was known about the Land of the Bubbling Mud but stories were told that it was a fearsome land where all that is acrid and wicked in the earth ascends to the surface and smokes its way into the sky. Some say that is where the clouds come from but the truth of that is not known. Men of the greatest wickedness have always been banished to the Land of the Bubbling Mud and are never heard of again. Much of this we learned later when travellers visited the area and brought the news back to us. They also told how the people of Bedosa began to leave the town to make their homes elsewhere.

Petronicus explained to me: "The town of Bedosa will probably be abandoned quite soon."

"But why is that, Petronicus? It is a big town and with the Ruler and his men banished it would be a good place to live."

"It is a big town and a well built town, child, you are correct. The bricks are made of the local mud and there is good stout timber in the hills around it for building. But Bedosa is a place of great wickedness and people will abandon it because the evil lingers in the air. If people breathe evil air they become wicked themselves. No, child, it is best abandoned and forgotten."

Very soon after the battle of Klynos, Petronicus said we had to return to the Mountain of the Year to replenish our supply of rare herbs and plants for our potions and cures.

We climbed to the burial place of Petronicus's master. Zilk was not allowed to accompany us because he was not a healer or a novice. He remained with the Revered One and showed great interest in the meeting place that the people were constructing. Petronicus and I looked down from the mountain and saw how it was taking shape.

Ten large upright stones, as tall as Zilk, were hauled by people and donkeys and placed in a half circle where the Great Council of Wisdom had been held. These stones were all about the same size, except for one that was larger, head and shoulders taller than Zilk. At the open end of the half circle, they placed a flat stone and we could imagine how the Revered One would sit on it with all the men of wisdom facing him.

On our return from the Mountain, the Revered One explained how Zilk had planned the layout of the half circle for him.

"Do you know that Zilk makes scratchings of the night sky on the ground?"

"We watched him doing that outside the cave, didn't we?" I said.

"Yes, Petronius, you remember. Zilk says that the sun begins its climb each day from a slightly different direction behind the

Pointed Rocks on the hill over there towards the encampment. That is why the half circle is where it is."

Zilk was watching us. He was smiling but I felt that he was frustrated at not having enough words to explain to us what he was doing. It would seem that he had spent a lot of time explaining to the Revered One how the sun rises in exactly the same spot on midsummer's morning every year. He had done this with sign language and scratchings on the ground.

"Now," said the Revered One, "look over at the Pointed Rocks. Zilk showed me that the sun would rise just above one particular stone on midsummer's morning each year. Look, can you see the stone shaped like a man's thumb?" Petronicus and I nodded but remained mystified.

We are all very familiar with Zilk's numberings now but it was quite new to us then. Everyone now knows that the shadow of the largest stone in the half circle falls on the stone seat on midsummer's morning each year, but you must remember that nobody had done anything like this before. We also have a big round stone, which can be moved quite easily by two strong men. This is moved from one big stone to the next as the years pass to mark off the years to the next Council of Wisdom.

I remember the magic in my mind as everything fell into place and the Revered One explained with great satisfaction: "Wise and learned men who visit the Mountain of the Year will always know how many years have passed since the last Council."

"And," I interrupted, "how many years to the next!"

"Yes, Petronius. Your youthful interest excuses your interruption."

I held my head down, but he looked at me benevolently. What wisdom would come of these numberings about the movement of stars and the sun I could not tell but, as Petronicus always said, we must continue to question. The Revered One let it be known that the meetings would commence when the sun was at the top of the day in future.

Everyone wanted to be at the Great Half Circle on the next midsummer's morning to watch the wondrous event that Zilk had predicted. In the few moons before that Petronicus decided that we should travel once again on the trail and earn our living as healers.

Petronicus said: "I think Zilk has been so confused with all that has happened since the Great Council of Wisdom that he needs to return to the trail with us and get away from our people for a while."

"Do you think Zilk was very frightened at the Council?" I asked.

"Yes, child, he was. Do you remember when he walked down the steps from the Temple of the Healers?"

"Yes," I said. "Everyone was watching him. Was he afraid?"

"His body was shaking like the grass in the wind. We must never forget that our world is as strange to him as his world would be to us."

"You are wise, Petronicus and you are right. Let us walk the trail again, all three of us together."

"We shall return to the Land of the Tumbling Waters," said Petronicus. "Zilk is familiar with that place. And the Tall People will be near; Zilk likes the Tall People. He can fish and learn more of our words."

"And we can learn more of his," I said.

We earned a good living in the next moons and returned, as midsummer's day approached, to the place of the Great Council. We had several good quality coins in Petronicus's pouch and we also had full bellies.

The word had spread far and wide about the forthcoming wonder that would be seen at the Stones. People came from many places, even as far as the Inner Lands and, some said, from the Far Country. Many had walked for a full moon to be there and to be able to return to their homes and tell their friends and families about what they had seen. I could not count the people who assembled just before the dawn on midsummer's morning; there were so many of them.

"It seems to me," I said to Petronicus, "that the whole world has come together."

"You know, Petronius, I think you are correct. Nothing like this has ever happened before."

The Revered One, who seemed to have made his permanent home in Klynos, was present and he sat on the stone in the middle of the half circle. And then miraculously, as the sun began its slow climb up the morning, the darkness disappeared into the earth and the light appeared. Everyone knows that the darkness hides beneath the earth when the sun rises and does not return to the land until the sun goes to rest in the Great Fires beyond the sea.

Petronicus and I stood with Zilk near the great stones and waited. It was cold in the early morning air so we wrapped our blankets and skins around ourselves. Zilk put his hand on my shoulder as we waited. I think he was very proud when we heard the people gasp in wonderment as a long shadow faded and slowly revealed the presence of the Revered One sitting on the centre stone. Many people thronged around him and it seemed that everyone wanted to rub hands with Zilk, who had worked out the numbers for the whole thing. Huge fires were lit around the stones that night and there was much shouting and celebration. The Revered One announced that a great feast would be held at Klynos to celebrate the end of the cataclysm and a return to the old thinking.

Klynos was crowded with people who had come from the towns and settlements nearby. The Elder Scribe of Klinbil was there with Kelkos who had defied the Bedosians from the stockade at Klinbil before the battle. Petronicus greatly respected the wisdom of Kelkos and told me to listen carefully to anything he said. Liminicus, who I had worked with in the House of Humility before the Great Council of Wisdom, was there and so was Kelcit, the Keeper of the House of Tablets of Klinbil. But Kelcit looked sad and mournful throughout the feasting. The town also seemed to be full of scribes and novices. Some of the people who had travelled from the Inner Lands and the Far Country to see the midsummer sunrise at the Stones also came to Klynos for the great feast.

The people of Klynos brought their herds down from the hills to provide meat for all the people. The townspeople wanted to thank everyone who had come to the town to help defend it against the Bedosians, and no coins were asked of anyone. The Tall People also slept inside the town stockade and that was unusual for them. Normally, if they came to trade, they left the towns before nightfall. The women of Klynos prepared bread sweetened with herbs that grew amongst the rocks. Petronicus remarked after the festivities were ended that rather more wine was drunk than was good for people.

The feast lasted three days and many trees were brought in to feed the cooking fires and the great town fire that was lit every night in the middle of the town. I remember well how we all lay down to sleep one night by the great fire with bulging bellies and a feel of wellbeing. It was a warm pleasant night and the Revered One, who normally slept in the house of the Elder Scribe of Klynos, came and lay down beside us. I felt so warm and safe with Petronicus, Zilk, the Revered One and Kelcit around me. Even the presence of the Elder Scribe of Klinbil who always seemed to look at young novices with disapproval did not disturb my feelings that night.

Petronicus was deep in discussion with Kelcit who had spent many days rummaging in the rubble of the House of Tablets in Klinbil, that the Bedosians had destroyed.

I could hear them talking and thought that Kelcit spoke very sadly: "So much lost ... so much lost. All the signs from the skies that marked off the years are gone. The words of the wise ones of

Klinbil all lost. Even the words from the only Council of Wisdom that the Revered One can remember have been destroyed."

I leaned over towards them and said to Kelcit: "But, Kelcit, Mentis of Bedosa found fragments in his House of Tablets. We must continue to look."

"But my eyes are old and tired, Petronius. Will you come and help?"

Petronicus turned to me and whispered: "I think you should, Petronius. We must never lose the words because we will lose the thoughts of the wise ones from long ago."

"But we must take the trail, Petronicus; we must earn our meat and bread."

The old man smiled benevolently and said: "Who do you think travelled with me before I found you? I am sure I will be quite safe on my own for a few moons."

We both smiled and that was the first time I remember feeling protective towards Petronicus; he was old and I was young and I felt I should be with him.

"But will Zilk travel with you?" I asked.

Petronicus was silent for a while. He looked over at the sleeping body of Zilk and whispered for my hearing alone: "There is much we can learn from Zilk and his people, but we have so few of his words and he has only a few of ours. Let him come to the House of Tablets in Klinbil and help you. If he listens to you and Kelcit speaking and reading the words he will learn our words and can then tell us more of his people:"

"And," I said excitedly, "he may learn to read!"

"Yes, that is what I was thinking," said Petronicus. I smiled, happy in the thought that the wisdom of Petronicus knew no bounds.

Twenty four

Our journey from Klynos to Klinbil took several days. The Revered One insisted on coming with us, which surprised me because he was so old and frail. Petronicus was concerned that his old friend would find the journey too tiring after all his exertions during the previous moons.

On the first night we made camp amongst some trees and lit a fire. We had plenty of food with us and there was clean water nearby. The Revered One lay down almost immediately and closed his eyes. I put my blanket over the old man and tried to make him comfortable.

"Thank you for your blanket, Petronius. My blood seems thin in my veins and makes me cold. Please rub my legs and arms for me and make the blood move again and I shall be warm."

The next day we waited until the sun was half way up the morning before moving on. We wanted the sun to be warm so that the Revered One would not feel the cold of the early morning. We moved slowly along the trail to Klinbil but the Revered One asked to stop just after the sun had reached the top of the day. He asked for Kelkos, Kelcit and the Elder Scribe of Klinbil to come to him.

"My friends, my body tires long before the day is done. I want you to continue the journey without me. Petronicus and the boy will stay with me and Zilk will lead my donkey."

"We will not leave you, old friend," said Kelcit. "Our work in Klinbil can wait a short while."

The Revered One appeared agitated and said: "No, Kelcit. You must get to Klinbil as soon as possible and search amongst the ruined tablets. And, Elder Scribe of Klinbil, you must finish writing down the words spoken at the Great Council of Wisdom and of all the events of the cataclysm before the memory fades. You have not completed that task; the scrolls remain unfinished."

"But, Revered One, my eyes tire and my head is like a leaf that has blown from its tree; things do not come back to me as readily."

"I know, old friend," said the Revered One. "The minds of old men are like a meadow much burrowed into by rabbits, they have holes of forgetfulness and much can be lost." The Elder Scribe smiled and nodded but did not answer. "You continue your journey," added the Revered One, "and try to finish the Great Work. I will follow and then I can read the scrolls and perhaps with both our minds they will be correct."

After a short rest the Elder Scribe of Klinbil left with Kelcit and Kelkos and continued their journey. We prepared our camp for the night and when we sat by the fire eating our food I said to Petronicus: "I think there is something troubling the Revered One."

"And so there is, Petronius. Can you think what it might be?"

"No, I cannot tell, but I know he has thoughts that make his mind heavy."

Zilk, who was listening to our conversation, said: "Revered One has pain. Tired and old. Zilk carry him in next sun."

Petronicus leaned over towards me by our sleeping place and whispered: "The Revered One is very worried about the accuracy of the words of the Elder Scribe of Klinbil."

"But, Petronicus, he is the Elder Scribe. His words are true," I said.

"But his memory is not, child. The real reason I want you in Klinbil is to help the Revered One check the words the Elder Scribe writes. The whole world knows that you stood just behind the Revered One when he spoke to the Great Council. You are young and things stay in your head longer." I was silent for a while and a little afraid, but Petronicus added: "I know what you are thinking, Petronius. You think the Elder Scribe will be offended if you check his words."

187

"Yes," I said. "I am only a novice and he may feel insulted."

"The Revered One and I have spoken together about that. But you see, Petronius, the words that will be remembered must be the complete truth. Scribes all over the world will be writing down what they think happened. Their words will be in the House of Tablets in many towns. The Revered One is concerned that there must be tablets that are accurate. He will let it be known that the words in the House of Tablets at Klinbil will be the correct ones. If there are different versions there will be doubt about what really happened. People who come after us will have argument and the words will be emptied of meaning." I smiled at him in the firelight.

Now I knew the real reason why he did not want me on the trail with him. I turned over to sleep that night a little afraid of the great task Petronicus and the Revered One wanted me to perform.

Many dark clouds passed through the night sky as I tried to sleep. Something was keeping me from drifting away to the land of painless dreams. It was a feeling that stayed just below my thoughts, something I could not put into words. And so I did what I have always done, I turned over and reached towards Petronicus.

"What is it, child? Hasn't sleep found you yet?"

"No, Petronicus. I think there is something deeply troubling you, something you have not told me about." Petronicus turned towards me and I could just see his face in the firelight. There was silence all around us, as everyone else seemed to be sleeping. "What is it, Petronicus? I am not a child now; I am old enough to know."

"You are correct, Petronius. You are not a child, so consider this. If the words of the ancient scribes that Mentis found in the House of Tablets at Bedosa could be falsified to suit the Ruler of Bedosa, so could the words the Elder Scribe writes now. We do not want wise men to be arguing over their meaning in future years."

"Yes, I understand that, Petronicus; you have told me that. But what else is it? I can tell by your eyes and the wrinkles in your brow that something pulls against your peaceful sleep."

"You are correct, Petronius, so tell me this; where is the ruler of Bedosa now? Where are the great blades they took from Zilk's people in the boat?"

"It is said that the Ruler and his people are banished to the Land of the Bubbling Mud and will never be heard of again," I answered. Then I asked: "Have we ever been to the Land of the Bubbling Mud?"

Petronicus shook his head. "No, and I know of nobody who has."

"But if we know so little about the Land of the Bubbling Mud, does that mean they could return with their great blades?"

Petronicus did not answer but there was a look of dread on his old face in the firelight.

The next day as Petronicus and I were about to lift the Revered One on to his donkey, Zilk stepped forward and simply picked up the old man and began walking towards Klinbil carrying him like a child. We knew that the Revered One could not walk far without someone supporting him. We also knew that he found sitting on a rolling donkey painful. Only Zilk was big and strong enough to carry him, and the nearness of Zilk's body helped keep the Revered One warm.

The sun climbed up the morning of the day and warmed our bodies as we went on our journey. We stopped now and then and I rubbed the legs and arms of the Revered One to make his blood warmer and make it move through his body and keep the cold away.

It was about the middle of the day that we saw the first group of people from Klinbil coming along the trail to meet us. Kelkos, who was much revered in Klinbil, had told them of our approach and many people wanted to come and welcome us. Some of them were carrying food to help us on our journey. They had pieces of roasted meat and fruit wrapped in large leaves. They had brought water with them in pig bladders and even blankets for the Revered One to keep him warm. The ones who had not seen Zilk approached him slowly at first. They wanted to rub hands with him because they had heard of his strange custom, but were afraid. Zilk put the Revered One down to the ground to rest and went amongst the people of Klinbil rubbing hands and smiling with them. Even more people came after the sun had reached the top of the day. Zilk had to let the Revered One down many times in order to rub hands with them. Our journey to Klinbil was much longer than we had planned and as we approached the town there was a whole throng of people walking with us.

It is a warm memory that I have of Petronicus and myself on the trail from Klynos to Klinbil, with Zilk carrying the Revered One, me leading the donkey and a large crowd of people all talking happily together.

However, my feelings of warmth and happiness soon changed when we arrived at Klinbil. The stockade had been thrown down and the great wooden gatehouse burned to the ground.

I remember feelings of both sadness and anger when we entered the town. The damage that the Bedosians had done to the town was wicked. Whole houses had been pulled down, the House of Tablets had been set on fire and they had even thrown dead animals into the town well. Many people had been injured when the Bedosian blade men had rampaged through the town searching out scribes and healers.

Now some people with broken limbs came to Petronicus and asked him to make them straight again. Petronicus, who was skilled in these matters, broke their limbs again with a large flat stone and set them once again in their true position. It was a painful procedure and I spent much time seeking out the herbs and lichen that would ease the people's pain. But there were many others whose broken limbs had set themselves in awkward ways and could not be straightened.

The town temple had been badly damaged and the Bedosian priests had told the people they must rebuild it in a different way. Just by the town gate was the scaffold that the Ruler of Bedosa had ordered to be erected. It had been on that spot that scribes and healers had been hanged.

Happily, some scribes and healers had escaped to the hills behind the town when the Bedosians broke into the town through the stockade. Slowly and timidly they had returned when they thought it was safe, and Petronicus and I were relieved to greet some old friends. There were also several healers who had journeyed specially to Klinbil to help treat the sick and injured. Petronicus was very concerned about the town well and told the people not to drink the water even after the dead animals had been removed.

"When will you leave for the trail, Petronicus?" I asked the first night we were in Klinbil.

"When I have written a scroll about how Zilk's people were washed ashore and how the Bedosians used that to enslave the people. I must tell how I found Zilk and how we began to learn his words. His words must also be written down. But this task will not take me long with you to help."

Twenty five

The Great Work of writing began within days of our arrival.

The people of Klinbil were inspired by the presence of the Revered One, Petronicus and Zilk. They held a town meeting around the great fire soon after we arrived.

Kelkos, regarded by many as the wisest man in Klinbil spoke his people. "My friends, people of Klinbil. We must provide food and shelter for our visitors who have come to write of these awful events. Future men of wisdom must know what happened and that will ensure that never again false beliefs and wicked thoughts return to harm our people and destroy our towns."

Nobody in the crowd disagreed. Several others rose to speak and said that people would come to Klinbil from places far away just to see the Great Work being undertaken.

"Yes," said Kelkos. "They will come to trade with us and we will prosper in peace. But first we must build a much larger House of Tablets where Kelcit can safeguard the Great Work. The Revered One will stay in the house of the Elder Scribe so he can confer with Petronicus, who is the wisest of men. And we must provide for Zilk and he can teach us many things from his world."

The next day I was put to work with Kelcit, sifting through the destroyed House of Tablets. We found many fragments and began to piece them together. Kelcit became less mournful as more and more of the old records were brought out of the rubble and reassembled. Almost immediately scribes from other towns came to Klinbil to watch us working and to read the fragments we had pieced together.

The people of the town made mud bricks and brought trees from the surrounding hills to construct a much larger House of

Tablets whilst the Elder Scribe sat in the sun by his ruined house scratching away with his rabbit bone on the scrolls. His novices were put to work making new scrolls from reeds that grew in the small ponds nearby.

Sometimes I worked with Petronicus but I was never invited to assist the Elder Scribe. The Revered One, rested, moved into the Elder Scribe's house as soon as it was repaired.

The next few moons passed happily for me. I was with my friends in a town that welcomed us and cared for us. The Revered One began to recover his health and I would often sit with him as he read the words the Elder Scribe had written that day. Sometimes I was able to correct what the Elder Scribe had written and I began to realise that the Revered One could not remember all that he had spoken at the Council himself. Petronicus finished his scrolls quite quickly. There were ten of them and he handed them over to Kelcit for safekeeping.

"But now," the Revered One announced, "the scrolls must be copied onto tablets and baked in the fire and they will last for ever."

That task was given to Kelcit of course, and the ovens were kept burning night and day as the ten tablets of Petronicus were baked. The people of Klinbil finished the new House of Tablets quite quickly and logs were brought in, smoothed down with sharp stones to make shelves to display the tablets.

Peace and goodness returned to the world; wise men once again discussed the great questions and as Petronicus often said: '*Whilst we discuss and question we will be free.*' He was absolutely right of course. The great question being discussed around the fires of the wise ones was about rainbows. Some said that all the colours in the world; the colours of the plants, the animals and all things that live and grow came from the rainbows. Petronicus wasn't sure about that and was content just to listen to what other people said. Some learned men claimed that rainbows lived during the night hours as well but that we just couldn't see them.

There is one night that I remember very well because it was the first time I argued with wise men other than Petronicus. It was a warm night and we all rested around the town fire. Once again the matter being discussed was the rainbow. I had also been thinking very deeply about Zilk and his numberings. Petronicus and I had talked about Zilk and his numberings but neither of us knew where it might lead.

I had not discussed it with Petronicus, but I felt old enough to intervene in the argument around the fire. The Elder Scribe of Klinbil was present and he always seemed to look with disapproval at young people. Kelcit was also there and I knew that he would be sympathetic to me. I was, after all, in my sixteenth year.

"But," I said nervously, "some very wise men say that all colours come from the rainbow. All the colours in the world, they say, start in the rainbow." I was hesitant and afraid they would laugh at me but I persisted just as Petronicus had always taught me to. "Colours do not disappear at night. The grass is still green only we cannot see the colour very clearly. And this fire is still red and the night is dark. Just because we cannot see the rainbow at night does not mean it is not there."

The Elder Scribe of Klinbil looked at me quite sternly and several other men did the same.

Kelcit said, however: "You have interesting thoughts. Tell us more, Petronius."

Liminicus was also nodding approval in my direction and Petronicus smiled encouragement and said: "Tell us your thinking, Petronius. Tell us what your mind is saying to you."

"Well," I said, swallowing hard. I was hesitant because I needed an example that none of them could argue with. And then a thought soared through my mind. "Just because we cannot see the rainbow at night does not mean that it is not there. We cannot see the sun at night when it rests in the Great Fire beneath the world but we all know it is there." The Elder Scribe of Klinbil looked agitated and clearly did not relish one so young questioning things. "Then there is Zilk's numberings. Surely, these numberings say that there is pattern in the world ..."

"Then it is the pattern of the gods and not for us to know," said the Elder Scribe.

He spoke in the tone of a reprimand and thought I would remain quiet after that but I saw Petronicus smiling at me so I continued: "Zilk has shown us that everything repeats itself, everything follows a course like the moon and stars in the sky. The flowers grow in the soil, reach for the light and die away and then their seeds come up again and the pattern is repeated. We do not know how or why this happens and often we cannot see the seeds in the ground but we know they make their lives again. Men do the same, they live, grow old and then return to the ground; we have always known that. The sun and moon follow the same pattern all the time." I stopped there because I had not thought far enough ahead about what I wanted to say.

Liminicus spoke next: "But are you sure about that, Petronius? Sometimes the sun makes short journeys and at other times long journeys. Long journeys in the summer when it is warm and shorter journeys when it is cold in the winter and it wants to get to the great fires more quickly. And the moon follows a slightly different trail in the sky as it grows from small to big."

"You are indeed wise, Liminicus," I said. There was silence around the town fire of Klinbil as they waited for me to bow my head and return to the silence, which is the rightful posture of youth. However, another thought came to me and I said: "I respect your wisdom, Liminicus, but is it not the case that the different patterns of the sun and moon are themselves a pattern? Are they not a course that is repeated each year and each moon?"

Silence descended around the town fire. The Elder Scribe of Klinbil looked at me severely. Kelcit nodded his head slightly and

Liminicus said thoughtfully: "Your thoughts follow a true course, Petronius. There is much to think about here."

I did not speak again but when Petronicus and I lay down to sleep by the fire he whispered to me: "Well done, Petronius. I was proud of you."

"I was very frightened," I whispered. "The Elder Scribe of Klinbil is a very learned man."

"Yes, but Liminicus agreed with you and he is a wise man and a healer."

"Yes, that is so. I worked with Liminicus in the House of Humility. He is a great healer. But the Elder Scribe is also a great man, is he not, Petronicus?"

"Yes, he is," said Petronicus quietly. "He reads the thoughts of the wise ones, men of the first thought, that are written in the tablets. But what if we removed the source of other men's thoughts from men like him? There would be no substance in their thinking. Don't you think we should distinguish between men who are wise and men who are merely learned?"

"I will ponder on that, Petronicus, in the moons ahead and speak with you again another time when I have given it thought."

My eyes were closing in the flickering firelight but I saw Petronicus smiling at me.

Twenty six

It was a sad day for me when Petronicus told me it was time he left on the trail again. He had finished the task that the Revered One had given him and there was nothing to keep him in Klinbil any longer. His words about the events leading up to the Great Council of Wisdom had been written on the scrolls and were now put on to tablets so they would last forever.

"We cannot expect the people of Klinbil to feed us much longer," he said. "They have a lot to do rebuilding their town. They will have to take their cattle and sheep to the high pasture very soon for grazing and food is always scarce at this time of the year."

"I will miss you, Petronicus. Will you return for me during the summer moons?"

"Zilk will stay with you. He is learning to speak our words very well now. Soon we will have long talks with him about his own world. You have tasks to finish and then you will be able to follow me."

Zilk and I walked with him down the trail for half a day before finally saying farewell. He embraced me and I noticed how sad Zilk was to see him go.

"Goodbye, child. Goodbye, Zilk. I will head towards the coastal towns and earn some coins for us. Meet me after five moons at the crossroads where the trail comes from Biltis and another leads to Bedosa. If I am not there I will leave my sign in the stones at the crossroads to tell you where to find me."

Zilk and I stood for a long time watching the old man becoming smaller and smaller as he walked along the trail. He turned just once to wave to us and then was lost in the distance.

A strange feeling came over me as I watched him go and I think Zilk shared it. It was a feeling of loneliness and dread – Petronicus had mentioned Bedosa!

"Petronicus gone," said Zilk. "Zilk out of happy."

I smiled sympathetically at him and said: "Yes, Petronicus gone. Petronius out of happy." I rubbed my belly and said: "Zilk in *sunka*?"

"Yes, Zilk in *sunka*. Petronius in *sunka*?" I rubbed my belly again and smiled. Maybe I realised for the first time that day just how lonely Zilk was. He must have listened to us all talking together so often and yet he was able to understand so little of what we said. From that time on I decided to learn as many of Zilk's words as I could.

We walked slowly back towards Klinbil collecting berries as we went. Clouds came over and darkened the sky and added to our sadness. But we were together and well fed with stalks and succulent mosses that grow in secret places that Petronicus had taught me about.

At length I turned to Zilk. "Petronius out of *sunka*."

Zilk smiled and said: "Zilk out of *sunka*. Zilk out of happy. Petronicus gone."

Later that day when crossing a small river, Zilk stopped and said: "*Kandis* for *sunka* when sun sleeps."

He speared a large fish with his great blade for our supper. We joined the others around the town fire that night and cooked the fish and it was so large that we shared it with Kelcit and the Revered One.

The Revered One turned to Zilk and said: "*Kandis* good. Me out of *sunka*."

The work continued during the next moon. Eventually the Elder Scribe of Klinbil finished his task of writing the words spoken at the Great Council of Wisdom. He had completed many scrolls, but the Revered One was worried because reeds crumbled very quickly when they dried. Kelcit was told he must be ready to put the words onto tablets and bake them in the fires as soon as possible. One day the Revered One took me into the house of Kelcit and together we read the final script written by the Elder Scribe. His words were true and accurate and it seemed the more the Elder Scribe sat quietly thinking about what happened, the more he could remember. He also consulted frequently with Liminicus and Kelcit but he never asked for my help.

"And now, Petronius," said the Revered One, "there is something you must also do. I want you to learn as many words of Zilk as you can and then write them on a scroll and put our words next to them. Do you know why I want you to do that?"

"No, Revered One," I said. "Petronicus and I have always tried to teach Zilk our words and learned only a small number of his. Surely it is more important that he learns to speak with us in our words than we learn of his."

The Revered One was quiet for a moment. He smiled at me and I thought he was going to do what Petronicus always did, ask me more and more questions until I came to the right answer myself. But he did not do that because as I realise now it was too important to waste time.

"Now supposing," said the Revered One, "that some of Zilk's people come to our world again."

"Again? But that would not be possible, they would be lost in the great fires if they tried to come here."

"Yes, that is correct. But they would not come here deliberately because they do not know we are here. But what if they suffered in storms like Zilk and his friends and drifted here and landed on our shores?" I thought deeply and a horrific thought came to me just as the Revered One expected it would.

"They would be thought of as gods?"

"No, not if the tablets are written and everything is known. But they may think we are enemies to them."

I felt my face warming into a huge smile. I could have hugged the Revered One but I had never done that. I only hugged Petronicus and sometimes Zilk. I spoke rapidly like a chattering bird: "But we could speak to them in their words. We could rub hands with them. We could give them *kandis* if they were in *sunka*. We could tell them of Zilk. Oh, Revered One, you are so wise."

"Thank you, Petronius. Before your master left we discussed it and that is the task we both desire of you and Zilk before you leave for the trail to join Petronicus."

"I wondered why he left me here when the Elder Scribe had nearly finished his task, and why he left Zilk with me. But Revered One, there is something troubling me …"

"Yes, I know there is Petronius. You came back from waving goodbye to Petronicus much troubled. What is it?"

"It is Bedosa. Petronicus said we would meet where the trails cross from Biltis to Bedosa. I fear that he might go to Bedosa to try and discover where the Ruler and the blade men are hiding."

"Petronicus is wise," said the Revered One. "He will not do foolish things. Besides, travellers have told me that Bedosa has been abandoned because of the evil air that is in the town and that the Bedosians have fled to the Land of the Bubbling Mud."

"Petronicus told me that towns are abandoned when great wickedness takes place and evil air remains to make other people wicked. Is that true, Revered One?"

"Yes, and not just towns. I know of forests and valleys where no man will go for the same reason."

"But, Revered One, great wickedness happened at Klinbil and that is not abandoned."

The old man smiled, paused and then said: "Your years with Petronicus sharpened your mind, Petronius. You question well."

"Then is evil air in Klinbil?"

"I think not, Petronius. The wickedness that took place in Klinbil when the Bedosian blade men broke into the town has been removed now. Can you think how that was so?"

I smiled inwardly. Yes, he was questioning me like Petronicus would have done. I was thinking hard and trying to put my answer into words.

The old man continued: "Go and look through the doorway and tell me what you see and then you might be able to answer my question."

I did as I was told and gazed out of the doorway. I could see the Elder Scribe of Klinbil sitting in the sun instructing his novice scribes. He had large piles of recently cut reeds drying in the sun ready to be folded into scrolls. I could see the new House of Tablets which was twice the size of the old one with ovens for baking the tablets and Kelcit buzzing around like a honey bee organising things and showing his novices what to do. I looked over towards the market place where the town fire was still smouldering from the night before. There were traders and travellers milling about. The stockade was being rebuilt and the wooden gatehouse was being made bigger than ever before. The gallows had been burned long ago. The whole town was a bustle of activity and happiness.

I returned and sat by the old man smiling.

"Well, Petronius, what do your eyes tell you?"

"There is great goodness in Klinbil now. There is happiness and hopes for better things."

"That is right. Evil doings can be undone by good things. And now there is a good thing that you must do."

"Write down the words of Zilk with our words?"

"Yes," said the Revered One. "One day every novice scribe when he studies his letters will learn how to say: 'Welcome people of Zilk. We mean you no harm. We will help you. We will give you food and shelter'."

"Yes, Revered One. That is a good thing we must do."

The next moons passed contentedly. I missed Petronicus greatly but found great joy in learning the words of Zilk and having discussions with him. We set about the task the Revered One had given us with great interest. Zilk was 'in happy' helping me because he must have thought about people from his own world being washed up on our shores again at some time in the future. I was also amazed how quickly Zilk learned to speak the words of our world and how happy he was to do it. Each day we tried to write down five words of Zilk each, followed by our word, which told of the same thing. Words about things we could see or hold in our hands were easy but other words were more difficult. We often had to use gestures and pretend actions to try and put the two words together.

We cut reeds to make large scrolls stuck together with sap from pine trees. The scrolls were big enough to wrap once completely around a man's arm. People often came to listen to us working and many found it quite funny, especially the young ones. But between us we completed nearly twenty scrolls of the words of Zilk, which Kelcit took for safekeeping in the House of Tablets. The Revered One said we had done well and copies would be sent to scribes in other towns to pass on to their novices. Eventually, the words would be baked onto clay tablets but that task would take years to complete. I don't think I had fully realised how important words were until we worked together on that great task. I had received words from Petronicus when I was a small child and the gods had given the words to men; everyone knew that. But why Zilk had different words, I never knew and I don't think Petronicus or the Revered One knew either.

"When we will go and find Petronicus?" asked Zilk one morning in late spring.

"Soon," I said. "Just one more moon must grow large and small and then we can go."

One night the Revered One called all the wise ones together around the town fire. Kelkos sat next to him with the Elder Scribe close by. Liminicus and Kelcit were also present as well as several other healers and scribes who had arrived in the town. Klinbil was becoming a great meeting place of wise men and many people wanted to come and speak with the Revered One.

Zilk and I were not allowed to sit near the wise ones that night but we were able to listen to their discussions.

The Revered One spoke first: "My wise friends, people of Klinbil, listen to me. There is something that must now happen." He turned to Kelcit and said: "The words spoken at the Great Council of Wisdom and the events that happened after have been written by the Elder Scribe. Petronicus has written about the events before that when our dear friend Zilk came to our shores with his friends and all these words have been put onto tablets and baked in the fires by Kelcit and his novices." There were shouts of approval and appreciation.

Kelcit and the Elder Scribe smiled and waved to everyone. "How many tablets are there, Kelcit?" asked the Revered One.

Kelcit stood up and held all his fingers up twice and said: "Two times a man's hand. Twenty tablets and that is more than I have ever heard of being made at the same time. And each the size of man's chest."

Again there were shouts of approval and appreciation and everyone around the fire seemed to be feeling happy and satisfied.

"But now," said the Revered One. "It must all be done again." The crowd was stunned to silence and Kelcit looked at the Revered One with some surprise. "Yes, friends, we must copy these twenty tablets and send copies to towns all over the world. The first copy must go to the Temple of the Healers at the Mountain of the Year and the next copy must go to Klynos."

There was general discussion around the fire. Many nodded an immediate agreement but others looked doubtful.

"But, Revered One," said Kelcit. "My scribes and I need help. There are only three of us and we need to earn our food."

Kelkos rose to speak: "Do not fear, Kelcit, we the people of Klinbil will provide for you. Klinbil will become an important town and people from all over the world will come here to see the Great Work being done. We will prosper in the trade of the world."

The Revered One had already spoken to Kelkos and knew what he would say. After a short pause to allow the townspeople to digest what had been said, the Revered One spoke again: "Scribes from other towns can come and help copy the tablets for their own towns. But they must copy from the first one and that way it will be correct."

Now even more people were nodding their agreement. The Revered One spoke further: "Never again must the Bedosian madness make our minds sick with false thoughts. The truth about Zilk and the 'gods' must be known to all men and all men who come after us must know the truth."

The Revered One sat down and the people of Klinbil nodded and shouted their agreement.

Very soon after that several scribes came in from Biltis. They sought me out because they knew I had learned my letters in Biltis. My time in Biltis now seemed like a lifetime ago. We exchanged stories about the town and laughed when we recalled having to tend the Elder Scribe's cows and sheep in the town pasture and how his wife would scold us for laziness and how hungry we always were. However, the most important thing for me was that they had news about Petronicus.

"He is a great healer and a wise man," said one of the scribes. "He remained in Biltis for a whole moon."

"And to where he go next please?" asked Zilk.

"Towards the morning side of the day," said the scribe. "There are many sick people near the Land of the High Valleys, people from Bedosa with broken limbs and all manner of infirmities."

Zilk was silent for a while and I could read worry on his face. The scribes went off to deliver their respects to the Elder Scribe of

Klinbil and to the Revered One. Later that day they went to see Kelcit and asked permission to begin making a copy of the scrolls for their town.

Zilk and I sat together in the afternoon sun. He was quiet at first and then he turned to me and said: "Petronicus *naptik* Bedosa?" Zilk often spoke in his own words when he was anxious or afraid. Fortunately I had learnt enough of his words to understand his meaning.

"Yes, Petronicus will pass near to Bedosa if he goes towards the morning side of the world from Biltis."

"Petronius and Zilk *naptik* Bedosa *leciman aroo* in Bedosa."

"Yes we can go to Bedosa if Petronicus thinks it is safe, but I do not know if your people's boat is still in the town. Zilk out of happy?"

"Zilk must go to boat."

Later that day Zilk went off to greet a trading party of the Tall People who had arrived that morning. I was feeling confused about what Zilk had said, so I went to see the Revered One.

"Why should you be surprised that Zilk wants to go and see his boat? His people's bodies might still be there."

"I am not surprised, Revered One, I am ... well, I feel ... as ..."

"You feel guilty because you never thought about Zilk and his feelings about his dead friends. Did you know that most of them were members of his family?"

"He told you that?"

"Yes, we speak together often. I do not understand what they believe should be done with their dead friends but Zilk is concerned that his people will be left to rot in the evil air of an abandoned town."

"I will speak to Zilk about it."

I slept little that night by the town fire. My guilt about not considering Zilk's feelings rose up within me and I did not have Petronicus to talk to about it. The next day I was resolved that although only four moons had fully passed we would set out on the trail and find Petronicus and then maybe we would all go together to Bedosa.

Zilk was 'in happy' the next day when I told him to prepare for our journey. We went to say our goodbyes to friends. They gave us food and blankets for our journey and many gave us messages for Petronicus. Kelcit was sad to see us go but he was busy preparing a new set of tablets to be sent to the Temple of the Healers at the Mountain of the Year so he had much to think about. His new House of Tablets now had many visitors who gazed in wonderment at the huge tablets being prepared. Many just wanted to touch them in order to return home and tell their friends they had done so.

"And then," said Kelcit, "as soon as that is finished, the Revered One wants another copy made for Klynos."

"Yes," I said. "Klynos must have a copy. It is an important town; men of wisdom and healers pass through there on their way to the Mountain of the Year."

"And now, the Elder Scribe of Biltis has sent scribes to copy the scrolls and then they can make their own tablets."

"Yes, you have much to do Kelcit. We will return when the leaves fall, and perhaps winter in Klinbil."

We went next to the Elder Scribe of Klinbil who bid us a formal farewell and asked me to convey his respects to Petronicus.

Finally we went to see the Revered One, who said: "Tell Petronicus that all goes well here and it is just how we both wanted it to be. Tell him that I will probably winter in Klynos so that I can be near the Mountain of the Year. Farewell my young friends; travel true and travel safely."

It was a sad parting and I noticed that Zilk was close to tears when we bid our goodbyes to the Revered One. Many friends came with us a little way down the trail. They gave us even more food and one of the Tall People gave me a beautiful piece of flint for the making of fire.

We did not look back but headed on down the trail. The weather was good and the sun was warm and we had a long trek to Biltis.

I said to Zilk: "Biltis *sitaki mabo kali febodis* Petronicus." It always pleased him when I spoke with his words.

"Yes," said Zilk. "You are right, we find Petronicus near Biltis."

We smiled together; we were learning each other's words so well and we both knew Petronicus would be pleased.

Twenty seven

We could see the crossroads long before we reached it. The country was quite flat thereabouts and you could see into the far distance. Petronicus once told me that you could see a whole day's walk away in the country near Biltis. I had really hoped to see Petronicus camped by the crossroads and I was very disappointed when he wasn't there. I reassured myself with the thought that we were a little less than a moon earlier than arranged.

Zilk put his hand on my shoulder. "Crossroads not at Petronicus."

"No," I said. "Petronicus not at crossroads. But the moon still does not shine its fullness; my master does not expect us yet."

"*Sitaki febodis* Petronicus."

I smiled at him and said: "Yes you are right, we will find him."

But I was disappointed and anxious. It seemed to me that Petronicus and I had been separated so often since the cataclysm began and I found it just as painful each time. We had often camped at crossroads when we were on the trail together. Travellers and traders in need of a healer often went to a crossroads in the hope of finding one. But on this occasion the crossroads were deserted.

We continued on our way but we slowed our pace, as we now had nothing to hurry for. In my awake dreams I had seen myself running up to the old man and embracing him lovingly. He would then tell me all about his travels and I would tell him all about our time in Klinbil and all about what had happened since he left. I would give him the messages from Kelcit, from the Revered One and from the Elder Scribe of Klinbil and we would have gone on talking and talking long into the night. But sadly it was not to be.

"Petronicus leave words in the sand?" said Zilk. "You know sand to look."

"Yes," I said. "Petronicus *milepos* in the sand." I looked around but I could not find the mark of Petronicus amongst the signs on the ground. There were signs in small stones of other healers who had passed that way but of Petronicus there was nothing. I began to despair and looked around anxiously. One trail led off towards the sea in the direction of Bedosa, another towards the morning side of the day to the Land of the High Valleys and another trail led to Biltis. But which way had he taken? Or had he even been here at all? We put our bundles on the ground and I continued to search for the signs of Petronicus. I was about to surrender my mind to complete disappointment when I saw an arabak tree growing just a short distance away from the trail that led to Bedosa. It was a huge tree and I knew that would be where Petronicus would leave me a sign. I ran over to it and looked down. The blood froze in my body. It became like ice on a stream in winter as a coldness swept over me and for a moment my body would not move.

"Zilk, come … look."

"What does the sand say to you, Petronius?"

"There, you see those five stones? That is the sign of Petronicus."

"That is *febodis* of Petronicus?"

"Yes." I paused and looked along the deserted trail to Bedosa. "He has gone to Bedosa and tells us to remain here and wait for him." I looked into the sad face of Zilk and said: "We must do what my master says. Let us prepare beds of moss and grasses and collect sticks for our fire. Then we must search for food."

Zilk was silent. He kept looking up the trail to Bedosa and I could see he was making words in his mind to say to me. When he was ready he said: "Petronius, Zilk's head says we go to Bedosa. Petronicus be hurt. Need us."

I looked at him in alarm. That would mean disobeying my master! That was something I had never done in my life before. But I was confused and uncertain. What if Zilk was right? Supposing Petronicus was sick or lying lame by the side of the trail? I turned away and let thoughts run through my head. Zilk had seen more of life than I had. He was older and had sailed the great ocean. I held my hands tightly with uncertainty.

My face must have told of the conflict within me. Zilk put his hand on my shoulder and smiled. But I had always obeyed Petronicus without hesitation. But … maybe … just this once? I looked at Zilk and nodded, but I knew he had more to say to me.

"Revered One says that Bedosa bad place now … no people."

"Yes, the town has been abandoned."

"Ab-an-doned?" said Zilk.

"Yes, abandoned. That means all the people have gone because great evil was there."

"Zilk's people there and will be in evil breath."

"Breath?"

"Yes, evil breath." He blew into the wind and waved his fingers to show he meant air or wind.

"I understand," I said. "The Revered One said that evil will be in the air at Bedosa. You are worried about the bodies of your people."

"Yes, they must become smoke and fly to the clouds in the breath of the wind and then they return to the land with the rain."

"I understand." I paced around for a short while as thoughts raced through my mind. And then I became calmer and said: "You are wise, Zilk. I will disobey my master. We must go to Bedosa."

We left the crossroads and headed along the trail. We seemed to be walking faster and faster and then we both began to run. How long we ran for I do not remember but we did not speak, as we needed our mouths to pull in the air as we ran.

Suddenly we found the trail barred. There was a stout wooden fence made from tree branches with large jagged stones on top.

Thorny brambles had grown in amongst the logs and there was a sign in the stones: *Place of evil – good men keep away.* I explained the words to Zilk.

We looked at each other fearfully and then Zilk said: "Come, Petronius, to Bedosa."

We scrambled around the barrier and continued on our way. Towards the end of the day we could see the town walls in the distance with the sea beyond. It was beginning to grow dark so we decided to hide ourselves in the trees, watch the town and enter the following morning.

We slept very little during the night. At first we took it in turns to try and sleep whilst the other watched the town, but the moon shone brightly and worrying thoughts stopped us drifting away to the land of painless dreams. We sat together for most of the night with our blankets and skins around our shoulders. The only sound that came from Bedosa was of wild dogs come to scavenge for any scraps of food left behind by the people. No fires were lit in the town so we were fairly sure that it was completely abandoned. As the night wore on we became very hungry. We had not stopped to forage for food since leaving the crossroads and the strength we had used in running had emptied our bellies.

"Bad is it to eat food from an evil place?" Zilk asked. I did not answer at first because it was such a difficult question.

"Truly, I do not know, Zilk. What does your head say to you?"

"My thoughts are empty but so is my belly. I am in *sunka*."

"I am not sure. If only Petronicus was here, he would know." How I wished my master were with us to answer Zilk's question for me. Petronicus could always answer questions, his wisdom told him everything. It was a strange feeling; Zilk asking me a question that I would have asked Petronicus. I thought for a while and then said: "Maybe he would say that food grown in evil air would have wickedness in it … but I do not know."

The night continued to pass over us. We spoke very little, each lost in his own thoughts. A wind got up and whistled through the trees. And then shortly before the sun stirred itself into wakefulness ready to climb into the morning, Zilk put his hand on my mouth and whispered: "Hush, Zilk smells smoke close by here."

I held my head towards the wind and nodded. Zilk stood up and began to look around. "Over by the rocks. I see a cave. Fire colour."

Zilk took his great blade and held it in front of him. This was the first time I had seen him prepared to use his great blade as a weapon. He led the way through the trees to a cliff that soared up in front of us. Before us we could see the opening into a cave. Zilk beckoned with his blade and entered the cave. I followed inside.

The cave was shallow and only just provided shelter for the sleeping figure we saw before us. He had a small fire, which still smouldered and cast a sparse light into the cave. I froze and gripped Zilk's hand; the man was a priest! He was sleeping and was completely alone.

Zilk kicked the man's foot and as the priest stirred into wakefulness he saw the point of Zilk's blade at his throat and let out a cry of fear.

I spoke first: "Your name, priest … who are you?"

"I am not a priest … I am not."

"You lie," I said. "You wear the robe of a priest. Priests are wicked. They have killed people and enraged the gods."

"How are you named?" demanded Zilk, pressing his blade ever closer to the man's throat.

"Please, please … I am not a priest."

"But you wear the priest's robes." I raised my voice and shouted: "You are a priest!"

Zilk raised his blade ready to strike death into the man, who scurried back towards the cave wall. Fear contorted his face.

Zilk hesitated as the man cried: "Please … Petronius … don't let him kill me."

Zilk turned to me in astonishment. "He has your name in his mouth." Zilk lowered his blade until it was just touching the man's chest.

"Petronius," spluttered the man, "I have been waiting for you. Petronicus told me to wait for you."

"Petronicus? What do you know of Petronicus?"

"He is the greatest of healers. You are Petronius his son and novice. And you are Zilk of the gods' people."

"Where is Petronicus now?" I demanded.

"He has gone to the Land of the Burning Waters."

"I do not know of this land," I said.

"Some call it the Land of the Bubbling Mud. He told me to wait for you here in Bedosa."

"You lie! Petronicus told me to wait at the crossroads from Biltis. I do not disobey my master."

"But you *are* here, you *are* at Bedosa."

Zilk now rested his blade on the ground. He turned to me and I saw the beginnings of a smile on his face in the sparse glow of the fire as he spoke:

"Petronicus is wise. Wisdom is in the knowing of people."

"Yes, Zilk," I said. I smiled to myself. "You are beginning to talk like Petronicus."

"Petronius, look closely at this priest," said Zilk. "My eyes see some of your face in him."

"Petronius," the man pleaded, "I am Bolga. We are of the same mother. Petronicus left words for you. There, over there by the cave wall. Please look and find a horn with a reed scroll inside."

"Take off that priest's robe; it is hateful to my eyes. If you do not speak the truth, Zilk will kill you."

Bolga continued to plead whilst I searched amongst his debris by the cave wall. Then he added: "Petronius, and he is a great man, told me to wait here for a whole moon and if you didn't come I must return and wait for you at the crossroads."

We fed new life into the fire and I sat down to read the message from Petronicus:

To my disobedient novice.

If you read this in Bedosa you have disobeyed me.

But you have disobeyed out of love and not from malice. Your brother Bolga will tell you all you shall know. If I do not return from this journey before another moon has waned you must return to Klynos and tell the Revered One that I am dead and that the Bedosians are still a danger to the world. Do not grieve for me. Let the gods guide your footsteps and thoughts. I will always be with you. I will be somewhere in the wind. I will be in the sky and in the trees – I will watch over you.

I felt tears coming to my eyes, but they were tears of anger as well as sadness. I did not read the message aloud but told Zilk later when we were alone. I carefully folded the scroll and put it into my pouch.

"Bolga," I said, "you have much to tell us."

And what a tale he had to tell. He was older than me, having seen about twenty summers. He could not count in numbers nor did he have the letters. He told how Petronicus had called at his mother's inn to tell her that I had survived the Great Cataclysm and was safely in Klinbil.

But sadly my mother was dead, having been killed by the priests when they heard she had harboured and protected me, a healer's novice. Bolga had not been at the inn when I rested there after the massacre in Bedosa but he had often heard tales from his mother about a lost child who was half brother to him. All she knew was that the child had been taken by a healer and never seen again. Who Bolga's own father was he never knew, but he was sure that he was different to mine. Our mother was a 'woman of the inns', Bolga said, who knew many men. Petronicus had explained these things to me as I grew. Bolga had been taken as a temple slave and had laboured on the new building for many moons. After the cataclysm he had returned to the inn, where Petronicus found him. Bolga was searching for some coins he believed his mother kept buried in the ground.

During the days we kept Bolga with us we heard much more of his story. But our most urgent need at that moment was for news of Petronicus. We were to hear later about the massacre of the priests when the blade men abandoned them. We heard how the temple slaves had hunted them down and killed most of them and that Bolga had stolen his priest's robe from a dead priest.

"Bolga," I said, "if you are truly my brother, if we are truly of the same mother, you will speak to me with truth. Where is Petronicus now? How long has he been gone?"

"Just more than a moon, brother. I took him along the trail for the days of one hand and a bit of the other. When we got to Trail End, Petronicus told me to return to Bedosa and wait for you."

"What is beyond Trail End?" I demanded.

"It is where no man goes. Beyond is the Land of the Burning Waters, which some call the Land of the Bubbling Mud. It is where fugitives go to hide."

"You have been to this strange land?"

"No," said Bolga. "But travellers and traders staying at the inn told stories and I remember how they told of the way."

"You will show us the way, Bolga?"

My brother nodded and we settled down to sleep for what remained of the night.

The next day the three of us entered Bedosa.

Twenty eight

No sound came from the town as we approached. The wild dogs scurried away as we entered through what remained of the town gate. The town was dead in its silence and the only things that moved were leaves and grasses blowing about in the streets. The roofs of the houses had fallen down and some houses had collapsed. Doors were hanging loosely on the leather straps and the whole place smelt of decay.

Zilk took the great blade that he usually kept tied on his back and held it in front of him. Bolga showed great fear and told us he had not entered the town since the cataclysm when the place was abandoned.

We continued our cautious and fearful way into the town. I saw the place where the scaffold had been and could see in my mind's eye the healers and scribes being hanged by the Ruler and his priests. I paused for a short while and looked into the House of Tablets and thought about Mentis lying dead on the trail where we had found him. The House of Tablets was a ruin.

We passed the place of the massacre where I had lain hidden under the bodies of the dead before escaping from the town. And then we approached the temple. I was tense with hatred and fear. Zilk put his hand on my shoulder because he knew of my fearful memories. This was the town where the father I never knew had been hanged for stealing food. Perhaps he was stealing food for me when I was a helpless infant, but that was something I would never know. I had never thought about him like this before, and then thoughts about my mother came into my head. She too had been killed by the Bedosians for sheltering me.

"Oh, Zilk," I said. "How I hate this place!"

"Is that the temple where my people lie?" asked Zilk. I nodded and we crossed what used to be the market place and approached the temple. It was truly the largest structure I had ever seen. So many slaves had worked on it under the rule of the priests. They had brought whole tree trunks and placed them on large stones to rebuild the place entirely. It was twice the size of the temple I remembered. Bolga stepped back, fearful of entering the great wooden doorway.

"Remain outside if you wish," I said, "but Zilk will need our help. He has to burn the bodies of his people."

Bolga hesitated and then said: "I will help. The bodies of the gods were put back in the great boat when we had finished. To see this place burn will bring joy to me. My back still aches from the building of it."

We entered and saw the chaos inside. The boat that had brought Zilk's people to our world was now covered in dirt and the place smelt of animals and filth. The temple roof had fallen in and rotting straw from the roof lay all around. The boat was badly broken and the large sailcloth had been stolen.

Zilk climbed into the boat and began to move the branches. I remained outside the boat because I sensed that Zilk wanted to be alone just then.

At length he returned to me and said: "My father, my brothers and my friends are all here but animals have torn their bodies. Their clothes have been stolen. They are out of happy. They must return home. Please help me, Petronius, and then make fire."

We worked silently together for a while collecting wood and kindling and piling it into the boat. Zilk was full of sadness but he smiled his thanks to me often. When we had finished we lit some kindling ready to make torches to throw into the boat.

"Zilk alone now. This is a son's to do."

Bolga and I went outside into the sunlight.

"Zilk is huge," said Bolga. "Is it true he is from another world as I have heard tell?"

"Yes, it is true but where that world is not even the Revered One knows."

"You have talked with the Revered One?" asked my brother in admiration.

Zilk came out of the temple and we could see small streaks of smoke creeping through the wrecked roof. We stood for a long time watching the fire take hold of the temple. And then it began to burn quickly as the fire ate up the dry wood and the smoke ascended into the sky.

"Come, Petronius. Let us leave this place," said Zilk.

Twenty nine

Zilk seemed more content as we left Bedosa and said that we must now spend all our thinking on finding Petronicus. We were following a trail, which kept close to the sea, and we kept going for most of that day. We wanted to put as much distance between us and that hated place as we could. Bolga led the way but complained he was hungry and that we should stop and search for food.

"No," I said quite sternly. "We must eat nothing so near Bedosa. Never eat food grown in evil air or evil will enter you."

That night we camped amongst the trees. We were a whole day's trek from Bedosa so I thought it was now safe enough to scavenge for food, but it was scarce. I dug into the ground to find roots to eat and Zilk managed to snare a rabbit but it was so small that it had very little meat on it.

The next morning when I awoke I saw Zilk standing looking out towards the sea. It was a bright morning and the sun was beginning to climb up the day. Zilk stood with his feet apart and the point of his blade sticking into the ground. He had his hands on the handle of his blade. I still found it astonishing how tall he was. I considered myself a man full grown in this my seventeenth summer but Zilk was head and shoulders taller than I was. I went over to him.

"See, Petronius," he said. "See how my people return home." I looked up and saw small clouds of pure white drifting across the sky and out to sea. "Soon they will return to my world in the rain and make the plants grow and bring all good things."

He turned to me and added: "Zilk in happy now."

We washed ourselves in a small stream but Bolga did not join us. I discovered during the next days that my brother seldom washed himself. We trekked all the next day towards the morning side of the world and when the sun was just beginning to fall towards the great fires, I asked Bolga: "How many days from here to what you call Trail End?" Bolga held up the fingers of one hand. I asked: "Why did you agree to guide Petronicus?"

"He gave me coins and said you would tell me where to find more coins if I stayed and waited for you in Bedosa."

"Did you not find the coins your mother buried at the inn?"

"No," said Bolga. "But Petronicus hid some for me and said you would know where I must look." I was silent for a while, but I was smiling; Petronicus had set me a puzzle. Zilk smiled with me.

"I understand the thoughts of Petronicus," I said. "And now tell us, what is beyond Trail End? Was that where you left Petronicus?"

"Yes. I was afraid to go beyond; I have heard such horrors are beyond."

Zilk then asked: "What heard? Tell of horrors." He turned to me and said: "Petronicus too wise to go into horrors."

"Many travellers passed through my mother's inn and told stories," said Bolga.

"What stories?" I demanded.

"The sea boils and white clouds rise up. Further out to sea there are mud flats where the mud bubbles and smells of burning death. Beyond that is Wretched Island, where bad men go to hide."

I was silent for a short while. I was wondering about his honesty and how true a course his thoughts took. He was three or four summers older than I was but he did not have the letters or the numbers. He had spent his life working at our mother's inn, and not in the company of a man of wisdom. I decided to treat him the way my master had always treated me. I would ask him questions to search his mind and tease the truth from him.

I looked at him with straight eyes and said: "Have you met and talked to travellers who have been to Wretched Island?"

"No! No one ever returns from there but they have seen it from the hills near the shore."

"Does any one live near the shore? How do the fugitives get to Wretched Island? Who guides them?"

"There are some eel catchers and people who trade in a yellow powder. They sell it to healers. A traveller once told me of a man called Mildos who knows the ways of the islands."

I thought quietly to myself. I remembered Petronicus taking some yellow powder from a sick traveller in payment for treatment. Petronicus knew what it was and we used it to treat mouth ulcers. It cannot be so evil, I thought, if it brings relief to sick people.

"Tell us more of this place," I said.

"The burning water scalds the feet and the clouds that hiss out of the mud is the breath of demons and evil gods who live beneath the world."

"Tales grow in their telling, Bolga," I replied.

Zilk smiled. "Now Petronius talks as Petronicus."

"The evil gods suck people down into the earth," said Bolga. "And they are never seen again."

"There are no evil gods, Bolga," I said. "It is the sun that sleeps under the earth in the Great Fires. Only men are evil sometimes, like the ruler and priests of Bedosa."

There was confusion on the face of my brother and he persisted: "The priests told us that if we do not obey them we will be taken down into the burning world below."

There was fear still in Bolga and, well, he was my brother, so I spent some time explaining things to him. I explained that when men die their bodies return to the earth and all that is good within them returns up through the plants and into the air. Men breathe the air and eat the plants and so the goodness of the dead comes to them. He looked very puzzled as I explained these truths but I was

221

patient with him; after all he had not spent his life being taught by a man like Petronicus. I told him that when we die our thoughts do not just end. They go to the Land of Wisdom where good men live with the gods.

Zilk and I discussed things later that night when Bolga was asleep. If it took Bolga and Petronicus five days to reach Trail End then we could be there in another three days.

"Petronicus is old," said Zilk. "And was taking a slow donkey. Petronius and Bolga and Zilk we are young and strong. We run. There in two days."

And so it was agreed. On the trail we learned more things from Bolga about what happened in Bedosa when the Ruler and his blade men returned from the Battle of Klynos. They were bleeding from their feet and full of wickedness and anger. One of the runners the Revered One sent out, a very young scribe, had reached Bedosa before them and spread the news. Several scribes and healers who had been hiding in the woods nearby came into the town and told the people of Bedosa to rise up against the Ruler. The people built barricades at the main gate and pelted them with sharp stones when they tried to enter. I smiled to myself when Bolga described the scene. Petronicus had been right all along; he said that it was only fear of the false gods that had enabled the Ruler and priests to control the people. The blade men had swirled their huge blades around so that the townspeople could not get near them but the townspeople wore the blade men down with stones and also let dogs loose on them in the manner of the Tall People.

Many priests had been injured in the fighting and several blade men had broken limbs. They were sick with hunger and no healer would go near them to treat their wounds. Eventually, after camping outside the gates of Bedosa for nearly half a moon, they set off towards the Land of the Bubbling Mud to escape the vengeance of the people.

Bolga took much satisfaction in telling us how the temple slaves had followed them at a safe distance and then massacred the renegade priests in the woods not two days distance from Bedosa.

We passed the place of the massacre on our journey and Bolga explained what had happened: "By then some of the priests had slipped away. They threw down their priests' robes and vanished into the forest."

"Did you hear where they all went?" I asked.

"No, it was not like that. Most of them travelled alone towards the Land of the High Valleys and I don't know what happened to them."

I noticed a disturbing look of relish on my brother's face when he explained the massacre and his part in it. He told us that most of the priests had been beaten by the blade men and left behind. The blade men no longer had any need for the priests. They saw them as a burden that slowed down their escape and they didn't want to share their food with them. The temple slaves found the priests late one night huddled around a fire, starving and exhausted. The slaves pounced on the priests and stoned most of them to death. They also robbed them of what little they had.

"And where are the bodies of these priests?" I asked. We were in a clearing in the forest where the massacre took place. The only sign of people was a burned patch in the centre where the priests had lit their fire.

"There was a wise man with us; his name was Nisla. I don't know where he came from. Do you know of him, brother?"

"No, I do not know a man of that name."

"He told us to put the bodies in a cave and block up the entrance with stones. I showed Petronicus the cave when we came here and he said it was the correct thing to do."

"Did he tell you why that was so?"

"The floor of the cave was hard stone. It was to stop their bodies returning into the earth and taking their wickedness with

them. Petronicus said, their wickedness would remain in the cave.
It could not get out."

"Petronicus is wise," I said.

Thirty

We reached what Bolga called Trail End in three days. We had been slower than expected because although Bolga was young and strong he was not used to travelling the trails for long periods. He complained constantly of hunger and seemed to want only to return to the inn to collect the coins that Petronicus had left for him. He was also very frightened of approaching the Land of the Bubbling Mud.

Later that day the three of us lay on the top of a low hill looking out towards the sea. The trail we had followed kept close to the sea all the way from Bedosa, with other trails leading off inland towards the Land of the High Valleys. There was nothing to mark Trail End except a very narrow path, which snaked its way into the distance. Beyond that we could see a large inlet where the sea had poked into the land; that was the Land of the Bubbling Mud. Further out still we could see islands and mudflats with hot white clouds hissing out of the sea. There was also an acrid smell blowing in on the wind towards us. The land close to the shore was flat, but we could not see where the land ended and the sea began for the forest of tall reeds that covered everything.

"Is this where you left Petronicus?" I asked Bolga.

"Yes, the last I saw of him he was leading his donkey towards the water."

"Did he say what he was going to do or where he was going?"

"No, he said nothing. He just told me to return to Bedosa and wait for you and you would tell me where the coins were buried."

"And this man Mildos, do you know where we can find him?"

"No. I know only what the travellers told me. Mildos, and I think his son, are the only people who know the secret ways of these islands."

I bade farewell to my half brother and watched him for a short while hurrying back along the trail. The last I heard of him was that he had left this part of the world and was seen on the trail to the Far Country.

His last words to me were: "My coins? Where will I find my coins?"

"Look beneath the arabak trees around the inn."

Zilk and I set off towards the sea. We walked close together for the comfort it gave both of us. We knew we were heading into a fearful place and our anxiety about Petronicus increased with every step. We passed some small mud houses but there were no people and it seemed to us that the houses had been abandoned and some of them deliberately damaged.

"The blade men do you think?" I said to Zilk.

"Yes," he said. "They take wickedness with them to all."

"But where is Mildos?"

Towards nightfall we found ourselves walking on very wet ground. We could hear the mud bubbling in the water just off the shore and sometimes our feet sank deep into the slime.

"We had better stop and wait until daylight," I said. Zilk agreed.

We ate the roots and berries we had collected and drank from a small stream, which emptied into the sea. We settled down to spend an anxious night with the sounds of hissing and bubbling all around us.

The sun disappeared into the Great Fire but it did not grow cold. Even the ground felt warm and we could hear the rumblings in the depths of the ground when we lay down. We tried to sleep but we could not drift away into the land of painless dreams.

At length Zilk put his hand on my mouth and said: "Zilk hearing something. Petronius hearing?"

"Only the sea bubbling," I said. "What do you hear?"

"Something moving … it is not far from us … Zilk cannot smell what it is."

Zilk sat up slowly and reached for his great blade, which was never far from his hand. We sat absolutely still and waited for the moon to shine between the clouds. Slowly the moon gave us a grudging light and we could see several paces in front of us. There was a large clump of reeds and a pair of dull eyes looking in our direction. I stood up immediately and ran towards the donkey that was watching us.

"It is our donkey," I shouted to Zilk. "Petronicus … Petronicus. It is us! Where are you?"

Zilk leapt over to me and began to stroke the donkey's head. It pushed its nose into me the way it had always done and I pulled its mane affectionately.

"But where Petronicus?" asked Zilk. "I see no Petronicus."

"Wait," I said. "Look!" The leather thong that the donkey had around its neck had been gnawed through. I felt its belly and could feel the ribs poking through the sagging flesh. "It is starved, Zilk, and Petronicus is not with it."

Zilk did not answer but I could see the look of fear on his face in the moonlight.

"Our donkey never strays far from us. Petronicus must be near," I said.

I have heard it said even by wise men that donkeys and other animals do not have the thinking men have. I had never really asked Petronicus about it but it seemed to me that if the donkey knew who we were, it must know who Petronicus was. Maybe it would lead us to him. The donkey lay down with us and I felt comfort from its nearness. Often in what remained of the night I reached out to stroke it. We had given the donkey what was left of the berries we had and then Zilk had crawled about and pulled grasses and leaves to feed to the animal.

"When the sun rises," I said to Zilk, "let the donkey lead us."

"Your head says donkey will find Petronicus?"

"We can hope. We know Petronicus is not behind us. We could not have passed him on the trail. And there is only one trail so he must be in front of us. The sun will rise shortly."

As soon as the sun sent streaks of light across the morning sky we left our sleeping place and tried to follow the muddy trail. The donkey stopped frequently to try and eat the poor grass at the side of the trail. I picked up some tufts and rubbed it in my hand; it was very coarse and brown.

"A donkey's belly soon empties if there is no goodness in the grass," I said. "There is little goodness in this."

"We must find grass for donkey soon," said Zilk.

We picked our way along what we thought was the trail but we could not see over the tops of the reeds. Even Zilk who was taller than me could not see beyond our immediate place. But towards midday we saw it, a strange wooden hut standing on four large thick poles. It was about the height of a man's chest above the mud. The donkey walked more freely as we approached it.

"You see, Petronius," said Zilk. "Donkey has been here before."

There were some wicker baskets and nets on a small platform outside the door of the hut. I had seen similar things before but not quite like these.

"What are these baskets, Zilk?"

He smiled and said: "In my world is a lot many islands. We take *kandis* for *sunka* from our boats. These catch *blaties*." He put his hand onto the mud and began to move his fingers as if they were legs, a bit like a spider."

"Crabs?" I said.

"Ah, you say, cr-abs." He smiled as he often did when he learned a new word. He pointed to baskets placed at the base of the reeds and made a slithering movement with his arms.

"Eels," I said.

Zilk nodded. "This must be the house of Mildos, the eel catcher that Bolga said us about."

But there was no sound from within. We climbed up onto the platform and approached the doorway. There was darkness inside, but as we entered our eyes made better use of what little light there was. In the corner we could see a pile of leathery fish skins and the whole place stank of dead fish.

There was a movement under the skins and the fearful sound of a terrified man.

"Please! Please do not hurt me. Don't hurt me again. Please, I am lame; don't hurt me," said the pathetic voice. I slowly pulled away the fish skins and looked into the face of a frail old man.

"Friends," I said in a gentle voice. "We are friends … have no fear of us. Are you Mildos, the eel catcher?" I smiled at him and touched his face tenderly. Zilk put down his great blade so that the old man could not see it.

"Yes, I am Mildos. I am the eel catcher. Who are you? Are you friends? Are you with the Bedosians?"

I knelt down beside Mildos and helped him to sit up. "I am Petronius. I am the son and novice of Petronicus the Great Healer."

Mildos threw his arms around my neck and hugged me close to him. He held me for a few moments and looked towards Zilk and asked: "And is this Zilk of the gods' people? I have heard about him."

"Yes, he is a friend; he will not harm you."

Zilk knelt down and stroked the old man's head. Mildos clung to us so tightly that his fingernails bit into our flesh. When he spoke, he spoke with the voice of a frail old man who had lived with fear for a long time.

"Are there many of you? Where are the men of Klinbil and Klynos? Are the Tall People with you?" I looked into his watery eyes for understanding. His thoughts were not straight, so I spoke to him very gently: "I do not understand, Mildos. What men do you speak of?"

"The army … the army sent by the Revered One to destroy the blade men. And the temple slaves? Are they with you? They hate the Bedosians."

During the brief time we spent with Mildos, we discovered how little he knew of the world beyond the Land of the Bubbling Mud. He thought of the Revered One as a great ruler commanding many men; his knowledge of the wider world was as limited as our knowledge was of his land.

"There is no army, Mildos. There are but two of us," I said. I felt the old man sink further into despair.

Zilk put his hand on the old man's belly and felt the slackness of his skin. "You are in hungry, Mildos. We feed you."

"But please tell us first," I said. "Have you seen Petronicus?"

"He was here," said Mildos. "But the blade men have taken him. It was Petronicus who told them about the army coming to destroy them."

"Where have they taken him?"

"Petronicus said many men will come with dogs and knife sticks to fight them. He said they will come when the harvest is in."

"Please, Mildos, tell us. Where have they taken Petronicus?"

"To Wretched Island," said Mildos. "They took my son as well and left me. I am lame and helpless. I am all alone."

Thirty one

Never in my whole life have I felt such anger gnawing at my body. That day I felt I could kill another man no matter how much I enraged the gods. The urge to kill swelled up in me until it clouded all my thoughts. But, I had to ask myself, was it wrong to kill wicked men to save a good and virtuous man like Petronicus? What a question that was! What a dilemma! How I wished Petronicus or the Revered One was here to answer it for me! My anger mellowed a little as I watched Zilk caring for the old man. I began to see Petronicus in my inner eye and he was saying: *'Do not let your feelings control your thoughts, child.'* Yes, that is what he would have said.

"We must think, Zilk. We must think more than we have ever done before."

Zilk went out and recovered the crabs and eels that were caught in the traps. He brought them in, cracked open the crab shells and fed small pieces to Mildos. The old man had not eaten for days. He ate ravenously and then became calmer when we sat close to him and held his hand.

"But you must go from here," said Mildos. "The blade men will return soon." Zilk sat back and leaned against the wall of the hut.

"If they return, Petronius, Zilk will fight them."

"But, Zilk! You cannot. You are but one man."

"But I am trained in the *fidik*; they are not. Think to always stand behind me when I fight them."

With food in his belly, and the feeling of safety that our presence gave him, Mildos stretched out and slept a little. He was barely able to stand and his lameness meant he could only crawl

231

about on the floor of his hut. Zilk and I lit a fire on a flat stone in the centre of the wooden hut. We feasted off the eels and crabs from the old man's traps.

We talked through all the things we knew. Mildos had told us quite a lot in his fear. We knew that the blade men had camped near the shore when they first came here. They had killed the few people who lived hereabouts and taken whatever they could, including the son of Mildos.

"They took Mildos' son to guide them to island," said Zilk.

"Yes, and that means they can come back whenever they wish with the son of Mildos to guide them."

"They will force him to guide them?"

"They won't have to force him. The son will want to return often to care for his father."

"Yes," said Zilk angrily. "They are clever in their wickedness."

"And they took Petronicus because they want a healer," I said. We both fell into silence. We looked at each other intensely and I think the same thought came to both of us at the same time. I spoke first: "Petronicus has sacrificed himself. He told the wicked ones that the men of Klinbil and Klynos are coming to destroy them, after the harvest maybe. He has made sure the blade men never return from Wretched Island."

Mildos had slept for a while but then lay in the warmth of the fire and our company listening to us speaking. He said: "They will return for firewood; there is none on the island. They will return to rob my traps, the traps my son sets for me."

The sun went down into the great fires beyond the seas. We could see little from the doorway of the hut because of the tall reeds that grew all around. We could still hear the distant bubbling sound and the occasional hiss of hot water that came up from the underside of the world.

We had been silent for a while and then Zilk said quietly: "Petronicus gave Zilk my life when I was nearly dead. I will give it for him now."

I smiled at him warmly in the dying firelight. We had become very close; perhaps he was the true brother I never had, a brother from another world.

"And so will I, Zilk. Petronicus gave me back my life as an infant left exposed on the town wall of Bedosa when they killed my father. They killed my mother although I knew nothing of her. I will also give my life back to Petronicus."

Zilk reached forward and took firm hold of my hand. "We must go to Wretched Island and bring Petronicus home."

We made our plans that night but we did not tell Mildos how we intended to do it. We thought it better to let him sleep and recover what little strength he had.

We knew from close questioning of Mildos that it would take us most of a day to reach Wretched Island. The two greatest dangers, Mildos told us, were tiredness and the biting fish. There was nothing on the island except a few very old huts that Mildos and his son had built over the years. Nothing grew on the island, and water had to be collected in pots when it rained. It was truly an island of wretchedness and none but the most desperate outcasts would go there. The blade men would probably be on the far side of the island, away from the huts, because that was where the fish ran close in shore. Sea fish did not come further in because the biting fish that lived in the mud beneath the waters attacked them. The eels could only be caught close inland where the water was kept warm from the breath coming from inside the world. The biting fish never attacked the eels but Mildos didn't know why.

"You must reach a small island hidden in the reeds before the sun has climbed to the top of the day," said Mildos. "That is when the biting fish come up from the mud to feed. They will eat any flesh they can find, except the eels; they do not eat the eels."

He told us of eel catchers in the past being driven mad in the water when the biting fish caught them unawares. Mildos pulled up his robe and showed us his legs; they were covered in small sores and scares. "When I was young the sores would heal, but not now I am old."

"Petronicus will know how to treat you," I said. "We will bring him back and he will treat you." Mildos told us we must be out of the water and on the small island by late morning and then stay there on the wet mud until the sun was sliding down the afternoon when the biting fish return to the bottom to sleep in deep cracks.

"How long will it take us?" I asked.

"You must leave at first light, as soon as there is a white streak on the morning side of the world. You must then get up onto the small island in the reeds and rest. You must then wait until the sun begins to sink. Take some meat. A dead rat, anything. Throw it into the water and if the biting fish don't come, you will know it is safe. Then you can get to Wretched Island before darkness comes."

"Can we return at night?" I asked.

Mildos looked doubtful and said: "It is possible, if there is a bright moon. I have done it in my youth, before I was lame."

"If cloud hides the moon can we take torches? Or will that bring up the biting fish?"

Mildos shook his head. "No, the biting fish do not know of fire; they come only in strong sunlight."

I remember looking at Zilk in some doubt. Were we strong enough to spend a whole day and night wading through deep water?

"Much deep is it, Mildos?" asked Zilk.

Mildos held his hand to just below his neck to indicate the deepest part. I was smaller than Mildos and knew that the water would come up to my chin. It would be a fearful crossing.

For the rest of that day we made our preparations. Mildos said we should take a small raft with dry blankets and food wrapped up in sealskin to keep it dry. This small raft would be floated behind us tied to a rope. He gave us sealskins to wrap around our legs because the water was very cold in some places but very hot in other places. Our plans and preparations were made and we settled down to sleep. We asked the gods in the Land of Wisdom to give us the strength to endure whatever the bubbling mud and the burning waters would bring to us the next day.

The last words I heard that night were from Mildos: "It is madness. You will never find the way. You will die tomorrow."

Thirty two

Zilk looked out through the doorway of the hut and said: "The sun is rousing itself from the Great Fires. It is making light on the morning side of the world. Come, Petronius, we must go now."

I roused Mildos. "Come, Mildos, you must guide us to Wretched Island."

"But I have no strength in my legs."

We had not told Mildos of our plan. We had discussed it in whispers whilst Mildos slept. Zilk lifted the old man on his shoulders so he would be clear of the water. And so with Mildos sitting on the tall shoulders of Zilk to guide us, and myself wading through the waters just behind them pulling the small raft we entered the water. Mildos looked fearful at first but did not protest when he realised how tall and strong Zilk was. I carried the great blade of Zilk tied across my shoulder. We each had a long pole to help keep us on our feet when the waters rushed past us. Mildos carried an even longer pole with a strand of thin leather about as long as a man's leg tied to the end. There was a small stone attached to the end of the leather strand to make it sink. This he held in front of him and allowed the stone to dangle into the water to show the direction of the current just below the surface.

"Stay always close, Petronius, and in deep water take hold of my shoulders," said Zilk.

By the time the sun was showing its full face in the morning sky we had left the shore far behind. The reeds were fewer but the going underfoot was very slippery. Sometimes I felt the water was hot and then suddenly it became cold again as it flowed along strange paths beneath us. We used our poles to steady ourselves and I gave as much support to Zilk from behind as I could.

Often he paused and said to me: "Please to push Mildos higher by my head."

I would then push Mildos up and tell him to hold his hands around Zilk's neck. But Mildos was directing his eyes always on the waters surrounding us. He would tap Zilk on one shoulder to indicate that he should turn in that direction. One tap meant half a turn and two taps meant a full turn. I was looking ahead but could see no reason for changing direction. Sometimes he called for a stop and held his long pole in front of Zilk to watch how the thin strand of leather moved. He was watching for slight changes in the direction of the waters before deciding which way we should go.

"The sea bed changes, and I have to be sure," he said. I began to feel the heat of the sun on my head and I kept looking into the water anxiously to watch for the biting fish.

"Mildos," Zilk shouted, "what is that?"

He was pointing to the water about twenty paces in front. The water was bubbling and splashing dirty mud into the sky.

"Do not fear," said Mildos. "It is only the mud bubbling up beneath the waters. It will not harm us because we do not go that way."

He tapped Zilk twice on the shoulder and we turned away from the bubbling waters but I could feel the heat on my legs. And then after a short while we seemed to be going back towards the shore. Zilk looked round to me and I saw doubts on his face. Maybe he had the same thoughts as I had, that Mildos was old and no longer knew the way. But about half way through the morning we seemed to be heading towards the sea once again. We had turned so many times that I was no longer sure which way we were going.

Zilk stopped. We were in some shallow water, which came just up to my waist.

"Mildos, I will stand you down here. I must rest," the big man said. He lowered the old man down and I put my hands under Mildos's shoulders to keep him upright. Zilk began to exercise his arms and shoulders. He would stretch out his arms, clench his fists and slowly relax again.

"Do you tire, Zilk?" I asked.

"No," he said. "Zilk is strong. We walk again now."

Mildos was looking at me anxiously. "We must hurry; the sun climbs high in the sky. Soon the biting fish will feel the sun and come out to hunt."

We set off again and found the going a little easier. The water remained shallow for a while, hardly covering my waist.

Mildos became excited and kept pointing the way ahead. "Look. In the reeds, the island. We can rest there. Hurry Zilk!"

At last we crawled out of the water, through the reeds and lay down on the wet slimy mud. We lay there until the sun was half way down the afternoon sky. Zilk cut the dead rat in half and threw some in the water. We watched in horror as the biting fish swarmed over the rotting flesh. I felt as if my own skin was being torn from my bones. We huddled together in the middle of the small island and watched as the water seemed to boil with ferocity. We waited until the rat had been devoured and the water became clam. After a while Zilk threw the remains of the rat into the water but no biting fish appeared.

Mildos watched the waters very closely and at last he said: "It is safe to go now. But leave the raft here until we return."

"How far is it now?" I asked.

"Not as far as we have come. We will be there before dark."

"The wicked ones," said Zilk. "Will they see us coming?"

"No," said Mildos. "The reeds are tall and thick this side of Wretched Island."

But the water was getting very deep. At times it was barely below my chin and I felt as if my feet were being lifted from the bottom and trying to float me away. Zilk saw my difficulties and told me to grasp hold of his shoulders.

We walked like that for a long time until Mildos called us to halt. "And now," he said, "the water runs swiftly. We must move in a different way. It is a way known only to the eel catchers."

I looked ahead and could see how the sea was pouring down channels between reed beds with great force. Beyond that we could see calmer waters but we were now in the most dangerous part of our journey.

Mildos explained that Zilk and I should face each other and put our hands on each other's shoulders. The water must be allowed to pass between our bodies and not press against our chests because it could push us over. He told us to keep our poles firmly in the soft mud on the other side of each other and we should then take one pace in turn. We tried it a few times before entering the rapids.

I felt the strength of the water immediately we stepped into the deep part. It seemed to be pushing me off my feet. Zilk would take one sideward step whilst I held him and then I would take a step whilst he held me. The weight of Mildos on Zilk's shoulders seemed to help keep us steady. I don't think our poles helped us much but Mildos told us to keep them firmly stuck into the mud beneath our feet when we were still.

Slowly we edged our way through the rushing waters. The gods smiled on us until we had passed the danger.

And just as the sun was about to sit on the edge of the distant sea we found ourselves pushing through tall reeds that slowed our progress but concealed us from any watchful eyes on Wretched Island.

Mildos whispered: "We must be quiet now. Do not snap the reeds. We are very close to Wretched Island."

Thirty three

The three of us peered through the reeds. We were about twenty paces from the mud bank that formed the shore of Wretched Island. Beyond that we could see three huts, one large and two smaller ones. There was also a small fire smouldering and two poles with a leather line between them for drying skins.

"If my son is confined," said Mildos, "he will be in the largest hut; that is the strongest. It has a log door."

"And the wicked ones?" I asked. "Where will they be?"

Mildos looked towards the sun and nodded slightly. "The fish run as the sun begins to rest," he said. "If they are fishing for food they will be on the far side."

"But Mildos," said Zilk. "Look past those skins. I see two men."

"Yes," said Mildos. "I see them too. I think they are preparing seal skins for drying."

Zilk and I exchanged quick glances. The silent decision passed between us and we moved forward. We left Mildos amongst the reeds on some fairly dry mud and crawled forward, Zilk in front with his great blade. I drew the small blade my mother had given me and we silently approached the largest hut. The two men were about forty paces away and as we got closer I could hear them talking quietly together. Zilk sniffed the wind. It was off the sea and would blow their sounds to us but not ours to them. He indicated that we should climb silently onto the platform by the door of the hut. The gods again smiled on us because the two wicked ones moved further away towards another pile of skins. They began laying them on the ground ready for drying. I noticed, however, that they left their two great blades sticking into the ground.

I crawled forward towards the door because I was the smallest. I was sure that if I remained low down on the platform the two Bedosians could not see me because they were lower down. I slithered forward towards the door of the hut. I glanced up at the two men and noticed thankfully that they were still busy arranging and rearranging the skins and did not look in our direction. Zilk stayed around the corner out of sight of the Bedosians. I found the door and I put my head close to the bottom of it and listened for any sounds of people within. Zilk still kept out of sight, watching with his great blade in his hand.

No sound came from within so I thought we should risk fortune.

"Petronicus," I whispered in the softest voice I could. "Petronicus, are you there?" I heard a shuffling within and nearly died with joy when I heard a fearful and despairing voice.

It was the voice of Petronicus: "Petronius? Is that you, Petronius?"

"Yes," I whispered. "And Zilk is here. Are you alone?"

"I am with the son of Mildos but we are tethered."

"Be patient, Petronicus. We are coming for you."

Slowly and with the utmost caution I began to remove the logs from the doorway. I watched the two Bedosians all the time hoping that I could lie flat on the platform quickly if they looked in my direction. I passed each log behind me to Zilk, who silently took it round the side of the hut and laid it down. I crawled into the hut. There was very little light but I felt the hands of Petronicus reaching out for me as I entered. The hands of my master were cruelly tethered at the wrists with thick leather straps.

"Child … child …" was all he could say.

He held out his hands and I cut the leather thongs that bound him. Then I cut the thongs that bound his legs. Petronicus embraced me quickly then leaned over to the other man and whispered: "Have no fear, Mildonius. It is friends."

The son of Mildos was more securely tethered than Petronicus. His knees were tightly tethered as well as his hands and feet. I had to work my blade vigorously to cut him loose.

"When we get out, be silent," I said. "Crawl along the platform and then run quickly to the edge of the reeds; your father awaits."

I helped Petronicus stand up but his legs and arms were stiff with being tethered for so long. He stood up painfully and then stooped down to pick up his medicine box. I took it from him, crawled to the doorway and whispered as loudly as I dared for Zilk to come and take it from me. And then all three of us stood close together in the dark hut and Petronicus began to rub his arms and legs vigorously. I did the same for Mildonius and then together we faced the door ready to leave.

But the man I saw in the doorway wasn't Zilk. Horror shot through my body like a red-hot stone and I was looking into a face I hoped I would never see again. I was looking at the face of the Ruler of Bedosa, the man I had seen slash a scribe with a great blade during the massacre.

I have never understood how my thoughts worked in that instant. My feet seemed fixed to the floor of the hut but my eyes and thoughts explored the face of evil confronting me. My blade came up in my hand without me making it do so and in the two paces separating us I fixed in my mind every feature of that evil face. I went for him with all the hate that belonged deep in the earth and flew at him like a dog at his prey. We grappled for an instant until I felt the huge hands of Zilk lifting the Ruler of Bedosa high above his head and hurling him off the platform into the mud. At the same time Zilk shouted: "Run all to the reeds. Zilk follow."

I picked up the medicine box and led the way with the son of Mildos supporting Petronicus as we went. We got to the edge of the mud bank and as I turned to look for Zilk I saw his skill with the great blade. It swished about in the air as fast as the wings of a bird and cut into the Ruler of Bedosa as he tried to escape. The other man came forward and tried to thrust his blade towards Zilk but in an instant Zilk had flicked the blade out of the man's hand and into the mud. The two men fled, cursing foully and with the Ruler of Bedosa holding his arm and dropping blood into the mud. They were shouting for the other wicked ones to come from the other side of Wretched Island.

"Quickly," I said to Mildonius. "Carry your father on your shoulders. We must get away as soon as Zilk reaches us."

I could see Zilk running with great strides towards us, his great blade still wet with the blood of the Ruler of Bedosa.

"Quickly!" Zilk shouted. "Show the way."

Mildonius with his father on his back began to pick his way through the reeds towards some open water. I followed, supporting Petronicus with Zilk behind me ready to defend us with his Great Blade if we were pursued.

After no more than twenty paces Mildonius paused breathlessly. "Friends," he said desperately. "I am weak with hunger. I cannot carry my father."

He began to sob and seemed to be floundering in the water. Zilk rushed forward and took the old man from him and told Mildonius to lead the way. It was getting dark but the further we got out into the water the less likely it was that we could be pursued. The stiffness in the muscles of Petronicus began to ease and he found pushing through the water less painful. I walked directly in front of him with our medicine box on my head. I told my master to put his hands on my shoulders for support.

Without the weight of Mildos on his shoulders, Mildonius recovered quickly. He seemed to know the way better than his father did and we moved more rapidly through the water and reeds. Behind us we could hear the curses and threats of the Bedosians as they tried to follow us into the water. We heard the screams of some of them as they were sucked into the bubbling mud. And then, there was silence behind us. The moon was watching us and pushed its face between the clouds to give us some light on the dark waters. We forced our tired bodies on through the water. I was really worried about Petronicus when we entered the deepest part of the crossing. I could hear him behind me coughing and spluttering as the cold water crept up around his throat.

He held tightly onto my shoulders and I kept saying: "Not long now, Petronicus. The water is shallower soon. Not long now."

When we came to the strong water we found it easier with four of us facing inwards with our arms on each other's shoulders. Mildos took the medicine box and sat high up Zilk's shoulders telling us which way to go. Petronicus slipped quite a lot and I could feel by his shoulders that he was getting colder and colder.

And then, after what seemed like an age, we staggered onto the island of reeds where we had rested on our way out. We lay down on the soft mud and let our bodies ease.

Petronicus lay down wearily but he wanted to hug Zilk and me very tightly. There were tears in the eyes of my master at that moment; I had never seen him like this in all the years we were together.

"Petronicus!" I said in alarm. "You have no leathers for your feet."

"No, child, the wicked ones took everything. Everything except the medicine box. They left me that so that I could treat them."

"You treated the wicked ones?"

"Yes, child. A healer must never refuse to treat sick men, no matter how wicked they are."

"But, Petronicus, they have enraged the gods!"

"Yes, child, I know, but if we treat their ailments with plants from the ground some of the goodness from the ground may enter them."

I nodded; he was right of course, but I was still overwhelmed with hate.

He smiled at me in the moonlight, put his hand on my shoulder and said gently: "You are full of hate, child. Hate is like a poison that runs through the body and brings sickness and death."

I put my face into his beard just as I used to when a small child and said: "I am sorry, Petronicus. You are the wisest of men."

"Healers must never refuse to help people. Even if they have no coins or anything to give in return. The plants we use come freely from the ground and our knowledge was given to us freely from our masters."

"And did that knowledge come from the gods?"

"Of course, where else would it come from?"

I took the leathers from my feet to bind them onto the feet of my master.

"No, child. I do not want your leathers. I will be all right."

"It is not fitting," I protested. "For a man of your years to be without leathers for his feet. It is for youth to be barefoot."

"You are kind, child, and I am too weary to argue with you."

I bound up his feet and then put the skins Mildos had given me for my legs on him. I could see how painful his ankles were from the tightness of the leather thongs that had tethered him for many days.

"My legs are young; they will heal quickly when we reach the shore," I said.

"How long can we stay here to rest, do you think?"

"Not long," I said. "Already I feel the coldness of the water creeping through my bones."

I took one of the dry blankets from the raft and wrapped it around his shoulders. And then it was time to move on.

"Light the torches," said Mildos to his son. "Petronius, your flint, please."

The torches that we had on the raft were made of dry sticks bound together with seaweed. On the ends there were pieces of fish skin covered with yellow powder, which seemed to burn very brightly.

We set off again with the medicine box lashed to the raft, Mildos holding a flaming torch high above his head and me holding one at the back. After a while we were told to stop whilst Mildonius crept forward to feel the direction of the water. We saw him bend right down and reach down the mud and then hold his hand just below the surface of the water to feel the direction of the waves.

It must have been extremely difficult for him to find his way in the dark but the gods continued to smile on us and began to take away the clouds to give us a full moon.

I remember saying to Petronicus as we stood in the cold water waiting for the signal to move on: "You said we should meet when the moon was big."

He smiled. "I have little breath for speaking, child, but as I remember, I said we would meet at the crossroads from Biltis when this moon was full."

We both smiled in the torchlight. Mildonius began to move forward again.

That night stretched itself cruelly onward and seemed to want to linger and torture us. But we forced our aching bodies through the water and when the first streaks of daylight stretched across the morning sky, we saw the shore in the distance. We struggled thankfully onto the shore tired, very dirty and cold.

We stayed several days with Mildos and his son. Petronicus needed time to recover and our donkey needed us to search far and wide for grass and forage for him. Petronicus sent me out each day to look for plants and herbs to replenish his medicine box.

"We shall have to journey to the Mountain of the Year soon or we will not have the means to earn our living," he said.

"Did the Bedosians take your little stones from your pouch, the ones your father gave you?" I asked.

"No, I told them they were healing stones and I would need them to treat their wounds and ailments."

"They are indeed stupid men, Petronicus."

He laughed a little and said: "Yes. They are of shallow thought. They took the coins I had earned on the trail and so, child, we have nothing left but our wisdom and knowledge."

"But, Petronicus, we have been poor before. Many times as I remember."

After a short pause I asked: "Why would they take your coins? Coins would be no value to them on Wretched Island."

"Greed," said my wise master, "has an appetite all its own; it gorges on itself. Remember that always, child."

I smiled warmly within myself. Petronicus was teaching me again.

When Petronicus and the donkey felt strong again we bade our farewells to Mildos and his son Mildonius and headed along the narrow path back towards Trail End. We travelled slowly because Petronicus was still weary and sore from the ill use he had received from the wicked ones. We passed silently by the place of the massacre of the priests and on towards Bedosa. We did not tarry but passed the deserted town as rapidly as we could.

One night, after we had left Bedosa at least a day behind us, I asked Petronicus: "Is the world safe now?"

He lay back on the ground and looked more peaceful than I had seen him for many days. "Yes," he said. "The Bedosians who did not die in the mud are now marooned. Nobody will go near them."

"There is only Mildonius who knows the secret way. You are correct, Petronicus; he will never cross to Wretched Island again."

"And think on this, Petronius. When the Bedosians die their bodies will rot in the mud. Nothing grows on the bubbling mud so their wickedness will die with them."

Zilk, who had listened to all our conversations with much more understanding, said: "Petronicus is the wisest of men."

"You have learned our words well, Zilk," said Petronicus.

"And Petronius has learned much of mine."

Later that night in the dying firelight I said: "Petronicus, how did you know we would come to Bedosa and not stay at the crossroads from Biltis?"

I could not see his face clearly in the half-light but I detected a smile.

"Because I know of your impatience. I knew you would leave Klinbil earlier than I told you to even if your tasks were not quite finished."

"But my tasks were finished and I could learn the words of Zilk just as well on the trail."

"You are correct, but you have always been an impatient child."

"I am sorry for my impatience, Petronicus," I said humbly.

"I understand, Petronius. Impatience is both a fault and a delight in youth."

And so we reached the crossroads where all the trails came together. It seemed to me that my happiness increased the further we walked away from Bedosa. We resolved that never again would we visit that hateful place.

I was so happy I ran ahead jumping and leaping along the trail. Zilk joined me and we laughed together. Petronicus laughed and shouted his joy to us. The world was safe, the wicked ones were destroyed and true thoughts ran once again through the minds of men. Soon we would be back with the Revered One and all was well with the world.

But above all, the four of us were all together again, Petronicus, me, Zilk and the donkey.

We set out with wind in our steps once again on the Happy Trail to Klynos.

Thirty four

The next few summers passed quickly. Petronicus and I travelled widely, and everywhere we went our fame went before us. It seemed that everyone wanted to meet and talk to us. They wanted to know everything about Zilk, especially the first meeting between Zilk and the Revered One in the cave by the Giant Rocks. They asked about his great speech to the Council of Wisdom and all about the battle of Klynos. Many asked for reassurance that the wicked ones could never return. I cannot remember how many times we told the story about our experiences in the Land of the Bubbling Mud.

I felt I was growing up very fast. I was now taller than Petronicus and could remember things that he sometimes could not. Petronicus let me treat sick people myself and just watched over me as I attended to them.

As the years passed, many priests who had not been with the Bedosians returned to the discussions and were accepted back into the company of wise and learned men. They eventually agreed that the gods were part of men but they would not accept that a small part of them remained in wicked people. The gods were fickle, they said, and would leave the bodies and minds of wicked men and expose them to sickness. But mostly, the priests contented themselves with caring for the temples, composing the prayers for the healers to use and attending to the ceremonies. Both Petronicus and I were overjoyed when we heard that the priests from the Temple of Healers had returned. They had long discussions with the Revered One and agreed to care for the meeting place that Zilk had erected.

Zilk did not always accompany us on the trail. In some ways I was sad and missed him greatly, but in other ways I was pleased because there was just Petronicus and myself and that was how it had always been. Zilk spent a lot of time with the Tall People. He discovered that some of their hunting calls were similar to those of his own world. But he returned to Klynos frequently to ensure that the Revered One was safe and well provided for.

Several well-known iron makers travelled in search of Zilk to discover how to make the great blades. Zilk looked at the iron rocks they used but saw how they crumbled and were of very poor quality. He shook his head and told them that the iron rocks in his world were much stronger. A story was told around the campfires that Zilk had let the ironers put his great blade into their ovens but that it was so hard they could not turn it into fire mud. The wise men of the world were relieved that our ironers still could not make blades longer than a man's finger.

Petronicus and I were very sad when we heard of the death of the Revered One. We were in the Land of the Whispering Rocks earning our living as healers, although many people consulted Petronicus for his wisdom. Petronicus was particularly sad because he and the Revered One had been friends for many years. We hurried back to the Mountain of the Year but arrived too late for the ceremony. The Revered One had asked his friends to bury his body high on the hillside of the Temple of Healers overlooking the place where he held the Council of Wisdom. Petronicus said it was a most appropriate place because the Revered One would be present at all future Councils to watch over them.

It was a sad time for us and I noticed that Petronicus never really recovered from the loss of his old friend. Increasingly, in the years that followed, Petronicus remained in Klynos whilst I travelled the trails earning our living. I always returned to Klynos for the winter, driving a few sheep and goats, which would provide for us in the cold moons. Zilk remained close by and I knew he would always be there to protect and provide for Petronicus during my absence.

I could not call myself a healer whilst Petronicus lived but simply being the novice of such a famous healer was sufficient for sick people to trust me.

One year, after a particularly wet summer, I was travelling the trail with our donkey, from the Land of the Tall Trees towards Klinbil when I found a message for me in the stones at the crossroads. It simply said: *Come quickly Klynos*. In my darkest thoughts I knew it was bad news about Petronicus who was now very old. I hurried my steps and did not stop to sleep at night, and arrived in Klynos at half moon. Zilk met me at the gates of the town because the Tall People had told him of my approach. He embraced me and we rubbed hands.

"Petronius," said Zilk, "come quickly. I have taken Petronicus to the House of Humility. He is very sick."

It was like being hit in the chest by a strong wind because the news blew the strength out of me. I was told later that Zilk had carried Petronicus in his arms all the way to the Mountain of the Year. It took him several days and he stopped for only short periods at night.

"The donkey is tired and hungry," I said to Zilk. "I will leave it with you and I will run to the Mountain of the Year."

"And I will follow with the donkey."

We parted. I took nothing with me, not even my blanket, and ran all that day and most of the night. The next morning I continued to run grabbing leaves and berries off the trees to eat. I rested only for a short time that night.

Petronicus lay on the floor in the House of Humility. He tried to raise himself up as I approached but his strength had left him. He held his hand up to me as I crouched down to him. I grasped his hand.

"I have been waiting for you, child. Only you know where I must lie."

"But you are sick, Petronicus." I said. "I will gather the herbs and plants we need."

"I am old, child, not sick. The ground beckons me. But I will die on clean straw as you always promised I would."

"But there is great sickness on the trail. The fruit has been bad this year and many people bleed from their stomachs."

I went to the storehouse and brought clean sweet straw for Petronicus. I took several blankets that the novices had washed in the stream and made Petronicus as comfortable as I could. "Tomorrow you will vomit for me, Petronicus, and I will see what ails you."

Petronicus smiled and said: "Yes, you shall, Petronius. You are a good healer."

But when morning came there was nothing in his vomit. His hands felt cold and his heart was slow. We didn't speak much to each other in the days that followed, I just lay along side him at night and sat by him during the day. Zilk arrived with the donkey and brought the medicine box for me. Petronicus had no other possessions of any value but he liked to have his box with him. Inside were all the small pouches of leaves and pollens that we collected on our travels for our cures.

I sat by Petronicus for many days but he seldom came out of his deep thoughts to speak to me, although I saw him looking at me on several occasions. Sometimes I noticed a slight smile on his old face and his eyes never lost their glint. Many people came to see Petronicus and brought food and milk for us, but Petronicus ate very little.

One night as I slept beside him a dream came to me.

I was small and slept in the folds of his blanket. It was winter and we lay by our fire. The donkey slept by us and I was stroking its head. Petronicus looked at me and smiled.

'Use the donkey to practise kindness on,' he said, *'and question, always question; that way you will live a free man.'*

We moved Petronicus closer to the big fire in the middle of the House of Humility and Zilk cut wood to keep it burning all night. The other sick people lying there were grateful for the warmth Zilk's great blade provided.

Many people died during the next few days but the sickness I had found on the trails seemed to die out and not many people were brought in. It was quiet at night, as the presiding healer and his novices insisted that no noise was made to disturb the sick and the dying.

One night, about half a moon after I had arrived, Petronicus seemed to be sleeping peacefully beside me. Zilk was sitting by the fire looking vacantly into it. I fell into a deep sleep. Petronicus returned to me in another dream.

I was a child again and he said: 'Make for yourself a trail of high regard and then you need not look behind you as only friends will follow you.' Petronicus and I were walking happily towards a town. In the centre of the town, by the market place, there was a temple with a wise old man sitting at the bottom of the steps. We went up to him and I knew it was Petronicus's father. 'And this is my son and novice, father; this is Petronius.'

I woke suddenly. It was cold in the House or Humility. The fire had died down and Zilk was asleep. Petronicus had his hand stretched out towards me. His face was turned in my direction and his face was frozen in a final smile. I knew then that life had left him.

I looked at his outstretched hand and saw it contained a small pouch. It was the pouch he always wore around his waist; it was the pouch his father had given him when he had sent his two sons off on their quest for wisdom.

Petronicus was now giving it to me.

I took it and emptied out the small stones into my hand. I never forgot the story of Petronicus and his brother and how their father had given one son coins and the other son stones to help them on their journey to find wisdom.

Petronicus was saying to me in his death that I would not need coins in my quest: *'Wisdom is in the seeking, child, remember that always.'*

Petronicus was placing the same trust in me as his own father had placed in him. My heart filled with pride and my eyes filled with tears. But I felt so alone – so very alone. That night in our solitary darkness I said my goodbyes. I buried my face in my master's long white beard just as I used to do as a child. And that was the last time I cried in this life.

Thirty five

Only Zilk witnessed our final departure to the Mountain of the Year. He had helped me to prepare thick leather skins to wrap the body of Petronicus so that my master would not be bruised as I dragged him up the slopes. It was the tradition for the novice to fast on the final journey with his master so I did not take any food. I left the donkey to graze at the foot of the mountain path and just took my blanket because it would be cold higher up.

Zilk was extremely sad when he said his goodbyes to Petronicus. He never forgot how Petronicus had saved his life when his boat was shipwrecked near Bedosa. Zilk also embraced me very tightly before I set off and seemed reluctant to let me go. He held me for a while and there were tears in his eyes when we finally rubbed hands.

I set off up the mountain. Just Petronicus and me for our last journey together.

All that day I heaved and tugged the body of my master up towards the snow line. It took all my strength and I saw it as payment for all Petronicus had done for me. This was the man who had taken me for his own, the unwanted child of a condemned thief who was hanged at Bedosa. I was a child nobody wanted, left to die exposed on the town wall. He had put me in the folds of his blanket and taught me his craft and shared his thoughts and wisdom with me.

Often his body got caught in the rocks and I had to stop and remove the rocks to make a path for him.

"The going is hard today Petronicus," I said. "But I remember how you smoothed the path for me all those years. I expect we will be there tomorrow or the next day."

As I struggled upward I was remembering the great joy I experienced when Petronicus first brought me to the Mountain of the Year. He had taken me into the Temple of the Healers and told the priests that I was good enough to be his novice. He told them to put my name in the scrolls of the temple for all to see. I remembered how he told me about the plants, how everything comes from the ground and everything returns to the ground. He showed me how to care for the plants and how to take just one small leaf so the plant would not be weakened and could grow again. In my mind I could still see him kneeling down and touching the small petals so gently with his finger. Oh, what excitement and joy there was for me that day.

We spent our last night together just below the snow line. I lit a fire and sat silently watching it flicker and grow as I put more dead wood on it. I pulled Petronicus near the fire and opened the leather skin so that I could gaze on his face for the last time. As night fell I began to wonder how many fires we had sat by together over the years. I smiled and looked over at Petronicus and wondered what he would be saying to me if he had breath to speak.

Early the next morning I finally dragged the body of my master to the place of his burial. The plants and shrubs grew strongly on the stones covering his own master's grave and I remembered how we had collected the most potent plants from that grave over the years.

I broke the ground with the blade my mother had given me and hewed out the soil and stones with a piece of jagged rock. I carefully placed Petronicus in the ground and piled earth and stones on top.

When I had finished my task I felt an overwhelming sense of loneliness. I rested and then walked a short way towards the sea and stood looking into the distance.

The sun climbed to the top of the day and I looked out and saw a small boat with a sail on its mast heading out to sea. I knew it was Zilk and I knew he was trying to return to his own world. He had told me that he was building a boat, cutting the branches off the trees with his great blade, but I thought it was for fishing. I never thought he would attempt the perilous journey to his home.

Zilk must have been watching for me. He saw me, stood up and waved his great blade. I waved back and then sat down and watched my dear friend disappear into the distance. He had stayed with us to protect and provide for Petronicus whilst I was away on the trails and now, having repaid his debt, he wanted to return home. As the darkness came I could see that Zilk was sailing in the direction of a particularly bright star. My fondest memories of him stirred deep in my mind and I prayed that the gods would guide him home.

That night I returned to the grave of Petronicus and lit a fire. I did not feel hungry; I was too deep in my thoughts to think about food.

There was a cold loneliness covering my body and I felt as if I was the last man in the world. And then as I looked up into the night sky I saw the star of Petronicus shining brightly down on me. The moon was small and did not fill the sky with light and, as I watched, my own naming star flickered into the view. It was always later than the star of Petronicus because it was further away. Petronicus said it was several days' walk away. Petronicus always knew about these things.

I am nearing the end of my story.

I returned to the foot of the mountain and then climbed the steps to the Temple of the Healers. As I entered I shouted: "I am Petronicus, the healer." I shouted it as loudly as I could and imagined my master smiling proudly in the Land of Wisdom where only good men live. The priests entered my name on the scrolls and on a clay tablet to be placed in the House of Tablets at Klynos.

So the story of my days with Petronicus is now over and I now travel the trails alone. But never really alone. I know that the plants will grow on the grave of Petronicus. They will grow strong in his goodness and the wind and the birds will carry the seeds all over the world. I will eat the food that grows in the soil and the goodness and wisdom of my master will multiply and become part of me and part of all that lives and breathes.

And now, my young friends, the sun has climbed to the top of the day and it is time to go.

Epilogue

Petronicus, who as a youth had been Petronius, but now known all over the world as the Revered One, emerged from the Temple of the Healers. His son, who was his novice, and many students who had travelled far to study his wisdom followed him. He paused at the top of the steps and looked down at the Stone Circle his friend Zilk had begun many years before. He saw that all the men of wisdom had assembled on this midsummer's day. The sun had reached the top of the day and it was time for the Council of Wisdom to begin.

The years now sat heavily upon him but he had been summer's child and had lived beyond the normal span of men. He needed the support of his son to descend the steps and once again the assembled people rose to their feet as he approached. This was the third Council of Wisdom over which he had presided and many great questions had been discussed and some resolved.

He had greatly expanded the Circle of Wisdom to allow students and novices to sit behind the wise ones and listen to their deliberations. He knew from his own training with Petronicus how important it was to teach the young. Petronicus often said: *'Wise thoughts nourish the minds of youth. Good men are not made with false thought.'*

Often, as he sat on the Centre Stone, his mind returned to that most famous Council of Wisdom held in his youth. He remembered how he had stood behind the Revered One and heard his great speech. He relived in his mind's eye the dramatic appearance of Zilk at the door of the Temple of Healers and how that great and powerful man had descended into the assembly with Petronicus. The events that followed at Klynos and in the Land of the Bubbling Mud have been told and retold by scribes, orators and dramatists many times.

But he was now the Revered One and he kept the discussions firmly under control in the Councils of Wisdom and allowed only one man to speak at a time. He remembered his own master saying: 'Wisdom must win arguments, not those who merely speak loudest and most often. Some who talk a lot really say little.'

In his twilight years, the Revered One often rode a donkey up the Mountain of the Year
to visit the grave of Petronicus.
He would spend many silent hours talking in his imagination with his dear friend and master.
And often he would go and look out to sea,
always hoping that his old friend Zilk might return ...

The End

Also Available from BeWrite Books

Crime
The Knotted Cord	Alistair Kinnon
The Tangled Skein	Alistair Kinnon
Marks	Sam Smith
Porlock Counterpoint	Sam Smith
Scent of Crime	Linda Stone

Crime/Humour
Sweet Molly Maguire	Terry Houston

Horror
Chill	Terri Pine, Peter Lee, Andrew Müller

Fantasy/Humour
Zolin A Rockin' Good Wizard	Barry Ireland
The Hundredfold Problem	John Grant
Earthdoom!	David Langford & John Grant

Fantasy
The Far-Enough Window	John Grant
A Season of Strange Dreams	C. S. Thompson
And Then the Night	C. S. Thompson

Collections/ Short Stories
As the Crow Flies	Dave Hutchinson
The Loss of Innocence	Jay Mandal
Kaleidoscope	Various
Odie Dodie	Lad Moore
Tailwind	Lad Moore
The Miller Moth	Mike Broemmel
The Shadow Cast	Mike Broemmel
As the Crow Flies	Dave Hutchinson
The Creature in the Rose	Various

Thriller
Deep Ice	Karl Kofoed
Blood Money	Azam Gill
Evil Angel	RD Larson
Disremembering Eddie	Anne Morgellyn
Flight to Pakistan	Azam Gill
Removing Edith Mary	Anne Morgellyn

Historical Fiction

Ring of Stone	Hugh McCracken
Jahred and The Magi	Wilma Clark
The Kinnons of Candleriggs	Jenny Telfer Chaplin

Contemporary

The Care Vortex	Sam Smith
Someplace Like Home	Terrence Moore
Sick Ape	Sam Smith
A Tangle of Roots	David Hough
Whispers of Ghosts	Ron McLachlan

Young Adult

Rules of the Hunt	Hugh McCracken
The Time Drum	Hugh McCracken
Kitchen Sink Concert	Ishbel Moore
The Fat Moon Dance	Elizabeth Taylor
Grandfather and The Ghost	Hugh McCracken
Return from the Hunt	Hugh McCracken

Children's

The Secret Portal	Reno Charlton
The Vampire Returns	Reno Charlton

Autobiography/Biography

A Stranger and Afraid	Arthur Allwright
Vera & Eddy's War	Sam Smith

Poetry

A Moment for Me	Heather Grace
Shaken & Stirred	Various
Letters from Portugal	Jan Oskar Hansen
Routes	Twelve poets. A road less traveled.
Vinegar Moon	Donna Biffar

General

The Wounded Stone	Terry Houston
Magpies and Sunsets	Neil Alexander Marr
Redemption of Quapaw Mountain	Bertha Sutliff

Romance

A Different Kind of Love	Jay Mandal
The Dandelion Clock	Jay Mandal

Humour
The Cuckoos of Batch Magna   Peter Maughan

Science Fiction
Gemini Turns   Anne Marie Duquette

Adventure
Matabele Gold   Michael J Hunt
The African Journals of
Petros Amm   Michael J Hunt

Coming Soon
The Drowning Fish   John G Hall
The End of Science Fiction   Sam Smith
Treason   Meredith Whitford
The Adventures of Alianore
Audley   Brian Wainwright

All the above titles are available from

www.bewrite.net

Printed in the United Kingdom
by Lightning Source UK Ltd.
102672UKS00001B/4-54

9 781904 492764